STORY LANE

BILL MCCAMBLEY

ISBN: 979-8-9872556-0-5

To my children
Without whom there would be no stories.
And no need

CONTENTS

ACKNOWLEDGMENTS

My heartfelt thanks to my beautiful wife, Pat, and our children, friends, relatives, Gary Zenker and other members of the Main Line Writers Group for their unfailing support and encouragement as I struggled in the wee hours to tell my stories. Special thanks, also, to Kate, Mary, Joe P., Aunt Joanne, Dennis, Carla, and Marta for their unwavering support at a difficult time. Greater love hath no man than I for you.

1

THE TIME OF YOUR LIFE

2016

Rain pelted a Rolls Royce parked in front of an old jewelry shop. L. Frank Webb III, sat in the back seat and stared blankly out at the drab strip of stores. This was the first time he had been back to the old neighborhood in over 40 years. He swore long ago that he would never return, but he permitted this one exception, for tonight he felt both vindicated and victorious.

Thick gray clouds made the summer evening both inhospitable and prematurely dark. The few landscape trees dotting the avenue swayed wildly in the gusts of driven rain.

Webb didn't care. He didn't even seem to notice the rain. Though stoic in appearance, as he believed any titan of industry should be, he was secretly euphoric, concealing a giddiness he could not remember having experienced at any time in his 64 years. Having just returned from Manhattan on the day he took his company public, he had just one more task on his to-do list: buy a watch.

Oh, but not just any watch. A Rolex – to signify victory. And not just any Rolex. The most expensive, ostentatious Rolex he could find in this jewelry store. And it had to be this store, the same shop his father had frequented to memorialize significant life milestones, such as they were, for the misguided fool.

The Timex pieces of crap the Old Man bought were appropriate to mark whatever minor achievement he might have happened to stumble across, Webb thought. He never bought into his father's tradition. In fact, he never believed much of anything his father held dear. This jewelry shop, for example, was a dump, and totally beneath the station Webb had achieved in life.

In fact, so was this whole crummy neighborhood. He did not understand what his father, and the current occupants saw in such an uninspired location and bourgeois existence. Bunch of idiots. What a waste of life.

He could not wait to return to his stately Jeffersonian mansion on the Main Line west of the city, swim a few laps in his Olympic-size indoor heated pool, and relax in the sauna before enjoying a proper, chef-prepared dinner while these poor schmucks dined on Big Macs or whatever it was they called food.

Still, there was one more item on his to-do list today, and completing it required he be here to symbolize victory over his father, his father's beliefs, and all the other naysayers who never believed he would amount to anything. Well, as of this morning, Mister L. Frank Webb III was worth more than three billion dollars, on paper anyway. He would return to this hellhole one last time, take the best it had to offer as his own, shake its dingy dirt from his imported Gucci leather loafers, and never return.

Webb's only regret was that his father had not lived long enough to see how successful he had become. It would've been great to see the shock on the Old Man's face as he watched his wealthy son being broadcast coast-to-coast this morning by all the major news outlets.

"So much for you and your sacred quantum physics. Being rich was so beneath you, huh? Up yours, Old Man," he muttered, stepping out of the limousine, clutching his coat collar to his neck as he walked a few brisk steps up to the jewelry shop display window.

He could afford to buy the most expensive watch in the shop. Hell, he thought to himself, as he looked through the window, he could afford the whole damn shop, as well as all the damn shops on the damn avenue, as if, short of having a massive brain fart, he would ever consider doing anything of the sort.

As he walked into the watchmaker's shop, little did he know he would never walk back out. His time was just about up. Had he heeded his father, he would have known.

1960

"AH, PROFESSOR LEONARD!" GOMEZ EXCLAIMED, AS THE TALL, thin, slightly stoop-shouldered gentleman entered the jewelry store.

"And good day to you, my fine Mr. Gomez," Leonard Webb responded.

"Well, I see you have brought young Leo with you today. It is not often that we get to see the little Albert Einstein. There is a special occasion, no?" Gomez asked.

"I suppose if anyone would know, you would, as many years as I've been purchasing watches from you."

"Correct, Professor! We each have much to be thankful for, do we not? And so, if I may ask, what is the special occasion this time? Have you found another piece of your puzzle, or perhaps the little genius did, eh?" he asked patting Leo on the head. "I would not be surprised."

"Nope, not today. Today we are celebrating something truly miraculous. Something much greater than work."

"Greater than a man's work? Que es?" Gomez asked, eyes wide at the thought.

"A little bird tells me there is a beautiful new member of the Gomez family."

"Ah, Professor. Bien. Si! I must show you. Sientese, por favor. You too, pequeno Leo, please sit with your father. I will get Elena y Lena," he replied in Spanish and English as he tended to do when excited, which was most of the time. "Dios es bueno, no?"

"Si, Senor Gomez, God is very good indeed."

"Este es el bebe Lena." Mrs. Elena Gomez returned a minute later with her beaming husband and presented her infant, less than a week old, to Leonard and Leo Webb.

"Oh, what a sweetheart," Professor Webb said, taking the infant and cradling her in his arms. Mrs. Gomez folded back the pink blanket so Leo could see the baby's face.

"Bebe Lena," she said softly to Leo, smiling.

"See, Leo," Mr. Webb said. "It's been eight years since you were this little. I'd forgotten how tiny infants are."

"See! See!" Mr. Gomez exclaimed, pointing. "Sonrie. She smiles. She likes you, Professor Webb."

"Oh she probably just has gas," Professor Webb chuckled, and the Gomezes laughed.

"Dad, can we buy the watch now?" Leo interrupted, as he got up off his chair and went over to one of the watch counters.

"No watches today, Leo. I told you we were coming to see Baby Lena."

"Can we go then? We saw her."

Sensing his friend's discomfort, Gomez interjected, "Well, young Leo, do you want to see a watch we have just for you? I think you will like it."

"Sure!" Leo exclaimed excitedly.

"Really, Mr. Gomez, that isn't necessary...."

"Oh, but I insist. A special watch for the special son of my best customer to commemorate the birth of Lena," he said, bending below the counter and pulling out a small watch box. He handed the box to Leo who opened it immediately.

"Wow, cool!" Leo exclaimed. "Mickey Mouse! Look dad, it's a Mickey Mouse watch."

"Mr. Gomez, really, it's not necessary…."

"Tut, tut, tut," Gomez replied. "It's not free. It's a very valuable watch. Therefore, I must insist on a very high price."

"That's better. How much?" Mr. Webb asked, looking back down at Lena and smiling.

"You will have to return my daughter to me," Gomez replied, as Elena giggled and punched her husband. "Como un payaso," she said, as she took Lena back from Professor Webb, and Leo wandered off.

"She says I'm a clown, but I definitely got the better end of that deal," Gomez said, watching his wife return with his daughter to the living quarters upstairs, above the store. "Plus, I think Leo is happy now too, eh?" Gomez said. Then, whispering, "God forgive me, Professor, but Leo took a ring off the counter and put it in his pocket."

"Ugh! Thanks, Mr. Gomez. I worry about that boy. Smarts aren't everything."

"Leo!" he called. We did not come here for rings. Put it back where you found it, now!"

"Ah, dad, it's just a crummy ring," Leo responded, digging in his pocket. "If he didn't want me to take it, he shouldn't have left it out on the counter."

"And if you want something, you can ask, mister. Give me the ring," he said, holding out his hand. "Taking things out of stores and not paying for them is stealing. We don't steal, do you understand me?" he continued, replacing the ring in its display slot. "Is this the way you say thank you to Mr. Gomez for giving you the Mickey Mouse watch? Now apologize to Mr. Gomez."

"Sorry, sir," Leo said. "Thank you for the Mickey Mouse watch."

"You are welcome, young Mr. Leo."

"Okay, son, let's go. Good bye, Mr. Gomez. You have a beautiful daughter."

"I will see you when you solve the next puzzle piece," Gomez replied.

"Hopefully I find it before Lena starts school."

"Of course you will, Professor. Vaya con Dios!"

"And may God continue to bless you and your family also, Mr. Gomez."

1969

"HI, PROFESSOR WEBB," NINE-YEAR-OLD LENA SAID AS HE WALKED into the jewelry store. "Who's he?"

"Well hello, Lena. This is my son, Leo."

"Dad, I've told you my name is Frank. Call me Frank. I hate Leo."

"Lena, I apologize. This is my son, Leo Francis Webb. He prefers to be called Frank."

"Oh, hi Frank," Lena said.

"Dad, can we make it quick?" seventeen-year-old Leo Francis asked, ignoring Lena.

"I'll go get Papa," Lena said, as she began to run to the back of the store. Just then her father came out of the back office.

"Ah, Professor Webb! What a sight for sore eyes. And Leo, my, how tall you've grown. I see your father often, but I haven't seen you in a long time."

"Hey, Mr. Gomez."

"Another puzzle piece?" Gomez asked hopefully.

"Indeed, my good man. And we shall mark the occasion in the customary way, with the purchase of your finest Timex," Professor Webb replied.

"Oh, brother," Leo Francis groaned.

"Tut, tut," his father continued. "It is a time-honored Webb tradition."

"No it's not. Grampa never did it. You started it."

"True, but traditions need to start somewhere."

"And end somewhere," Leo Francis snorted, as he plopped down in a chair.

"Timex makes a very fine watch, Leo," Gomez interjected.

"Come on. A Timex? No sale. They're so cheap."

"If they're so cheap, perhaps you will buy it," his father said.

"Don't expect me to waste my money on cheap watches."

Lena saw it all, heard every word, and remembered. After Professor Webb purchased his latest Timex watch and left with his son, she spoke to her father about what it all meant.

"Papa, that man, Professor Webb, why does he come in every year to buy a new watch?"

"Lena, Professor Webb does not buy a watch every year. Sometimes he buys twice a year, other times once a year, and sometimes a year or two will go by when he does not buy a watch."

"But why so many watches, and why are they always Timex watches?"

"Lena, darling, it is a long story...."

"Oh, goody, Papa. I love your stories."

"Well, this is a true story. Professor Webb and I have been friends for a long time. He was one of my first customers when I opened this shop long before you were born. In fact, we are the same age. The first time we met, in 1944, we were both twenty-five years old. He first came into my shop with his father, who was also named Leonard Webb."

"Wow, three Leonard Webbs: Professor Webb, his father, and his son."

"That is correct."

"They must like the name Leonard."

"It's just a tradition. Sometimes the son is named after the father."

"And sometimes the daughter is named after the mother, like me and mama, right?"

"Yes, that is right. Anyway, Professor Webb's father only came in that first time. He never returned."

"Why not?"

"I'm not sure, but I don't think he liked it here."

"Leo . . . um, I mean, Leo Francis, doesn't like it here either," Lena noted.

"You see that too, do you? Well, I suppose you are correct. Professor Webb's son and father seem to have that, and some other things, in common."

"What other things?"

"Well, you know how Professor Webb likes to buy a watch whenever something good happens in his work or in his life?"

"Yes. I think it's sweet. It's a great idea."

"I agree. He is a good and creative man, I think, and very, very smart, which is why he is a famous professor in a big university, The University of Pennsylvania. Penn is one of the finest universities in the whole world."

"And Professor Webb teaches there?"

"Yes, he does."

"Wow. He must be a genius."

"I think he is, but he says his son is an even bigger genius."

"Really?"

"Yes."

"Professor Webb is really nice, Papa, but Leo Francis does not seem so nice."

"Now, Lena, enough of that. Mama is right when she says not to say bad things about people. It doesn't do any good."

"Professor Webb is very patient with Leo Francis."

"Yes. I think that's because Professor Webb's father was so tough on Professor Webb. Professor Webb's father drove him very hard. He pushed him to excel in school, which he did. Professor Webb's father wanted Professor Webb to go into business and make a lot of money, but Professor Webb did not want to go into business."

"Why not? Did he want to be a teacher?"

"Well, yes, a teacher, and a scientist."

"Wow, a teacher and a scientist? He must be very smart."

"Yes, Professor Webb has devoted his life to science. He loves physics, which is the science of how things move and how the world is built. But his father did not care about any of that. He just wanted his son to make a lot of money."

"Is Professor Webb poor?"

"We should be so poor. No, Professor Webb, I think, makes a very good living. He is not poor at all, but he is not very rich. His father wanted him to be very rich. Professor Webb knows his father was disappointed in him, which makes him sad."

"Professor Webb is sad?"

"Sometimes. Sometimes he will come and talk to me after I close the store. We will just sit and talk in this office. That's how I know he is a good man, and how I know he is sad sometimes."

"So, he's sad because he thinks his father doesn't like him?"

"No, his father died many years ago. Professor Webb is sad because his son shares his father's beliefs."

"You mean Leo Francis likes money more than science?"

"Yes, and Professor Webb thinks that Leo Francis will go into business instead of working with him on his big science puzzle. It is his dream to solve the puzzle with his son."

"What kind of puzzle?"

"I don't know. He tried to explain it to me once, but I really don't understand it that well. He calls it the Unified Theory, but I don't know what it means. I just know no one can figure it out and they have been working on it for almost fifty years."

"Wow, fifty years! It must be a huge puzzle."

"The hugest, which is why Professor Webb wants Leo Francis to help him."

"Why won't Leo Francis help his dad solve the puzzle?"

"Lena, my darling, I do not know. It seems that Leo Francis will have to figure things out as he grows up. Maybe he will work with his father one day. I hope so."

"Me, too."

"But, whether he does or not, I bet Professor Webb will figure out that big puzzle anyway."

"Because he is so smart?"

"Because he is so good."

"Papa, you forgot to tell me why he always buys Timex watches."

Gomez paused before answering. "I really believe buying watches is an excuse to visit here and be close to friends. I think the Timexes mean he has solved a little piece of his puzzle. If he ever comes in here and buys a Hamilton...." Gomez smiled at Lena.

"Yes?" Lena asked, expectedly.

"It would mean something very good for the world."

1972

GOMEZ RECOGNIZED THE NOW-FAMILIAR LIGHT TAP-TAP-TAP ON THE front door of the jewelry store, just two minutes after he locked up and turned the window sign to "Closed."

He hurried to unlock the door. Professor Webb was standing in the doorway.

"Ah, Professor. Good to see you again. Please, come in, come in."

"It's not Professor anymore, Mr. Gomez."

"Excuse me?" Gomez asked as they walked, yet again, to the back of the store.

"They canned me. I wasn't publishing enough. But, they're right. I knew I needed to publish more but, well, I was so close. So close…." he repeated as his voice trailed off and he plopped down in the chair in Gomez's rear office.

"Would you care for something to drink, Professor? Scotch?"

"Excellent. Yes, that would be excellent, my old friend. You know, you should have been a psychologist, the way you read people."

"Ah, that is nice of you to say, Professor. But, trust me, I have my hands full just fixing these newfangled watches coming out nowadays. Can you believe, electronic? Blip, blip, blip. No moving parts. What is there to fix? No. I am afraid these electronic watches will be the death of me."

"All the more reason to move into medicine. People will always break down, as I have."

"Now, now, now, Professor you are not broken. You just said you are very close to solving your big puzzle."

"Yes, so, so close. I think anyway, but I can't really say for sure. I mean the puzzle pieces aren't all the same size. The last piece may be so huge that it represents 99% of the puzzle. I may think I'm close, yet I might still be a lifetime away.

"Unfortunately for me, that's just a little too large a commitment for the university to make. They need me to publish. Without that last piece, there is nothing I could publish that would make any sense. It's all up here," he continued, pointing to his head.

"But it is all so very conceptual. Publishing anything, without knowing the final solution, would not make any sense to anyone who has not invested a lifetime into the arcane corner of the universe which I alone, apparently, inhabit."

"Can your son help you?" Professor Webb's wince let Gomez know he had hit a nerve.

"Not in my lifetime," Professor Webb replied. "He has elected to major in computer science, of all things. It's all very cutting edge, he assures me. That's where the future is, computer science. Well, at least it's science, I guess. There may be something to be said for that.

"It's just that he's so focused on making money. Money, money, money. That's all that boy thinks about. Is that what it's all about, Gomez? Having the most stuff? Whatever happened to making the world a better place?"

"He could make the world a better place. Perhaps he will make a wonderful computer."

"Computers are just big calculators. He won't be advancing science. He'll just be perfecting calculators."

"But, Professor. Can't better calculators help scientists work faster or better?"

"Yes, I suppose you may be on to something there. I just hope he doesn't become blinded by the money, that's all."

"Maybe he can be both wealthy and a scientist, no? Maybe his computers will let him make big discoveries, no?"

Professor Webb took a long sip from his glass, then sat up straight, looking at Gomez eye-to-eye.

"If he advances science, it will be by accident. And he's too gifted to rely on serendipity. If he would choose to advance science, there is no doubt in my mind he would. The world needs people like my son, truly gifted people, to get serious about using their talents to help the world, not to enrich themselves.

"Maybe he can do both, you may be correct. He will definitely achieve one or the other – great scientific discovery or great wealth, depending which he chooses to focus.

"From where I sit, he will focus on wealth, so he will be wealthy. The world does not need for him to be wealthy. The world needs for him to use the gifts God has given him for the benefit of all, not one."

Professor Webb slumped back into his chair and rubbed his eyes. A few minutes of silence passed before Gomez broke the silence.

"Your son sees you, you know. He sees how hard you work, and he knows, as I suspect you do, that you will never be wealthy. He has never struck me as one who is going to sacrifice, as you have."

"Yes, he is my father's grandson. Where did I come from?"

"I let you in the front door, remember?" Gomez smiled.

"Nice try, my old friend," Professor Webb said, as he chuckled and stood. "Yes, maybe you're right. I cannot expect him to sacrifice. That has to be his choice. He is growing up and has to make his own choices now. In the meantime, I am going to have to find a place to conduct my experiments, as money also seems to be important to folks at the university."

"You will be fine, Professor. You are a good man and a great friend. You will figure out your puzzle."

"Yes, God willing. But will I ever figure out my son?"

1981

"PROFESSOR WEBB, HOW NICE TO SEE YOU AGAIN," LENA CALLED across the store as Professor Webb entered.

"Likewise," he replied. "You look more and more beautiful each time I see you. How are you, Lena?"

"I'm very well, thank you. Guess what?" she smiled at him from behind one of the store counters.

"What?"

"I graduated, see?" she said holding up her school ring for him to see.

"Well, well, now. I would have expected nothing less of you, young lady. Does this make you the first college graduate of the Gomez family?"

"It does. Papa is so proud. Mama would have been too."

"Indeed she would have been. I am sure she smiles down on you every day. So, have you gotten a job with your brand new college degree?"

"I have, and that's the best part. Next week I start working for one of the biggest accounting firms in the country. It's going to be great. I will get so much experience working in all kinds of client businesses. I can't wait to get started."

"And who is going to help your father in the shop?"

"Papa agrees that we will hire a worker or two. We can afford it now that I will be earning a salary. In a few years, after I gain some experience and know more about business, I am going to franchise Papa's business so he can retire."

"Professor Webb!" Gomez exclaimed, coming into the store from the back office. "What brings you to our little store?"

"My dear Mr. Gomez, Lena here tells me your little store may be one of many in a few years."

"From your lips to God's ears," Gomez replied, shaking the professor's hand warmly in both of his. "And what is it that you have in the bag there?"

"This, my good fellow, is a little something we can drink to celebrate Lena's graduation from college," he said, pulling a bottle of red wine from a shopping bag.

"Oh, Professor Webb, how wonderful!" Lena exclaimed. "I'll get some glasses," she said, running upstairs.

"Wait a minute," Gomez said. "Something's not adding up. You didn't know Lena graduated until you walked in here and you already had the wine."

"You are a wise old coot aren't you?" Professor Webb laughed.

"Don't forget, Professor, I'm younger than you by four days," said Gomez, pointing up at the professor.

Lena returned with three wine glasses and a corkscrew and began to uncork the bottle of wine.

The Professor thought for a minute and then confessed, "Well maybe we can celebrate something else at the same time."

"More good news?" Gomez asked hopefully. "They gave you your job back, finally?"

"Better than that. Much better," Professor Webb replied.

"What could be better than that?" Gomez asked, spreading his arms wide.

"I'll tell you what. Today, Mr. Gomez, in addition to Lena's wonderful graduation from college, we celebrate my very first purchase of a Hamilton watch, right here in your store. How's that?"

Gomez thought for a moment. Suddenly his eyes went wide.

"Madre de Dios!" Gomez exclaimed. "La ultima pieza del rompecabezas. Usted encontro, no?"

"I'm sorry, but I don't understand."

"Papa asks if you found the last piece of the puzzle."

"Lena, your Papa is a wise old coot, after all. Thirty-seven years ago, I first walked into this shop and purchased my first watch. Do you know why?" he asked both of them.

"Because that same day, the day in 1944 I first met your Papa, Lena, I started working on that puzzle. I was so excited. As excited as you are now to begin your professional career. But yes. Now, after all these years, I have indeed finally found the last puzzle piece. The puzzle is complete."

Later, after Gomez had turned on the music, and they had danced in pairs – first Lena and her father, then Lena and Professor Webb, and finally the two men – after they had finished off the wine, and after Professor Webb had received his first Hamilton watch, a gift from Gomez to mark the occasion, it was then that the two old friends sat down on the back patio yet again, as they had many times over the years, and talked. And, for the first time, Lena was with them.

"I returned from California a few weeks ago," the professor began. "I visited my son, who now refers to himself as L. Frank Webb. He has divorced himself from the name Leonard, it seems. I suppose I should be happy that he kept his last name. But it is clear to me that, in name and location, he wishes to be as far away from me as possible, and that's okay. I understand.

"But there's good news with this. The good news is that he and his wife have a newborn baby boy, my grandson, Michael. Oh, and what a sweetheart he is. I wish my wife had lived to see her grandson. She would have loved him. And smart? I think Baby Michael received the absolute best of the Webb genes. If I'm right, and I am sure I am, then he's going to be even brighter than his father who is brighter than me."

"I'm not so sure your son is brighter than you, Professor," Lena interrupted.

"It is true, Lena. I have always known it."

"But, Professor, really, you solved the puzzle. How much smarter could he be?"

"That's the sad part, Lena. What he could have achieved in science – oh well, let's not go down that old worn path again, shall we? It's a tired lament and worrying about it won't change anything.

"But each generation in my family, for some reason, is smarter than its preceding generation. That is crystal clear to me, make no mistake about it.

"So I hold out great hope for Michael, for that reason; but, especially for another reason. In looking at my father, then me, then my son, and now my grandson, do you see a pattern?"

"Hate to say it, but bad-good-bad-good comes to mind," Lena replied.

"Well, I wouldn't put it that way. I was thinking more along the lines of capitalist, scientist, capitalist, scientist – hopefully, this last is correct, though we will have to see with Michael. If he doesn't become a scientist, then I will defer to the sequence you note, Lena, and conclude that Baby Michael will someday, I hope to God with all my heart, be a very good man.

"In the meantime, there is something very important I need to talk to you and your father about. It relates to my puzzle.

"My son moved to the west coast to seek his fortune in computers and, it appears, he has been quite successful in that regard. He and his friends from college are involved with what they call software. They actually started their own company and have many employees. Don't ask me where they came up with the money but, apparently, California is a good place to have a software company. He tells me there are special people, venture capitalists, who helped him with the money."

"That's good, no?" asked Gomez.

"I suppose," Professor Webb replied. "I just know that my son will always be pursuing money – more and more money all the time. He will never think he has enough. That troubles me. It troubles me so much that, on the plane ride back, I made a very, very important decision which involves you and your daughter."

"Us?" Lena asked, surprised.

"Yes, Lena. You. You and your father are the best friends I have ever had. You are honest, hard-working people who are very interested in others. That is why you are so successful with this business. People like coming here, and coming back, because of the way you make them feel, and because of the way you show an interest in them. That is a very special quality which comes naturally to you both.

"And since you have been so good, and so accommodating to me over the years, I find that I must ask a very big and very important favor of you.

"Lena, I have solved what's called the Unified Theory. It is the most important scientific discovery in history. Thousands of teams of scientists have been working at it for about sixty years now, but God has seen fit to allow me to understand the final answer. And, since I understand it, I know how wonderfully good it can be. It can be good beyond all telling.

"I also understand how dangerous the solution can be, were it to fall into the wrong hands. It could end life on this planet, and many planets, forever. Therefore, I cannot permit it to fall into the wrong hands.

"Now, I have consulted a very famous attorney and we have talked extensively over the past few weeks. I am very certain of what I must do. Initially, this attorney advised me against what I had in mind but, after a while, he saw how unyielding I was, and he advised me how to protect my interests, and legally do what I believe is best for all.

"First, you must understand that I discovered the secret by myself, without any outside assistance at all. The attorney did not believe me at first, saying I must have had help from people at the University, so that my discovery would be the property of the University, even though the University and I parted ways almost ten years ago.

"I assured him of this truth: everything we did at the University to solve the Unified Theory was a waste of time. We were going down dead end after dead end, always thinking we were making progress or understanding a little more. It was at those times that I would come in here to buy a Timex watch.

"However, after I was let go, I was literally like a man without a life raft, adrift on a huge ocean with no means of support. At the time, I was devastated and began to have bad dreams at night. There were times when I would not sleep for days on end. I was an emotional train wreck, as they say.

"One night I had a dream I will never forget. I was in my shop at home, working on my puzzle when, suddenly, there was a young man there with me. He looked to be in his early twenties or so. I know that I had never seen him before. Then he asked me a question. He asked, 'Why do we do this?'

"Well, I didn't know what to say. I looked down at my hand-written notes and charts and equations and saw that I was holding a watch in my hands, except the back was off the watch, so we could see the internal mechanisms. I said, 'It is what we must do. We must use our gifts.'

"Then there was a tremendous crashing sound like an explosion and I awoke in a cold sweat. My heart was racing. I had no idea who that young man was. I knew only what I had to do, and that what I had to do to solve the puzzle involved measuring time.

"That same day, after many months of self-doubt, fear, and lone-liness I began to pull myself together emotionally and vowed to continue my work.

"With my wife's blessing, I poured our life savings into my research. I began a period of extensive reading. I dug heavily into what others were doing in the field. Scientists all over the world seemed to be attacking the problem from new and unique perspec-tives. Many of these approaches were, on their face, vastly different, one from another.

"Mine was an exceptional vantage point. It was as if I were sitting in the Colosseum watching the warriors below slugging it out, except, from where I sat, I could see all the errors of logic, the false starts, the weak hypotheses, the feints, bluffs, and misdirec-tion. I could see who was strong and who was weak.

"I classified the strong into three separate categories, based upon the very distinct paths they were pursuing. Doing so permitted me to see a commonality in the approaches that none of the individual participants could see. They were too close to the forest to see the trees, as it were.

"In the end, I knew which direction I had to pursue. I knew it was a long path, even were I to find help. Given the paucity of resources at my disposal, it would be that much longer. The question I faced was, would I have enough time? Would I be able to finish the work I was to start? I didn't know, but I did not waste much time worrying about it, because I didn't have much time to waste.

"In the end, I was successful. I wish my wife were here to share our success with me. That is one regret: that she did not live long enough to see the good all her sacrifices accomplished. Another regret is that my son did not help me. Perhaps it is for the best, though. He is happy and I have solved my puzzle."

"And what is the solution, Professor?" Lena asked.

"Lena, on the advice of my attorney, I cannot say. You see, someday, when the solution is made public, there will be an investigation into who knew what and when. There will likely be claims that this solution belongs to the University, or to some other organization, either claiming to have helped me or claiming to be primarily responsible for deriving the solution.

"My son may even sue to own the solution. Anyway, that investigation may involve you and your father, Lena, so the less you know, the better off you will be."

"Us? Why would they investigate us?" Lena asked.

"Because it is possible that you may end up owning the solution someday."

"Excuse me?"

"Right now the solution is written down in my journal which is being kept in a locked vault by my attorney. In my will I state that all rights to the solution and the journal notes will belong to your father and you, under a specific set of circumstances.

"If, in your opinion, my son has turned his life around in such a way that you believe I would approve, then the solution becomes his. If he does not, if he remains selfish, self-centered, and focused on amassing wealth, then ownership will pass to his son, Michael, but only if Michael is a good man focused on the needs of others. And, having now seen him with my own eyes, I strongly believe Michael will be a very good man."

"Bad - good - bad - good," Lena recalled. "Like father, unlike son."

"But, if I'm wrong about Michael, Lena, then the answer will legally belong to your father, then you, and then to any children you may have someday."

Professor Webb paused now and looked at Gomez and Lena. "So, my two good friends, is this acceptable to you?"

"Yes," they replied. "We love you, Professor," Lena said, reaching down now and hugging Professor Webb, as he sat in his chair.

"Es cierto," Gomez agreed. "It's true. We do."

"Good, in that case, perhaps there is one more thing you can do for me."

"Name it, Professor," Lena said.

The professor reached into his pocket and pulled out a small box. He opened it to display a Timex watch.

"You purchased that here. That is our watch box," Lena said, seeing the "Gomez" label on the bottom.

"Correct, but I have made modifications to the mechanisms inside the watch. It has something to do with my discovery," he said, before explaining the watch's new capability to Lena and Gomez whose eyes went wide when they understood.

"Madre de Dios," Gomez whispered his oft-used prayer.

"Madre de Dios," Lena exclaimed, blessing herself.

2005

THERE WAS JUST ONE MORE STORE HE NEEDED TO VISIT BEFORE leaving to catch his flight back to the west coast. None of the five jewelry stores in eastern Montgomery County, Pennsylvania, provided him with the answer he sought. Still, he felt certain that his was the correct course of action.

As a newly minted Wharton School MBA, he knew it was decision time. It had come down to this. He had to make a decision among three different career opportunities. He could accept the position Goldman Sachs had offered him, which, if he did, would almost certainly assure him of tremendous wealth and his father's admiration.

Or, he could accept a management position in his father's extremely successful software company back West which, if he did, would almost certainly assure him of tremendous wealth and his father's admiration.

Or, three, he could follow his heart, which would guarantee his life would have purpose. And decision number three's future was looking ever more tenuous, the longer he went without finding that one particular jewelry shop.

He had two hurdles to overcome in his quest to locate that store. First, he had absolutely no idea where the shop was, other than a vague feeling that it must be near his father's birthplace – Hatboro, Pennsylvania. Second, he had less than three hours to find it and get to his departing flight.

He parked his rental car, fed the meter, and walked up to what he felt was possibly his last opportunity for happiness: Gomez' Timeless Jewelry. His heart sank, however, for he knew that Gomez' Timeless Jewelry was one of the biggest franchise jewelry chains in the country.

The odds were slim that this was the quaint little shop he envisioned. Still, the store was in a strip of stores which were all decades old, so he entered the store with some hope.

There were, easily, a dozen customers in the store at this mid-afternoon hour. Entering, he looked back and up at the bell that jingled as he entered the store. Quaint. And the display counters and vinyl tile floor, though clean, were dated. Not big or corporate at all. A good sign.

"Hello, may I help you?" the young man asked. He appeared to be in his late teens, and sported a name tag which read simply, "Win."

"Win," the man replied, pointing to the name tag, "is that...."

"My name," the teen replied. "I apologize for interrupting, but I get that all the time. It's short for Winnie or Winston. I guess one of these days I'll break down and get a new name tag."

"Winston, huh? I guess your folks were Winston Churchill fans."

"Actually, my grandparents were Churchill fans, and my mom was a fan of my grandparents. Hence," he said, pointing to his nametag, "I didn't get a vote."

The man chuckled. "Interesting watch you have under the glass there. It doesn't appear to be working, there's no stem to wind, and it is permanently encased in a box without access," the man said.

"Oh, it's working alright," Win replied.

"Are you sure it works? The second hand is not moving."

"It is moving so slowly you cannot see it move. It is not actually a second hand."

"What is it then, if not a second hand? It sure looks like a second hand."

"Sorry, I don't have a clue. All I know is it's a very special, one-of-a-kind piece. It's for show only, not for sale. My mom had it installed there permanently in 1982."

"Is your mom here? May I speak to her about it?"

"She's out now, but we expect her back shortly. Would you like to wait?"

"Yes, I would, but I can't. I have a flight to catch. By the way, what does that inscription say?"

"It says, 'Leonard Webb II 1919 – 1981. The Greatest Man in the History of Time.'"

The young man looked stunned.

"You okay?" Win asked.

"Did you know him?" the man asked Win.

"Long before my time," Win replied.

"Me, too."

"Did you know him?" Win asked.

"No, but he was my grandfather. Thank you, thank you so much," the man said, as he grabbed Win's hand in both of his and shook it. "And thank your mother for me, will you? I have to go."

The young man rushed out the front door. He had received his answer, and he now knew what he must do. He jumped into his car as Lena stepped out of her car.

Seeing his mother arriving, Win ran to the front door and called after the man as he drove away, "Wait! Wait! My mom's here," he shouted, too late, as the man hurried away in his car.

Win walked up to Lena. "You'll never guess who that was," he said.

But she had seen the young man's face. He resembled his grandfather not only in physical features but in excited countenance. There was no mistaking that.

"Oh, I know who he is," Lena replied. "That is Michael Webb."

2016

L. Frank Webb III stepped into the store, out of the cold, driving rain to the tinkling of the bell above the door. The first thing he thought was the establishment lacked an electronic alarm system. "Foolish," he muttered as he shook his raincoat, spraying water onto the floor.

He noticed that the store was bright and clean, though dated. There were no other customers at this late hour, given the stormy conditions outside.

As he walked further into the store, he noticed a middle-aged woman sitting behind one of the counters. She was holding rosary beads in her hands, praying.

She looked up, put the rosary into her pocket, stood and asked, "May I help you?"

"I suppose you were praying for customers. Well, here I am. The answer to your prayers," Webb snickered dismissively as he looked down at the display cases, not making eye contact with Lena. "I want to buy the most expensive Rolex you have. Where do you keep them?" he continued.

"I'm sorry, sir, but we do not carry Rolexes."

"What? What kind of self-respecting jeweler doesn't carry Rolex?"

She ignored this. "We do have some very fine Longines and Hamiltons."

"And do they still come in those silly egg-shaped silly putty cases?" he asked, looking up and making eye contact for the first time.

Lena gasped and raised her hand to her face. "Madre de Dios," she whispered, when she recognized him.

"Hey, do I know you? You're, wait, wait…Lisa, right?"

"Lena," she whispered.

"Hah! Lena, yeah, that's it. I never forget a face."

"Excuse me, sir. The phone's ringing," she lied. "I will be right back," she said as she ran to the back of the store.

"What should I do? What should I do?" She was frantic. "How could this be happening, after all these years? How could it be that he shows up now, right now? Mother of God, help me. My God! My God!"

She was pacing now. "Should I call 9-1-1? If I do, what happens when they get here and nothing has happened? What happens if I don't call? What to do? What do I do?"

She stopped pacing, took a deep breath and decided. "I must call." She quickly dialed 9-1-1. Then she walked back into the store.

"So, Lena, tell me. You've never left this place? You've never left Hatboro?"

"No, sir." She was scared.

"Too bad. You could have had a great life, like I did."

"We have managed nicely, thank you, sir."

"Uh-huh. Nice, not great. You can drive a Mack truck through the difference you know."

"Yes, sir. I suppose."

"Guess that explains why I have lost more Rolexes than you have ever sold."

"Perhaps I could size you for a smaller band," Lena said.

"Uh-huh. Very funny, but I don't think you catch my drift. By the way, why is this watch locked in a case here?"

"It is a special watch. Your father gave it to my father and me."

"Really? Well isn't that interesting? A cheap Timex, I see. Really cheap. There's no winding stem. No battery either, I guess. It has stopped working – stuck at one second to twelve," he said, staring intensely at 'the commemorative plate in front of the watch.

"'The greatest man in the history of time'? Are you serious? My father? He died destitute, and because of him my mother died poor also. He accomplished nothing in his sorry life."

"Don't you say that, Mr. Webb!" Lena said firmly. "Don't you dare say that. Your father was a great man. The greatest of all time, for his discoveries."

"Discoveries? What discoveries? He discovered nothing. His life was a total waste," he laughed at her. "My father couldn't discover the moon with a telescope."

"You see that? You see that watch?" Lena shouted now, pointing at the Timex enclosed in the case. "That proves otherwise."

"How? It's a broken Timex. That's all it is. A broken down piece of worthless crap."

"That broken down piece of worthless crap is tracking your life, Mr. Webb. Your broken down, worthless crap of a life which, when that second hand reaches twelve, will end. I was praying the rosary for you when you walked in."

"Save your prayers, bitch. I can buy and sell you a million times over, so you'd do better to pray for someone who needs it, like yourself! Do you really believe that voodoo garbage? Do you? You think my father could invent a time machine? Are you that gullible? My father died poor. Poor!" he screamed.

"I have more money than I could spend in ten lifetimes and you say my life is crap? I'll tell you what's crap. My miserable son-of-a-bitch father's life, your life, that idiotic misguided soft-headed lunatic son of mine's life, and the life of every other weak-minded, blue collar sap who lives in this God-forsaken wasteland of a town.

"And I'll tell you another thing. I'm sick of it all. Sick of you, sick of my father, sick of my son. The whole sorry bunch of you can just go rot in hell! Bunch of losers. Losers! That's what you are!" he screamed.

As he headed for the door Lena asked, "And how are you going to take it all with you, all that money that you can't spend in ten lifetimes?"

He looked at her with contempt, as the second hand struck twelve and the alarm sounded on the Timex, the first and last time it would ever sound.

As he reached for the door handle he turned to face Lena. "I'll see you in hell. Look me up. I'll be the one wearing the Gucci...."

He never finished the sentence. A massive coronary claimed his life. He was dead before he hit the floor.

Lena rushed to grab him as he fell. The police rushed in and saw her cradling L. Frank Webb's lifeless body in her arms as she wept. The rosary had fallen out of her pocket and was draped across his Gucci leather loafers.

2016 (Three Days Later)

LENA ATTENDED THE FUNERAL OUT OF RESPECT FOR PROFESSOR Webb. Win attended the funeral out of respect for his mother.

She was dreading the funeral, as she really would not know anyone there. The only person she knew, even remotely, was the deceased, Leo Webb, or L. Frank Webb III, which is the way the obituary and Wall Street Journal headlines referred to him. And, other than the few minutes before he died, she hadn't seen him in decades, when she herself was quite young.

As a successful, wealthy, and well-educated Latin American franchise entrepreneur and business owner, Lena was accustomed to attending large public affairs – such as this funeral Mass at the Cathedral of Saints Peter and Paul was likely to be. Still, she was pretty certain she would not be hob-nobbing with the Fortune 500 captains of industry who regularly associated with L. Frank Webb III.

She was not nervous about conversing with any of these luminaries, as she was quite an accomplished public speaker and sought-after lecturer.

She was not intimidated by the overflowing crowd, lengthy procession, television cameras, reporters, or by the fact that the Cardinal himself was saying mass. (Ironically, Webb's company had contributed well to the church for the honor.)

She was not uncomfortable speaking to a family she did not know, as her own faith was quite strong and her condolences evidenced that.

She was nervous about meeting Webb's son, Michael, who surely would attend his own father's funeral.

As she and Win stood in the pew, watching the procession of the casket up the center aisle of the cathedral, she wondered about Michael. She wondered if he had become the good man Professor Webb believed he would become. She had few facts to go on, for, try as she might, she could find nothing published about Michael. Google returned no search results. He did not even have a Facebook page.

His father was unhappy with him, apparently, so she took some hope from that. Perhaps Michael was not the money-loving capitalist his father had become. This would have pleased Professor Webb, she knew.

Still, she had read nothing about Michael pursuing a career in science either, and Professor Webb felt certain that Michael was to be the smartest of the Webb clan.

So, what had become of Michael after he ran out of her store eleven years ago? And why had he been there in the first place? These are questions she had not been able to answer.

As the procession came to a stop in the front of the church, the Cardinal consecrated the soul of the deceased.

It was now time for Mass to begin. The Cardinal walked up the steps to the huge main altar, bowed, and walked over to his chair, where he stood momentarily and announced that he would be concelebrating this mass with the decedent's son, Father Michael Webb.

And Lena knew, in that instant, that the prayers of Professor Webb had indeed been answered.

2016 (Continued)

Two nights later, as Lena was closing the store for the day and locking up, there was a gentle tap-tap-tap at the front door. Lena opened the door to see Father Michael Webb standing there.

"Hello, Mrs. Gomez," he said. "I am Father Michael Webb. I think you knew my father and grandfather."

Lena smiled, "Indeed I did, Father. Won't you please come in? We have much to talk about," she said, clasping both of his hands.

"I want to thank you for tending to my father in his final moments. The news reports said this is where he died," he said, stepping just inside and motioning to the floor where he stood. "I was hoping you might be willing to talk to me for a few minutes."

"Please, Father, you must be tired. Come to the back. We can sit in the office and talk."

As he followed her to the back of the store, he noticed the watch and plaque were still where he remembered them. "The greatest man in the history of time," he said. "Perhaps you will explain to me why you believe that."

In the back room they each took a seat and Lena began.

"Father, your grandfather and my father would sit in this office, in these same two chairs, many a day over the years and discuss many things. Although from vastly different backgrounds, and with vastly different gifts, they formed a long and deep friendship.

"Your grandfather was gifted. There can be no question about that. But, he was also deeply troubled. He was most concerned with his son, your father. They just never saw eye-to-eye."

"Tell me about it," Father interrupted. "My father was at odds with most people."

"Yes, well, after many years of sorrow, your grandfather decided that there was not much he could do to make his son be the scientist he had hoped he would become."

"Really? Grandpa wanted Dad to be a scientist? I didn't know that. My dad never told me that – although, truth be told, my dad never talked much about Grandpa or growing up."

Lena continued. "It was evident to my father and me that your dad, even when he was a boy, was going to be a handful. If Professor Webb said right, he'd go left. If Professor Webb said it was raining outside, he'd say it was sunny. They agreed on nothing."

"Yes, dad was headstrong, to say the least. You either agreed with him or you were out; he'd have nothing to do with you."

"I am sorry to hear that."

"I am sorry to have to say it."

"Your grandfather suffered in other ways also. The University released him in the middle of his career. That was a big blow which set him back financially and in a lot of other ways. Ironically, though, as he explained it to us, it was probably the biggest factor in his success."

"And what success was that?"

"My father and I believe your grandfather started trying to solve the Unified Theory around 1944. He didn't succeed until 1981 about the time you were born."

"Wait. Did you say my grandfather solved the Unified Theory?"

"Yes."

"That's impossible. That theory is unsolvable with current levels of technology and understanding."

"Father, really. I would think you of all people would know that nothing is impossible with God. And your grandfather definitely had God's ear and His blessing. I believe your grandfather was a holy man, sent by God, for a definite purpose.

"Your grandfather referred to it as his puzzle. He was always trying to solve pieces of his puzzle. And whenever he felt as though he had found another piece he would come in here and buy a Timex to mark the occasion.

"One day, after many years, he came in to purchase a Hamilton.

That is the day we knew he had solved his puzzle. One month later he died of pancreatic cancer at the age of 62. It seems, you see, that God gave him just enough time to do what he had been given to us to do."

"And what, exactly, did he discover?"

"I do not know. He did not want to tell Papa and me, because he thought it would jeopardize us if we ever came under investigation. But, he did tell us one of the stunning implications of his findings. It took our breath away when he told us."

"Okay, you have my interest. I'm all ears. Does it have anything to do with that watch out there on the counter?"

"Yes, it does," Lena replied. "That was just one of the many Timex watches your grandfather had purchased here over many years. But he modified it – customized it actually. He customized it to track your father's life. In fact, after sitting quietly in our shop for thirty-three years the alarm sounded only at the precise moment that your father died."

"What?" Father was incredulous.

"Yes, I swear to you. I heard it with my own ears. My heart almost stopped, I was so afraid for your father. That watch was tracking your father's life."

Father Michael's eyes went wide at this revelation. "I hope you are not saying that Grandfather's watch could determine my father's date of death."

"No, not determine. The watch did not decide when your father would die. That is ridiculous. It merely measured your father's life. It kept the time of his life."

"But, how could Grandfather calibrate it to end on the day my father would die? That implies that he could see into the future."

"No it doesn't. It just means that your grandfather's discovery involved a more precise measurement of time. I can assure you that your grandfather did not believe in determinism. He very much believed in free will. He also knew, however, that our understanding of how the universe works is incomplete.

"Whatever piece of the universal puzzle he discovered, it was the piece that shows, among other things, I am sure, the length of time allotted to each one of us. That doesn't determine what we can or can't do. It just measures how much time we have to get it done."

Father studied Lena, puzzled. "But he never published his results. Trust me, if Grandpa had made a huge scientific discovery, my father would have made a fortune out of it. But my father never mentioned it."

"That's because your grandfather told no one except my father, me, and his attorney. He feared the consequences of his discoveries being made known to the general public. He felt certain your father would attempt to use his discoveries for commercial gain, and he was absolutely firm in his conviction that great good would come from his discoveries, but that, in the wrong hands, great evil was also possible.

"He prayed for guidance, conflicted as to what was in the best interests of humanity. He gave strict orders not to disclose any of his journals, notes, or proofs, and believed God would reveal the proper time to disclose his discoveries in due course – perhaps not to him, but to someone."

"Then why are you telling me, if this information is confidential?"

"It was confidential, pending certain conditions that, in my opinion, have been met."

"What conditions?"

"In his will, your grandfather granted power-of-attorney over his discoveries to my father and me, until such time that we determined you had not followed in your father's money-loving footsteps. I suspect your vow of poverty qualifies you on that score."

"And had I followed in my father's footsteps?"

"Then legal ownership would have passed to me and my assigns."

Father Michael stood now, running his hand through his hair, soaking it all in. Finally he said, "Wow. I am more like my grandfather than my own dad."

"Indeed you are. You even look like him."

"I do?"

"Yes, and you move like he did also. Looking at you in here takes me back years, to when I would sit and watch Professor Webb and my father talk."

"So, what would you do now with my grandfather's works, if you were me?" Michael asked.

"I think your grandfather's discoveries need to be turned over to the United States government," Lena said. "For better or worse, we must trust in our leaders and in God."

"Yes, I agree."

"I will have your grandfather's law firm contact you, Father. I suppose we will have to meet with the attorneys and the government and the church officials to effect a legal exchange. I can arrange that, if you agree."

"Yes, I think that would be best. But what about you?"

"What about me? I have complied with your grandfather's wishes and I am happy to do so."

"But there ought to be something for you in all this."

"I seek nothing, Father. Truly, your grandfather and my father were great men. I am happy to honor their memories in this small way. But, do you mind if I ask you a couple of questions?"

"Please, fire away."

Lena inhaled deeply and exhaled slowly as she thought. There were just a few things she could not understand. A few pieces of her own personal puzzle on which she hoped Father Michael could shed some light.

"When did you decide to become a priest?"

"That final decision was made the day I first entered this shop eleven years ago and saw my grandfather's watch, and your inscription about him being the greatest man in the history of time. That made a definite impact on me. I took it as the sign I was seeking – a sign from God that I must do what in my heart I knew was right for me, rather than what was right for my father."

"Fair enough," Lena said. "But what made you come to this shop? How did you ever find it?"

"I was going through an extremely difficult time, trying to decide what to do with my life. I felt so conflicted. I had gotten this wonderful education at Wharton, and had two tremendous job offers. Big bucks stared me in the face everywhere I looked.

"The pressure from my father was tremendous. I knew I would succeed in business, however, because, well because I was just a heckuva lot smarter than everybody else. Plus, my dad was a great role model for succeeding in business.

"It's just that I wasn't happy. I couldn't imagine being any more different than my father. He was mean, really mean. Tough. But he had to be to get as far as he did and achieve what he achieved.

"It just wasn't for me, though. I really wanted to be a priest. And it was the best decision I have ever made. I love the church and the teachings of Jesus but, believe me when I tell you I came this close to making the wrong decision," he said holding his thumb and index finger a half inch apart. "If I hadn't seen that watch I would not be a priest today."

"Are you saying you searched for a watch you weren't sure existed?"

"Yes. I did not know if it existed, or where it was if it existed."

"Then why were you looking for it in the first place?"

"Well, like I said, it was a difficult period for me. I couldn't sleep at night. I would wake up in cold sweats.

"One night I had a dream, and I will never forget it. I was in a workshop of some kind. Suddenly, there was an old man there with me. I know that I had never seen him before. So I asked him a question. I asked, 'Why do we do this?'

"I looked down at his handwritten notes and charts and equations and saw that he was holding a watch in his hands, except the back was off the watch so we could see the internal mechanisms. He said, 'it is what we must do. We must use our gifts.'"

At the same time Father Michael said these words, Lena said them also and blessed herself.

"You have had this same dream?" Father Michael asked.

"No," Lena replied. "Not me. Your grandfather. He told me this same dream he had many years before you were born, when he was trying to decide what to do. He, too, had reached a crossroads and was searching for direction, just as you were many years later. The only difference was he told the dream from the perspective of the old man.

"You see, Father Michael, your grandfather was the old man in your dream. The watch he held in his hands told him what he must do with his life. He interpreted this dream. I remember very well what he said to me. He said, "I knew only what I had to do, and that what I had to do to solve my puzzle involved measuring time.""

"It seems that the Lord does indeed work in strange ways." Father Michael smiled kindly when he said this. "He used one dream to deliver two different messages to me and my Grandfather."

"No, Father Michael," Lena said, shaking her head. "The message was the same. He was saying the same thing to both of you. I think He was saying, 'I have given you great gifts. Follow your heart in the service of others. Use your time wisely, not as others would have you do, but as I would.'"

FATHER MICHAEL WEBB WAS A GOOD MAN. HE ALSO PROVED TO BE a very wise man, as his grandfather had predicted.

His grandfather, who was dying as he finished his notes, knew that he could leave his discoveries only to someone who would put the welfare of others first. He trusted his old friend Gomez – or his daughter – to either find, or to be, that person.

Upon reading the notes, Father Michael realized the global implications of the discoveries, for both good and evil.

Among the good: unlimited fuel, unlimited food; not just accurate weather forecasting, but optimal weather engineering; genetically enhanced learning and intelligence; rapid, comprehensive knowledge acquisition for all; starships and interstellar travel, leading to colonization of Earth-like planets in other galaxies.

And among the evil: the ability to create the ultimate nuclear weapon capable of disintegrating the entire planet in an instant.

Father Michael faced a gut-wrenching decision. If properly managed and equitably distributed among all the world's populations, his grandfather's discoveries would eliminate the need for nation-states, geographic boundaries, and all location-based governments.

Such awesome power could not be entrusted to any one government. To best serve the interests of God and mankind, Father Michael knew he would have to devote all his abilities to the management of his grandfather's life work.

Originally, when Father Michael became a priest, he had aspired to be a parish pastor. Instead, the burden of controlling the dissemination and development of his grandfather's discoveries for benefit all fell upon him. His parish became the planet Earth, and he would be remembered throughout all of recorded human history simply as Father Michael.

Professor Leonard Webb's discoveries comprised the undisputed greatest individual contribution to the advancement of science.

Historians generally credit him with being the first of the great

Unified Scientists, whose inventions would include full-body non-invasive surgery, rapid error-free genetic engineering, plentiful renewable energy from crystals and non-carbon sources, anti-gravity cars and planes, long-term cryogenics, greatly increased average human life expectancy, rainfall initiation and control; elimination of tornadoes, hurricanes, earthquakes and tsunamis; cures for every type of cancer, eradication of famine; and, of course, accurate time to live (TTL) calculations, to name just a few.

For his discovery of The Law of Unification, and its subsequent impact on human development, historians dubbed Professor Leonard Webb the Father of The Great Earth Renaissance.

And although L. Frank Webb III was far wealthier than his son and father combined, neither he nor his wealth were ever recorded or remembered by historians. It was as though he had never lived.

2

A CHRISTMAS LEGACY

December 27, 2018

"Look, Doc," Tom said. "I know you don't like to do this, but I've been coming to you for a year and a half. Things are not going the way we'd hoped. I understand that. But, I have to put you on the spot, because I need to know.

"I have other things going on in my life other than cancer, and it would be helpful, for planning purposes, to understand how much time I likely have. And I'm not asking for any kind of guarantee. I understand that you can't say for sure how long I have, but you have a lot of experience with this stuff, so I'm pretty sure you have a good idea.

"Should I move to North Carolina to be close to the grandkids, or not? Should I trade in my car? Should I schedule a family vacation for next summer? Stuff like that."

"Well," Dr. Grant began, "it truly is difficult to say. Your body has rejected two chemotherapy treatments already. That's not good.

39

But there is a third we can try. And how much longer you live will depend upon whether the new chemo will stop the growth of the tumors."

"Okay, let's assume it does stop the growth of the tumors, does that mean I will be on the chemo indefinitely, for the rest of my life?"

"Yes."

"Okay, so I will never be chemo-free?"

"Probably not."

"And I'm a candidate for surgery?"

"No, due to the placement of the tumors, surgery is not an option."

"Well, that sucks, but it's helpful information. So, if the new chemo stops the growth of the tumors, how long will I have?"

"One to two years, probably, but no more than three."

"Well, okay. And if the chemo doesn't halt the tumors?

"Less than a year."

"Well, I made it to this Christmas. Think I'll make it to one more?"

"It depends."

"How about Hanukah? Does it come early next year?

Doctor Grant smiled, but said nothing.

"Mmm…seems like I'm in miracle territory."

That night, Tom dreamed, once again, of his miracle – the one miracle, perhaps of many in his life, that he could point to with absolute certainty as a miraculous gift from God; the one time he knew he had been touched by an angel. It was December, 1973, two months before his twenty-first birthday.

In the dream, he stood dumbfounded, speechless. This "angel" was stunning, gorgeous, and he could not take his eyes off her. Nick Bellamy was at his side, saying something, but the dance music was loud and Tom was mesmerized.

The angel was tall, blonde, and unbelievably graceful as she danced. It was a pre-Christmas dance at LaSalle University. Tom and Nick were juniors who had decided, at the last minute, to forsake bowling this Friday evening and head to the dance instead. Why not? Might get lucky. Can't rule out luck.

In that moment, though, Tom knew he would need more than luck. He would need some serious help. She was having a grand time, apparently dancing with one of her girlfriends. Tom had never seen her on campus before. He was certain of that.

She spun now, in tempo with the music, and glanced his way. He looked down, not wanting to appear to be ogling, which he had been, and saw that Nick had been shouting at him. But he remained transfixed. It was her…maybe, or something otherworldly. He looked up again. She smiled at him before looking down, grabbing her friend's two hands, and continuing with their jitterbug.

Go, he thought. *Move. She smiled at you.* But had she? Perhaps she was just smiling because she was having a good time. Perhaps he had misinterpreted a coincidental glance for an intentional one. He may have stayed there, anchored to the floor like one of the nearby basketball posts, for too long. Other guys were coming in. Some of the players from the men's basketball team who, like him, were tall. Competition.

"Go!" Nick shouted above the din.

"Huh?"

"Go! Go get her. She likes you."

"Who does?"

"Who does? Who do you think, Numbnuts? Grace Kelly over there, that's who," he said, with a nod toward the stunner.

"You think?"

Nick rolled his eyes and started clapping his hands.

"What's that mean?" Tom shouted, pointing. "Why are you clapping?"

"It means, Tinkerbell, that I want you to live. To fly! Go! Go, fly!" he said, finally, pushing his friend out of the periphery and into the nearby dancers. "Go. Do your thing. Wow her. You can do it. Men, worldwide, will celebrate this moment someday."

"They will?"

"Absolutely. Mythological. Classic." Tom rolled his eyes. Nick, an education major, was always quoting the classics.

Nick waved him on. "Go! She's waiting."

She's waiting, he thought. He hesitated. The music suddenly faded. The room seemed to grow dark. He couldn't move. He still needed help.

She's waiting, he thought again.

For what?

January, 2019

"Just two tonight?" Julie asked.

"Just two."

"From now on." Nick added.

"Why? Where's Walt?"

Tom and Nick looked at each other, before looking down. Neither could face her.

"He's not with us anymore," Tom said, after a pause. "I'm guessing heaven."

"He died?"

"Definitely heaven," Nick said, looking up. "He was a good guy. The best."

"Oh my gosh, no," Julie said. "When? You three were in here just last week."

"Buried him yesterday," Tom said. "Massive brain hemorrhage last Thursday. Nobody was home. His wife found him on the garage floor when she returned home from the supermarket."

"Oh, that's horrible!" Julie said. "I'm so sorry. I had no idea he was sick."

"Neither did we," Nick said. "Nobody knew, not even Walt or his wife, Arlene. Apparently, he had just finished with some yard work and had been standing on a ladder to hang the leaf blower up on an overhead hook. Arlene found him face-down on the garage floor. The ladder fell on top of him and the leaf blower lay in pieces nearby."

"That's so sad," Julie said. "I mean he was younger than you guys, right? He was the youngest of the group, wasn't he?"

"He was," Tom said. "He was sixty, five years younger than me and Nick."

"Oh my gosh, I'm so sorry," Julie said. "If there's anything I can do…."

"Just keep him in your prayers," Nick said. "That's all any of us can do for him now."

Julie took their orders, brought their glasses of water, then disappeared into the kitchen. Nick and Tom looked out the plate glass window of the diner to the airbase across the highway.

"Then there were two," Nick said.

"Yep. We were up to seven regulars for a long time, not including the subs. How many years has it been?"

"Twenty-six, officially, as far as the group goes. Remember? It was 1993. The week of the church carnival. That's when Joe and Lou and Stan joined us."

"Yeah, but you and I go back to, what – 1971?"

"Yes, forty-eight years. We were the first two. Now we're the last two."

"The first shall be last."

"Lucky us. I guess."

"Not feeling so lucky right now."

"I hear ya."

"Still, forty-eight years is a pretty good run."

"True."

"And, the others were all older than us."

"I know. It makes sense, I guess. I guess I always figured we'd outlive the others, but I never figured I'd outlive Walt. Man, sixty. That's way too young."

"Poor Arlene. It must be tough on her."

"Yeah, it'll take time. The kids will help, though."

"Right. Still, we should probably go see her once in a while. See if she needs anything."

"We will."

"Nick, you know…I just want to say…."

"What?"

"I just want to thank you for hanging in there with me."

"What are you talking about?"

"You know, with my cancer and all. Driving all the way up here every week, visiting with me, going to this godforsaken diner…."

"Tom, come on. It's what friends do."

Tom looked at Nick. Serious. "It's what *good* friends do, and don't think I don't appreciate it."

"Yeah, well, you know, the boss practically kicks me out of the house every Tuesday night. Says I drive her nuts with my political talk."

"Well, thank God for Laura, that's all I have to say. Tell her I said so, will you?"

"Sure."

"And for you too. Thank God for you too, Nick. You've been a real friend."

"It's the Christian thing to do, Tom. Were roles reversed, you'd be there for me."

"I know."

"The way you always have."

"Hey, everybody needs a good electrician."

"And a good accountant," Nick added, drinking his water.

The two old friends continued to stare out the window at the sun setting on the distant horizon.

"Pretty sky," Tom said.

"Kind of reminds me of heaven – or makes me think of heaven."

"Yeah, I guess."

"Do you suppose Walt is there?"

"No friggin' way," Tom said. "I'm guessing his constant adolescent sexual innuendo isn't nearly as highly valued in heaven as it is in other places."

Nick laughed. "How about the others?"

"I don't know. Debbie, probably."

"Yeah, definitely Debbie."

"And Ed. Maybe."

"Right. Mister Notre Dame."

"Stan has a shot," Tom said.

"Yeah, it's a good bet. He actually entered the seminary after Vietnam."

"Why'd he leave the seminary?"

"I think he needed to take care of his folks and his siblings after his dad died."

"Wow. Vietnam. The seminary. And taking care of his family. He definitely punched his ticket."

"We are so screwed," Nick said.

"Well, we'll probably run into Joe and Lou again anyway."

"Yep. Joe will still be flipping overly well-done burgers, no doubt."

"Charred burgers."

"Like I said, so screwed. Do me a favor," Nick said. "Pray for me after I'm gone. Look in on Laura once in a while. She'd like that."

"What are you talking about?" Tom said. "I'm the one with cancer."

"Don't matter. I'm going first. I've always known that."

"Ain't no way. You're healthy as an ox. I'm lucky if I get another six months."

"Even with the new chemo?"

"Ain't gonna be no new chemo. I'm done with it. It's no way to live. No way at all. Not for me, anyway. Not anymore."

"Really?"

They said nothing for a minute. Then Tom said, "I guess that makes me a quitter, huh?"

"You're no quitter. You've never been a quitter. I respect your decision. You've been through a lot. Way too much. I wish things could be different, but I respect your decision. It's been a tough year."

They sat in silence a while longer, each lost in their own thoughts. Finally, Nick said, "Yeah. A tough year."

"Anyway, odds are I'll be going first," Tom said.

"Nope. I'm going first, my friend. Trust me."

"Why would you say a thing like that? You know I'm stage four. Terminal. It's just a matter of months, thanks to that stinking super fund site across the street there. Polluted all the water around here for years. Took Ann. Now it's going to take me. You lived down in the city, not out here. You're good to go."

"Don't matter. It's karma."

"Karma? What the heck you talking about? We're Catholic, Nick. We can't believe in determinism."

"Not determinism. Karma. There's a difference."

"What's the difference?"

"It's just a feeling I have. I've had it for many years. Ever since we met, I guess, you and me. I always knew I was going to go first."

"Here's your soup, guys," Julie interrupted, placing bowls of chicken rice soup in front of each of them.

"Take his back," Tom said. "He's full of soup already."

Julie smiled. "Can I get you anything else?"

"No, we're good, "Nick said. "Thanks."

"By the way, Bill, the owner, is buying your dinners tonight," Julie said. "On the house. He wanted me to tell you."

"Why?"

"Walt's passing, I guess. Tradition. Your group has been coming here every week for years."

"Nice. That's very nice," Tom said. "Please thank him for us. And thank you, Julie."

"Don't forget to help yourselves to the salad bar," she said before turning and walking away.

"Look, Nick, you can't go before me. Remember, the final bucket list."

"Yeah, well I could drive you down."

"Nick, I am in no condition. You know that. The drive down might kill me. Seriously. I'm just way too weak now. If my bladder ruptures again...."

"Okay, okay. Sorry."

Tom seemed lost in thought. Nick sipped his soup, waiting.

After a minute, Tom said, "Plus, I haven't danced in many a year. Except in my mind. In my mind, the music has never stopped. Promise me, Nick. Promise me you'll complete my bucket list, the last bucket list item. We've completed all the others. There's only one left. Mine. But I can't do it anymore. You'll have to."

"Go to the university?"

"Yes, the old gym. Where Ann and I first met. You were there with me, remember?"

"Of course, I remember. The Christmas dance."

"A wise man once said, 'Men worldwide will celebrate this night someday.'"

Nick smiled at his old friend, before looking down. "Not sure how wise he was."

"He was right, though. You were right. And you are wise. You've always been. *Si monumentum requiris, circumspice.*"

Nick smiled. "The only thing we take with us is that which we leave behind.' You use my words against me."

"Correction, my friend. I cite your legacy. I use your words in testament to you, to the friend you have been, to the man you have become."

"Fancy words for diner patrons."

Tom smiled. "Be that as it may, my old friend, and I emphasize old, I trust you will not fail me in this, my last request. Go back, Nick. Look. Let me see it through your eyes one last time."

Nick took a deep breath, reflecting. Apparently, this topic had come up before. "Tom, I'm not so sure...."

"I am, Nick. I am."

"How can you be so sure?"

Tom hesitated then, turned, and gazed out the window. After several long seconds, when he seemed to be attempting to come up with an answer that made sense, he turned back, looked at Nick, and said, "Karma."

"Ah," Nick said. "You're definitely using my words against me now."

"More your philosophy, as flawed as it is." Then, after the two friends stared each other down, Tom said, "Will you, Nick? Will you do this for me?"

"Sure," Nick said, half-heartedly.

"Nick, we've been through so much together. We actually grew up together, in a way. And still, here you are. Here we are. Through thick and thin and you've never let me down. Never. But, Nick, this is the last favor, and there are none I consider more important."

"Tom, I just don't see how...."

"Promise me, Nick. It's important. It's important to me."

Nick looked at his friend, shook his head before looking down at his soup. "Okay, I promise. For you. Come on, let's get some salad."

As they rose from their booth and approached the salad bar, Nick said, "We should get some pickled beets in honor of Walt. He always had the pickled beets."

"Probably cause brain hemorrhages," Tom said.

"There's no science to prove that."

"As opposed to the years of scientific karma research."

December, 2019

TOM WAS AFRAID. HOW COULD HE NOT BE? HE WAS IN HOSPICE, and he fully understood the reality. A man of faith, to be sure, he also had hope. Hope that he would be going to a better place. A place of no more pain, suffering, bleeding, vomit, or tears. He wasn't sure what heaven would be like, other than it would be good. Something good. He also hoped that he would see Ann. That she would be waiting for him. Would be there for him at the hour of his death and say yes to him one last time, the way she first did on the dance floor forty-six years ago.

But, he worried. Would she want him again? He had made so many mistakes. She was in heaven. Of this he had no doubt. And heaven, by definition, is perfect happiness. If Ann was perfectly happy now, and resting in peace, would she go out of her way to walk with her flawed husband? He didn't know. He hoped, but he didn't know. And he would not blame her. Not one bit.

She had already given him everything she had when she was alive. Forty-two years of marriage. Forty-four years of her life. Four children, for whom she sacrificed her career to raise. Five grandchildren. A great legacy of love, laughter, family, grace, and faith.

What more could he expect? Nothing. He had no right to expect anything more of his saintly wife.

Still, he hoped. And prayed. Every day. "Wait for me, Ann. Please. Be there for me at the hour of my death. Say yes to me once again as you first did forty-six years ago on the dance floor. Let us walk together forever, Ann. Tom and Ann. Ann and Tom. Two peas in a pod. My soulmate. Forever."

So, this was the end. At least they had honored his request and put him in the same room where Ann had passed away. Room 314. The next-to-the-last room in a row of seven private rooms on either side of a long corridor. It was here, in this room, in this very bed, that he had watched Ann take her last labored breaths, and shed her last tear. His eyes welled up now, as they always had, with the memory.

"Wait for me, Ann," he prayed softly, almost to himself. "Just a little longer."

The pain was tremendous now. He had forestalled the morphine drip, understanding from Ann's experience, what the implications were. It was, to his way of thinking, a form of euthanasia, albeit church-sanctioned, as near as he could tell. It would take away the pain, but it would also take away his consciousness and his body's desire to keep fighting, to keep breathing.

With or without the morphine, however, the end was certainly near now. Still, the pain was excruciating. He would not be able to tolerate it much longer. He had fought the good fight, but his time was at hand, and he knew it.

What he did not know, because he had not opened his eyes for several hours, was that his daughter, Mary Kate, sat at his side. She had been sitting there all day, watching her dying father's labored breathing, holding his left hand in her hands.

He hadn't seen her sitting there when he last opened his eyes. But she had seen his eyes – jaundiced, ghastly yellow. He had opened them for just a couple of seconds, but saw nothing.

He was also unaware that Mary Kate held his hand, was sitting next to his bed, or that she had, at the recommendation of the attending nurse, approved the morphine drip just four hours earlier after seeing his eyes and leaving his side to cry in the hallway.

His breathing was now becoming quite labored, increasingly intermittent, and scary. It was almost as if there were tiny little balls bouncing around and clacking in his throat or lungs. Mary Kate questioned the nurse about this. "That's what we call a 'death rattle'" she said.

"Go, Dad," Mary Kate whispered now, leaning in close to her father so that he might hear. "Go to her. Go to Mom. She is waiting for you. Don't be afraid. She forgives whatever you think needs forgiving. She loves you, I know she does, and she will be there for you."

It was too late, however, to tell her father the shocking news about his friend, Mr. Bellamy. She had received the text from Mrs. Bellamy within the last hour. It was certainly going to be a long, sad, painful week for many people.

Mary Kate, overcome with grief, had fallen asleep in her chair next to her father's bed, holding the rosary beads which now dangled from her hand over one arm of the chair, so she was not awake to see him when he suddenly sat up on that bed and said, "Enough already."

Feeling better than he had in a long, long time – absolutely pain-free with a high degree of energy – he sat on the edge of the bed and looked at Mary Kate sleeping.

"You rest," he said, kissing his daughter on her cheek. "I've got something I need to do now. One final thing."

He couldn't believe how good he felt. He wasn't sick at all. Not one little bit. It was a miracle! Miraculously, too, he was no longer tethered to the catheter or any of the several bags of medicine hanging from the pole, whatever they were.

He scanned the room for his clothes and was trying to figure how best to minimize the chance of Mary Kate seeing him naked, when he noticed he was already completely dressed, head to foot. He was dressed in his usual casual outfit – blue denim shirt, jeans, Bomba socks, his 'Jesus' necklace, watch, and even the loafers on his feet and the Irish jeff cap on his head. He checked his pants pockets. His wallet, car keys, and cellphone were there.

"When did all this happen? Looks like I was going out in style."

He tossed the blanket and sheets aside, and somehow knew he had to hurry, so he wasn't going to sweat the details. The clock on the wall read 7:25 and it was dark outside.

"There's still time," he said, walking to the door of the room and opening it. Before stepping into the hallway, he turned and saw Mary Kate sleeping in her chair.

She had not stirred at all – had not woken or spoken. Still, he heard her clear as a bell.

"Thanks for everything, Dad. Please wait for me."

Tom understood her meaning. "I will, Mary Kate. Mom and I will always be there for you." He started to leave the room then, but turned back. "And, don't forget. One good joke a week. It's important."

"I love you, Dad."

Tom, sensing he could no longer disturb his daughter, walked over, hugged her and kissed her cheek. "I love you too, Baby Doll. I will wait for you. I promise. Be good. Be great."

Mary Kate did not respond, but continued to sleep deeply. Tom left her then, walked to the door, and exited the room.

Looking down the hallway, he noticed there was just one nurse at the nurses' station.

"A quiet night in the old hospice," Tom said to himself. He pulled the jeff down low on his forehead, bowed down, and hurried past the nurses' station, hoping he could do so unseen. He did.

Out in the elevator lobby he pushed the down button and rode the elevator to the first floor. There was a security guard stationed at the main entrance, but Tom was pretty sure the guard would not recognize him as a patient.

"Good night, my good man," Tom said, doffing his cap as he passed the guard and entered the revolving glass door. But the security guard never looked up from the newspaper he was reading.

Outside the hospice, Tom couldn't have been more surprised or pleased by what he saw. In the roundabout sat a brand new, gleaming, gold 1971 Dodge Dart. And, standing next to the car on the passenger side was Nick Bellamy.

"Took you long enough," Nick said. "Been waiting here half an hour."

"Karma," Tom said softly, realization dawning.

"Told you," Nick said and smiled.

Tom ran up to Nick and hugged him. "Nick! I can't believe it. How could you have guessed?"

"Child! You cut me to the quick!" Nick said. "Professor Marvel never guesses. Professor Marvel knows!"

"Oh, Nick. You nut!" Tom said, releasing him and standing back. "Man, it's great to see you. You look great! You're like, what? Forty-eight?"

"Exactly. Same as you," Nick said, pointing.

"Really?" Tom said, looking down at his own hands, seeing the age spots were gone, removing his cap and running his hand through a full head of hair. "Nick…how?"

"I don't know. Look, don't look a gift horse in the mouth. Let's just go with it, okay?"

"Right…right. I agree. Let's just ride this pony for all it's worth." Tom turned from Nick and looked at the car. "But how can we be forty-eight and this gorgeous 1971 Dodge Dart be brand new? If it's 1971, we're only eighteen."

"I don't know what year it is for us anymore," Nick said. "If I had to guess, I'd say this baby isn't new, but restored. You know, kind of like…like we are, I guess."

"Right, right," Tom said, running his hand over the brown vinyl roof. "Man, she's a beauty."

"Speaking of beauties, we better get going. The clock's ticking. Come on. You drive," Nick said, hopping into the passenger side.

"I drive? But, it's your car isn't it?"

"When was it ever my car? It's always been your car. You always drove. I always rode shotgun."

"But, I don't have any keys."

"Check your pockets," Nick said.

Tom reached into his pants pocket and pulled out his car keys. Indeed, they were keys to a Dodge. But he hadn't driven a Dodge in decades.

"How is it possible…?"

"Man, for someone not looking a gift horse in the mouth, you sure do ask a lot of questions."

"Right, right." Tom ran around to the driver's side and hopped in, closing the door. He put the key into the ignition and started the engine, which purred like it was brand new.

"Man, listen to that, would you, Nick? That baby's a slant six. Best engine ever built." Nick nodded his agreement. "So, where to?" Tom said.

"Dude, it's your bucket list. If I had to guess, I'd say we're not going bowling. You know where to," Nick said, turning on the radio. Gladys Knight was singing "Midnight Train to Georgia."

"Okay," Tom said.

"And step on it. We're late already."

As the Dart roared out of the driveway with the two old friends inside, they sang right along with Gladys Knight, with the windows down, just as they always had when they had commuted to college. Tom sang the lead. Nick sang the backup. But, in this song, they both knew, the backup was the coolest part:

And I'll be with him (I know you will)

*On that midnight train to Georgia (Leavin' on
    the midnight train to Georgia)
I'd rather live in his world (live in his world)
Than live without him in mine (Her world...is
    his, his and hers alone)
He kept dreamin' (dreamin')
Ooh, that someday he'd be a star (A super-
    star, but he didn't get far)
But he sure found out the hard way That
    dreams don't always come true (Dreams
    don't always come true)
Oh no(Uh uh) uh uh (no, uh uh)*

A short while later, or at least what seemed a short while even though time seemed to have lost all meaning, Tom pulled into the parking lot at LaSalle University. "It's packed," he said.

"Yeah, it's the dance," Nick said. "Looks like a good turnout."

Tom parked the car. They got out and began walking toward the old gym, pulling their jacket zippers up to shield them, some-what, from the mid-December evening wind and cold. The campus was decorated with Christmas lights, Christmas trees, wreaths and a large, lit Nativity scene. If Tom and Nick had arrived late, they weren't the only ones. Dozens of college-aged students also were walking to the dance. "We'll be the oldest ones here," Nick said.

Tom looked at him, stopped walking, and said, "Nick, man, you're getting younger. You look like you did when we were back in college."

Nick looked at Tom. "Huh, really? You too."

"Weird," Tom said, as the students hustled past them.

"Yeah, it is. You complaining?"

"No."

"Me either. Come on. Let's go."

They continued walking, but Tom was slowing. "Come on," Nick said. "What's the matter?"

"Nick, I don't know. What if…what if…."

"Tom, stop. Come on. It'll be fine. You'll see. This whole night will be fine. It has been so far, right?"

"Right."

"So what makes you think the dance will be any different?"

"I…I don't know, Nick. I guess…I guess…I just don't know."

"Yeah, well, that's why I'm here."

"Huh?

"That's why I'm here. That's why I was here the first time, and that's why I'm here again."

"*Semper fidelis*," Tom said.

"That's right, my friend. *Semper fidelis*."

"But, how can you be so sure?"

"I don't know. But, I am," Nick said.

Tom stopped walking, turned, and looked back.

"You thinking about quitting now?" Nick asked.

"No, Nick. I guess not. I don't want to go back. I'm just afraid."

"Of her saying no?"

Tom was stunned. He looked at his friend. "How did you know?"

"Like I said, I don't know. Maybe…maybe…I've been given a grace. Maybe it's not me who knows, but someone seems to, I'm pretty sure. Someone wants me to help you. Someone wants you to walk into that dance."

"Who?"

"Dunno. God, maybe. His angels? I'm not sure."

"But what if she doesn't want me, Nick? What if I hurt her so badly she just can't forgive me? What if this is like…like…her chance at a mulligan or something?"

"Mulligan?"

"Yes, mulligan. Her do-over. What if she knows if she says yes to me again, it will only lead to more heartache? More disappointment? But, if she says no, she is free to…to do whatever she wants. To be whoever she wants. Not my girlfriend or wife…just…just…happy."

"Dude, come on," Nick said, grabbing Tom by the arm. "Let's go. You're way over-thinking things. Plus, we have a bucket list to complete. We can't turn back now."

Tom pulled back his arm. "No, Nick. I'm serious. What if she says no. I don't know if I could take it. What if this is her heaven, but my hell? What if this is how all my sins come back to haunt me? Forever?"

Nick let out a deep breath, exasperated. "*Carpe noctem.*"

"Seize the night?"

"Seize the night, Tom, I don't know where you come up with these ideas. I've known you my whole adult life and I have to tell you, if I never have before this, that you are a great blessing to me. You've always been. To me, and to many people. You and Ann raised a beautiful family. You had a beautiful home, a successful career. I know the end was difficult for you and Ann due to your cancers, but you had four decades of what looked to me to have been pretty good, happy, and loving lives.

"Were you perfect? No, of course not. Did you hurt her? Probably, in some way, shape, or form, but I dare you to show me the husband who hasn't hurt his wife at some point, and vice versa. Plus, by turning around you are not giving Ann the opportunity to tell you how she feels.

"If she is resentful, okay, at least you'll know. Do you really want to go through…through…whatever this is we're in, eternity I guess, not knowing? Do you really want to not know now? Aren't you tired of not knowing? Plus, what if…what if…she says yes to you? Do you want to risk missing that? Are you so risk-averse you would miss hitting the greatest game-winning grand slam in history? Remember what Wayne Gretzky said."

"You miss 100% of the shots you don't take."

"Now you're talking. That's the clean-up hitter I know."

"That's exactly right. Nothing ventured, nothing gained. Except, in this case, we're talking about eternity. You're being given a great gift here, Tom. The chance to know, finally, once and for all, and for all eternity, if Ann loves you. How can you walk away from that?"

"I can't."

"Didn't think so."

Tom put his arm around Nick's shoulders. "Thanks, Teach. Come on. Let's show these kids how to dance."

Christmas Eve

So, HERE THEY WERE ONCE AGAIN. AND THERE SHE WAS, JUST AS HE remembered her.

Nick waved him on. "Go! She's waiting."

She's waiting, Tom thought. He hesitated. The music suddenly faded. The room grew dark. Why was that so eerily familiar? Why was that so important? He couldn't move. He still needed help.

She's waiting, he thought again.

"*Carpe Noctem.*" It was Nick, at his side. But, when Tom looked, Nick was no longer there. There was no music. No lights. No dancers. He was suddenly, inexplicably, alone.

Then, just as all seemed hopelessly lost, a floodlight illumined a five-foot diameter circle on the dance floor, about thirty feet distant, near as Tom could tell. In the circle, dressed in a white gown, was Ann. She was looking down and did not see him. But, he could see Nick had been right. She seemed to be waiting.

"Go, Dad," Mary Kate's words came to him. "Go to her. Go to mom. She is waiting for you. Don't be afraid."

Tom smiled. He had many angels this night, it seemed. "Thanks,

Mary Kate," he said.

He hadn't seen Ann since she passed away two years earlier. The cancer had not been kind to her, and she had suffered greatly. He prayed every day, every single day since, to ask her to wait for him, not knowing if she could. Not knowing if she would. Not knowing if she forgave him. It seemed as if he was about to find out. He took a deep breath and, for the second time in his existence, feared her rejection.

And for the second time in his existence, he took his first tentative steps toward her. Even from this distance he could see, once again, that she was stunningly beautiful. There was no cancer anymore. She did not suffer anymore. Of course not. She was in heaven. Would she risk heaven for him?

He walked up to her and stopped just two feet away. Now they were both in the spotlight. She looked up at him. Looked him right in his eyes. He felt the tears coming to his own eyes. She was so gorgeous.

"I waited," she said, and smiled at him.

He wiped his eyes and smiled at her. "You are so beautiful. You look like when we first met forty-six years ago."

"Twenty-one. You see me how you wish to see me," she said. "And I you."

"Is this heaven?" he asked. "Are you in heaven?"

"I am now," she said, touching his face. "We are."

"Forever?"

"Yes. Forever."

"Ann and Tom?"

"Tom and Ann," she said, touching a white hanky to his eyes. "There are no tears in heaven, by the way."

"Back there, just a little bit ago, Nick said someone wanted me to come here. He didn't know who."

"It was me," Ann said.

He smiled and took her to himself in a bear hug. "Oh, Ann.

Ann. You have no idea how much I have missed you. How much I have longed for this minute. I didn't know if you would forgive me. If you would want to be with me."

"I know, Tom. I know," she said holding his head into her shoulder. "I knew it would be difficult for you. You were always so responsible. You blamed yourself for everything, even things outside of your control, like my cancer. But, Tom, know this. I always loved you and I always will. And I know you have always loved me, and always will. We will walk together in eternity."

"Really? In eternity?"

"Yes, in eternity. In love for eternity. That is your heaven and that is my heaven."

"Thank God almighty."

"Yes. Thank God and His son and Mary and Joseph and the angels. You will love them. But first, I believe there is a question you need to ask."

He stepped back, held her at arm's length, as she held him, and he said, "I haven't danced in many a year."

"That makes two of us."

He smiled. "Wanna dance?"

She stood on tip toes and kissed him. "I've waited a long time to hear those words. Yes, Tom, my love. I would love to dance with you. Come on," she said, leading him by the hand.

The dance floor, and dancers, and 21-year-old versions of Nick, Joe, Lou, Stan, Debbie, Ed, and Walt, who were all there to share in this, the final bucket list, appeared as "All I Want For Christmas Is You" by Mariah Carey started playing.

"Your favorite song," Tom said.

"Of course," Ann said. "After all, this is heaven."

"Come on," Tom said. "Let's show these kids how to jitter bug."

Back in the hospice, alone, Mary Kate wiped the last tear from her father's cheek

"Cut a rug, Dad," she said. "Merry Christmas."

3

THE RISER

I t was another quiet night on the ward, with even fewer visitors than usual, which was fine with Nancy O'Driscoll, RN. Visiting hours would be over in an hour. The last of her colleagues from the day shift had gone, leaving the floor under the watchful eyes of just her and Therese Allen, RN, another night hawk, another lonely soul.

Nancy studied the chart for the next patient on her round before entering his room. She shook her head slowly, imperceptibly, and sighed. LeSean was a sad case. Even Nancy, hardened by life and the losses of loved ones, was not so inured to misfortune that she couldn't empathize, if barely, with the young man who lay dying on the other side of the door and who, seemingly as an act of will, had stymied some of the best doctors in the hospital.

Well, if he was so intent on dying, maybe he should get on with it. There were others who could use his bed. Others who were fighting to live. She closed her laptop and berated herself, mentally. *Shame on you! Be kind.* She placed her hand on the door, pushed it open, and entered the room.

He lay still, ignoring the football game on the wall-mounted television, the arrival of his caregiver, and the world around him. His roommate in the semi-private room had been taken to surgery that morning and was recovering in intensive care.

For the time being, LeSean had the room to himself, though it would have been news to him, dismissive as he was of his surroundings and the few people there. He was confined to his bed in one of the largest hospitals in the city, as he had been for the past five days, post-op and post-ICU. Yet he was where he wanted to be – a few steps from death's door and getting closer.

Soon it would be over – the pain, the sorrow, the inexorable Fate that seemed to have dogged him all sixteen years of his short life. If one of the five bullets that had accidently found him had entered his body a fraction of an inch higher, it would have all been over by now.

Regardless, it would be over soon enough. All he could do was wait for the inevitable. Wait for Fate, which had stalked them in the inner-city slum he inhabited with his mom ten days ago, before the sixth bullet had taken her. Now he had nothing. All the hope, all the love, all the family – all gone.

Taking his wrist, Nancy said, "Let's check your pulse, shall we?"

No "Hello, how are you doing this evening, dear?" which was just as well with LeSean. He didn't know what this woman's problem was, and he didn't care. It was obvious to him she was going through the motions. She had never displayed any discernable empathy. He let her check his pulse, but did not respond.

He never responded. Never made eye contact. He felt certain she didn't care one way or the other if he lived or died.

Not that Nancy O'Driscoll, R.N. mattered to him. He didn't despise her, didn't hate her, he just didn't consider her. He had dismissed her days ago. They had been thrown together by Fate, his mortal enemy, and he didn't appreciate, as he lay dying, her attitude, presented like some kind of toxic cherry atop death's lethal dessert.

Clearly, she didn't care for him. So, to hell with her. It would've been nice if she cared. But, then again, a lot of things would be nice.

LeSean closed his eyes to dismiss her from his field of vision and, hopefully, his thoughts. His world, what was left of it, was between his ears. Remembering his mother and how she loved him was all life held for him now. Everything else was hopeless. Fate had beaten him. At age sixteen, he was done fighting. He had lost. First, his older brother, James, lost to drugs, leading his father to leave, and now his mother, his rock, his best friend and fan, lost to Fate.

They had been in the wrong place at the wrong time, sitting at the kitchen table, working together on his civics homework, when a gang from another neighborhood decided it would be a good time to shoot up the house of a drug kingpin who lived next door. Except they shot up the wrong house.

His mother had always been there for LeSean. She had always forced him to be the best student he could be, and the best athlete. Since James had died, she wanted LeSean to be the first in the Lance family to go to college. And he wanted that too. Or had. Now? Now, what was the point?

His mother took him to church every Sunday and did his homework with him every night. She had taken such pride in his excellent grades and in his intelligence. He would make something of himself, make a good life for himself and escape the 'hood. She would see to it.

Except, now, she wouldn't. Suddenly, recognizing the silence around him, he opened his eyes and saw the door closing behind Nancy O'Driscoll, who never saw the tear that trickled down his cheek.

———

He wasn't sure how long he had dozed. It could have been fifteen minutes or fifteen hours. The sedative and pain killers constantly dripping in his IV connected to his arm were as effective at dulling reality as they were at dulling anxiety and pain.

The window shades were drawn, the overhead lights were on, but the TV was off. He guessed it was evening because the food tray next to his bed smelled more of meat and potatoes than of pancakes and bacon. No matter. He hadn't eaten in days.

He knew he was dying, even if the medical professionals hoped against hope on his behalf. He was still amazed each time he awoke, always having assumed he had closed his eyes for the last time. But, there was always another time. The body didn't give up easily.

Still, he knew his body was fighting a losing battle. He could feel it. It was no longer a matter of days, but hours. He would not be here tomorrow night. Thank God, it would be over. His miserable life would finally be over. He would be with his mother and James again. They would be reunited. He was certain of it.

LeSean wrinkled his nose at the foreign, faintly foul odor accosting him. No, not foul exactly, but… not pleasant either.

He did recognize the smell, which, though not fragrant, not even close, was not unwelcome. It was…was…familiar, somehow – something that brought his father to mind.

How could that be? He hadn't thought of his father in years. But what was that odor? Lemon Lysol? Mixed with the pungent smell of the tannery next to the baseball field? Or, was it both? The scents were part of his past. And, though each was in its way unpleasant, together they held a positive association for him, of a time when his family was whole and happy.

His father had been a maintenance man, and one of the perks of his job was the ready availability of cleansers and cleaning materials in their little row home, which he had always taken pride in keeping spotless. He was good at it, too.

Lemon Lysol was a reminder of those good times long past. The same could be said of the tannery odor. No one in their right mind would ever consider such a stench pleasing, except by association with some pleasant childhood memory. Like the inner-city ballfield, so-called, where he had played baseball.

Overgrown with weeds, without lighting or drainage, located in a flood zone and more often underwater or muddy than playable, it was home to his most happy memories. Of good times when his family witnessed his many heroics as a young athlete.

LeSean could "do it all" James used to say. He *has all the tools*, James would proudly proclaim to their parents. LeSean's lips arched upward, slightly, at the suddenly resurrected, long-latent memory.

"Good job, my man. I'll take it from here."

LeSean opened his eyes, half expecting to see a maintenance man cleaning the floor. Instead, he saw the door to his room close behind the maintenance man, and a visitor sitting in the chair next to his bed, a man he had never seen before.

The man smiled. "Forget smelling salts," he said. "Lysol does it every time, eh?"

LeSean looked from the stranger to the door and back.

"Nurse O'Driscoll has given me fifteen minutes before I turn into a pumpkin," the stranger said, continuing to smile.

"Do I know you?" LeSean said, ignoring the stranger's attempt at humor.

The man continued to smile. "Interesting question. If time is the playground of miracles, tense is the sliding board." Then, seeing LeSean's obvious distress, he continued. "No, not yet. You don't know me yet. But, I am a friend. I'm here to help."

"You a doctor? Another doctor?"

The stranger looked down, shaking his head. "You do ask some marvelous questions. But no, I am not a doctor, not a medical doctor anyway."

"What kind o' doctor?"

"It's unimportant. A doctor of life, perhaps. But, enough about me. Let's talk about you. How do you feel?"

"I ain't talkin' to you. Who the hell are you?"

"I'm a visitor, and there aren't too many of them here, if you'll forgive the impertinence. Someone who cares about you, maybe the only one left now, and we only have a few minutes, so if I am to help you, we can't be wasting what little time we have. So, let's begin again, shall we? How are you feeling?"

LeSean closed his eyes and turned his head away. "What do you care?"

"I'm here, aren't I?"

"I don't know. I don't know if you're here, for real. Half the time I don't know if I'm alive or dead. It's these stupid drugs they keep pumping into me. I smelled Lysol and I thought I'd see a guy cleaning the floor. Instead I saw you, whoever the hell you are. Why should I tell you anything? There's such a thing as patient privacy. Maybe I should just call the nurse and have her kick your sorry black ass outta here."

Two minutes passed in silence. LeSean turned his head back and opened his eyes, expecting the visitor, the intrusive apparition, to be gone. He was wrong.

The stranger looked at his wristwatch. "Ten minutes," he said. "That's all the time I have to do my job."

LeSean looked at the stranger more closely now. "My old man used to say that."

"You remember?"

"No. My mom told me. He was a maintenance man."

The stranger seemed comfortable letting the conversation go where it may. "Why would a maintenance man say he only had ten minutes to do his job? He'd work all day, right?"

"Yeah, but he worked all day and came home tired all the time. He'd say he only had ten minutes a day for me and James."

"Your father was a good man."

LeSean's eyes widened. "For real? You know him?"

"Not well. I know of him."

"He left, that's all I know. He weren't nuthin'."

"He didn't leave," the stranger said. "He was killed."

"Man, you got the wrong dude. My mom said he left us."

"She was young and afraid. She didn't want you to suffer from the truth. She was doing her best to protect you from an ugly world."

Another tear escaped LeSean's eye and ran down his cheek. He brushed it away impatiently with his hand, stunned, disbelieving.

"She coulda told me," LeSean said. "I'm old enough now."

"Yes, she would have. She wanted to. But, as is too often the case, she ran out of time."

"You say he was killed. How?"

"It was late at night. He was leaving the bank he cleaned to go to his car. No witnesses."

"He suffer?"

"He did, for a few minutes."

"How much they take from him?" LeSean asked, immediately regretting the question.

"There isn't enough money in the universe to justify taking a man's life. The important point is your dad was a very good man. He gave his life trying to provide for his family. He loved you and your mother very much. You were his whole world."

LeSean wiped away another tear, roughly. The stranger handed a tissue to him. "I'm sorry to be the one to have to break this to you."

"Dude, who are you? Why you messin' with me?"

The man handed him another tissue. "Here, blow your nose. I'll be gone in five minutes."

LeSean did as he was told, pushing himself to sit up now, with new-found agitation if not strength. The man then handed him a glass of water. "Good. Good," he said. "Relax. Have a drink. I'll tell you."

He wore cordovan wingtip shoes, a blue pinstripe suit, a white oxford shirt, a red tie with navy blue stripes, and a red satin pocket handkerchief. He rolled a fine fedora in his hands as he sat, leaning forward, elbows on knees. He was calm, composed. To all appearances, he was well-to-do.

Once LeSean had finished blowing his nose, taking a sip of the water, and placing the drinking glass on the side table, he focused on the stranger, hopeful for the first time in almost two weeks.

"In a sense, your father gave his life for you. So, too, in a different way, did your mother. And not so you would choose to die. They sacrificed much that you might have a good life. James squandered his chance. So you are their last hope. They gave up everything for you. Don't you see how your giving up dishonors their memory?"

"Giving up? Man, I was shot five times. Ain't my choice. I can't even breathe sometimes."

"I know. I know. But, you've got to fight. You can't let the 'hood win. You can't let them take your life from you. Your father suffered at the end only because he wanted desperately to live. Had he just given up, he wouldn't have suffered. In the last few minutes of his life, he really, really tried to get back to you. He didn't give up at all. But the opportunity was denied him."

"You were there?"

"No."

"Look, man, who are you? What's with the hat?"

The man looked at his wristwatch. "Three minutes to pumpkin," he said. "My dad is a famous pitcher, the most famous closer in the major leagues, 'The Riser.' The hat is a fedora. My dad wears them when he's not pitching. He says they bring good luck, so I wear one too."

"'The Riser'? Never heard of no 'Riser.'" LeSean said.

"He has two notable sayings," the stranger continued, ignoring the comment. "People ask him how he throws a riser because, technically, it's impossible. Everybody knows no pitch rises. Because of gravity, every pitch drops, even if a little bit. But the big league batters swear he throws his fastball so hard it rises. All these amazing, professional hitters, some future Hall of Famers, who could hit any pitcher, can't hit him, the greatest closer who will ever live. People ask him how he does it. Why do hitters see the ball rise? He always says the same thing: 'Perception is reality.'"

"Perception is reality," LeSean said, mesmerized.

"That's right. 'The Riser' believes we are the master of our own reality. The only one who can craft the life you want is you. Only you. No one else."

"Only me," LeSean mimicked, trance-like.

"Have you ever seen a great magician and wondered how he did a particular trick?"

"Yeah."

"Do they ever tell you how they did it?"

"No."

"Why not?"

"I dunno. Don't want you to know, I guess."

"That's right. They have altered your reality. They have made you see something you really didn't see, and it became reality for you. 'The Riser' does the same. He makes hitters see what he wants them to see. They see the ball rise and they swing and hit only what's there: air, but never the ball."

"The Riser," LeSean said, softly, to himself. Then, shaking his head, "Never heard of him."

"Trust me, you will. Everybody will. All you have to do is get up out of bed and live your life so as to honor the memory of your family."

LeSean wiped at his eyebrow with his palm, agitated, recovering from his trance, as the stranger stood. "Wait, man," LeSean said, "why did you come here? Who are you?"

The stranger smiled. "If you could, knowing what would happen to him, what would you tell your dad on that last day, before he went out to clean the bank?"

"I'd tell him don't go."

"Would he listen to you?"

"I…I don't know. I hope so."

"That's right. You don't know. No guarantees. The best you can do is try. Create your own destiny." Then, he put on his fedora and stood. "The nurse is coming. My time's up. I've got to go."

"Wait!" LeSean cried. "The other thing. You say he said two things. What's the second one?"

"My father?"

"Yeah."

"It's what he always told me: 'Ten minutes is all the time I have.'"

"Just like my old man," LeSean said.

"Just like everybody, really," the stranger said. "Maybe especially for closers because that's about all the time they get in a game. But each of us shape our lives in all the little decisions we make, or fail to make, in ten minutes or less, every day."

"Will I see you again?" LeSean asked, suddenly panicked. He had so many questions. He did not want the man to leave.

The stranger paused with his hand on the door handle. "As you have said, 'I hope so.'"

And, with that, the door opened and Nancy O'Driscoll entered, walking directly toward LeSean without acknowledging the stranger. The man doffed his fedora at LeSean, and addressed Nancy O'Driscoll's receding form, "Take good care of him," he said. Then, he departed.

Nancy O'Driscoll stopped walking, waved her hand in front of her face as if to ward off a fly, and looked around. "Strange," she said, almost to herself.

"What's strange?" LeSean said, immediately understanding that the stranger had not been visible to her.

She turned her attention to her young charge. "Well now, look who's decided to join the living!" She resumed walking over to him and reached for his wrist. He put his arm up to her. "Oh, nothing," she answered his question. "Thought I heard something. Happens a lot, the older I get."

LeSean was beginning to understand the reality of what he had just witnessed: time really is the playground of miracles. He played his hunch. "Didn't you tell a man a few minutes ago that he could only stay for fifteen minutes?"

"What man? There haven't been any visitors on the whole ward tonight," she said.

"A man was just here. Didn't you see him?"

Nancy looked around. "Here? Tonight?" before turning back to LeSean. "You okay?"

"Yeah, for a bullet goalie. But if you didn't talk to any visitors, how would he know there were only fifteen minutes left?"

Nancy looked askance at him, concerned. She knew there were no visitors, but decided to play along. "I suppose the large signs in the elevator, the waiting area, and the hallway might have tipped him off. I mean, if he had been here to see them."

LeSean smiled, recalling the visit. Just as he associated the scent of Lemon Lysol and the tannery with a happy past, he suspected he would come to always associate fedoras with good luck, a happy future.

Wow, a happy future! Just a few minutes ago he had been staring at no future at all. Something weird had just happened here. But it had been a good weird, for sure: The stranger had been granted a wish in time and had delivered a message to his own father.

In that moment, all the pieces of the puzzle automatically clicked into place and LeSean smiled, in awe of the great gift he had been granted. One day, he now knew beyond any doubt, he himself would bring 'The Riser' to the world. "Perception is reality," he said for the second of many times in his life.

"Is it now?" Nancy O'Driscoll said, checking his pulse, relieved at LeSean's interaction with her. If all it took was an imaginary visitor, who was she to complain?

"Yeah. Hey, how you think I'd look in a fedora?"

What an odd question! Nancy thought. "Better than you'd look in a coffin, I suppose."

"Yeah, that's what I thought."

Nancy looked at him quizzically. "Kids," she said, shaking her head.

"What d'ya mean?"

"They, you, make no sense. You'll see someday, assuming you decide to live long enough to get out of here and have kids of your own."

LeSean smiled, recalling the stranger. "My kid'll be cool."

"Your kid? So, you've decided to give up this bed, is that what I'm hearing?"

"Yeah, I'll be going home soon," he said, smiling for the first time she could remember.

"That's the spirit. And where's home?"

"Don't matter. Ain't got no family now. You like baseball?"

"No time for baseball," she said. "I work nights."

"Who watches the cat while you work?"

"How did you know I have a cat?"

"Just guessed," he said, smiling, choosing not to mention her age and lack of a wedding band.

"Wiseguy," she said. "That's just what I need now. Another ungrateful mouth to feed."

But, for the first time in a long time, she permitted a smile to cross her lips, as she blushed.

Nancy O'Driscoll, R.N., to her credit and eventual good fortune, and her cat, were destined to become lifelong baseball fans because of a life-changing decision she would make in the next ten minutes.

And, somewhere in time, the stranger – and his 'Grammy' – smiled.

4

______

UP ICE

rad Tourneau descended the rear staircase, walked briskly through the cooks' galley, and down the basement stairs. He passed the walk-in freezers and his father's collection of exotic motorcars. Checking his watch, he punched an eight-digit code into an electronic keypad on the wall next to a large glass door, which slid aside, permitting him to exit into the cabana area behind the main house. Once outside, the large plate glass door slid closed with a soft swoosh behind him, the only sound he heard in the pre-dawn dark.

He grasped a large, hard-rubber-coated iron hand hold that protruded waist-high from a bluestone retaining wall, and began a series of squats, preparatory to his jog.

Brad loved this time in the early morning, alive, alone, and awake before just about anyone else in the surrounding county. It was a cool, clear, crisp May morning, perfect for jogging, with mist swirling in a wispy cloud six feet above the surface of the Olympic-size pool in front of him and the crystal clear water it contained. Although not clearly visible in the dark, Brad knew the water was pristine. His father demanded it.

Unlike many teenagers, Brad exercised without listening to music. When he ran, he preferred to be aware of everything around him, rather than be buffered from it. For as long as he could remember, he had been able to detect all action going on around him, action that most people missed. He enjoyed being so aware, so in-tune, so connected, especially in the wee hours when distractions were few.

Competing sounds did not mitigate his keen sense. Rather, they heightened it, sharpened it, so it could, at times, be a burden, a curse, unbearable. His parents' dinner parties, and school dances, for example, were so challenging that, oftentimes, he would retreat outside, or to a quiet place, where he did not hear and see everything.

All those simultaneous conversations demanded his attention at the same time rather than combining to form a background hum, as is true for most people. He heard all those discrete conversations, and saw each of the participants, with clarity, even those on the far side of the room. And, because he could see them all at the same time, his eyes worked very hard. His eyeballs scanned the room rapidly, seeing all; his brain, processing all. It was only a few years ago that the headaches had finally stopped.

None of that now, though. Not here, as he stretched and crunched in the dark, with the stars twinkling brightly an hour before the early morning sunrise. His legs and respiratory system would soon be taxed as he jogged five miles, but his brain would be at ease, relaxed. He lived for the quiet, the clarity. It was his music.

Warmed up now, he started out as he did every morning: around the pool, inhaling the cool humid air, and along a slate path that ringed the periphery of his father's rear meadow, then through the black iron gate in the hedgerow at the rear of the property, about three hundred yards from the main house.

He ran along the shoulder of the dimly lit county road a short distance, then turned right onto a street through a housing development. Half a mile later, he entered onto the black macadam county power line trail, which ran the entire length of the local township, beneath the high-voltage power lines high above.

He jogged past the rear property lines of several local farms and county ball fields, and through some wooded areas and wetlands maintained by the county as preservation lands.

The trail was unlit, but it didn't matter. The horizon was already turning light pink and there was enough light to see by, barely. Some Canada geese honked overhead, as they descended into one of the harvested cornfields that had not yet been replanted for the coming season. The only other creatures up at this hour along the trail were a few squirrels, some deer, and some field mice.

And Tony Bench.

Tony Bench wasn't his real name. It was what Brad called him. Joe Billingsley, Brad's best friend, was a firm believer that everybody needed two names: their real name and a nickname. His nickname for Brad was 'B-rad.' Joe claimed 'B-rad' was the perfect nickname because it was actually Brad's real name hyphenated, and Brad, whose parents had planned every aspect of his life, couldn't be radical if his life depended on it.

'B-rad' both said something about who Brad was and who he was not at the same time, and was, therefore, a great nickname. Brad was not the nickname impresario his friend was, but he wasn't above dabbling. Tony Bench was Tony because he wore his long gray hair pulled back in a ponytail, and Tony rhymes with pony. He was Bench because he sat on a bench at the halfway point of Brad's run.

His sitting there was a recent development. Why Tony sat there so early every morning, Brad couldn't say, as they had never spoken. Which was fine with Brad. The fewer distractions, the better.

Jogging strongly, stepping high on the balls of his feet, Brad's footfalls on the black macadam, wet with dew, were the only sound accosting his otherwise tranquil, meditative state as he focused his attention on what he wanted to do with his life. High school graduation was just a few short weeks away and his life would change dramatically, no doubt. His parents had sent him to exclusive Saint Joseph's Prep and he would graduate near the top of his class. He had already been accepted into The University of Pennsylvania on a full scholarship, so his future was bright.

Still, he was troubled. He looked down and saw his feet practically floating over the macadam as he effortlessly and gracefully picked up his pace near the halfway mark. Tony Bench came into view, just over a small rise, sitting on his bench at the end of the trail. He was sitting perfectly still, hunched forward, leaning on his old wooden walking stick, as always.

Focusing again, Brad wasn't so sure if his future was as bright as the one his father envisioned for him. For many years, his father had been very clear about Brad's career path, as sole heir to the great Torneau legacy. Brad would be a pre-eminent investment banker, every bit as qualified, intelligent, and, eventually, as connected to the movers and shakers of this world, as was his father. It all sounded so good, really. Brad was an extrovert, after all. He loved meeting new people and he was not averse to becoming a power broker, a leader.

Still….

Brad approached Tony Bench, who continued to peer straight ahead, as always, giving no indication that he even saw Brad, or saw anything at all for that matter. As he jogged by, Brad looked over, wondering if there would be any eye contact today. There wasn't.

He continued down the trail fifty feet or so before turning and starting back. Coming upon him again, Brad saw that Tony remained as statuesque as ever: leaning forward, chin on his old hands atop the knotty club head of the walking stick, as Brad passed a second time, returning home.

His dad taught him that he could choose to be a leader or a follower, and there could be no mistaking what choice he expected of his son. Brad checked his watch and ran onto the wet grass bordering the trail, just as two bikers raced up from behind and almost lost control of their bikes, swerving at the last minute to avoid hitting him.

"Sorry, man," one biker shouted, after they had raced by. "We didn't see you."

Brad re-entered the trail before he heard the laughing in the distance behind him. He turned and saw Tony Bench dancing around, whooping and hollering like an old fool, shouting and pointing at him.

"I knew it! I knew it! You saw 'em, eh? Ha-ha! Woo-hoo! You saw 'em. You saw 'em. Ha-ha! I knew it! I knew it!"

Brad smiled. A dancing Tony Bench was a sight to see, comical, but he didn't go back. He was late. Glancing at his watch again, he said to himself, "Crazy old fool," before resuming his jog home.

Putting Tony Bench out of his mind, for the moment, Brad tried to refocus and think through his dilemma. Anyone in his right mind would prefer to lead than follow. That was obvious. It was a rhetorical question.

Still....

Damn! What was it? What was eating at him? It was so simple, really, wasn't it? The answer to his father's question? Of course he wanted to be a leader. Of course.

Of course.

He continued to listen to his footfalls and his own breathing and heartbeat. He turned and stole one last glance at Tony Bench, now way in the distance back there. But, he could still hear him laughing and hollering, if only very faintly.

Brad turned forward again and entered the last leg of his journey home, without any new answers but with two new questions. Did he want to be a leader or not? And, who the heck is Tony Bench?

THE HANDS-FREE CALLS NEVER STOPPED. MR. TOURNEAU WAS either calling, or being called, the entire trip.

He and Brad drove to Philadelphia together in his "work" car, a late-model Mercedes Benz, as they did most weekdays. He would drop Brad off at St. Joe's Prep enroute to his office in center city. The steady stream of early morning phone conversations was a daily occurrence.

Brad knew he would be "working" his father this morning. He hated the thought, but he had been schooled well by the old man. Leaders lead, after all, and leading basically is manipulating people to achieve a desired outcome. Brad had heard this sermon many times. Being manipulative did not come naturally to Brad, who was more instinctive, reactive, and less calculating, all of which was anathema to his father.

"Act in haste, repent in leisure," the old man had warned numerous times. Better to lie in wait, prepared, and let them come to you, those who want something. Know what they want before they ask it. And always, always, get something in return.

With much practice over a period of years, this is a desirable skill that can be learned, his father assured him. The tricky part, the piece of the equation that separated the men from the boys, was to get what you wanted without giving up anything of value. This was the mark of a true gamesman, a true leader. The best, most noble and highest pursuit known to man, his father taught, was to get something for nothing, repeatedly. That is the road to true wealth; the sign of a true winner. Trading well required – no, demanded and deserved – excellent planning and execution.

Know your opponent, his weaknesses, his needs and desires, set the lure, and leave your heart at home. Never negotiate for the other side. Be prepared and time your offensive with precision. If it was easy, everybody would do it.

No, the true masters practiced these tactics repeatedly, over a long period of time and with many audiences. Every relationship, every encounter with another human being, was a war, some bigger and more important than others, admittedly, but make no mistake, if you're not winning, you're losing and Tourneau's do not lose. Ever.

But, his father would lose one little battle this morning. While his father was focused on other things, Brad was focused like a laser on just one thing, a hockey game. Brad looked out the window. They would soon be at the Prep. It was time.

"Dad," he started.

"Brad, please," his father warned. "I'm on the phone."

Brad smiled. He had counted on that response.

"Dad…."

His father held up the palm of his hand to Brad, giving him a stern look.

Setting the lure.

Mr. Tourneau pulled the sedan up to the curb in front of the Prep and parked there.

"Thanks, Dad," Brad said, gathering up his books and preparing to exit. As he reached for the door handle, his father spoke up. Right on time.

"Brad, good luck today, and don't forget you're coming to my office tomorrow, so let your teachers know."

"Yeah, Dad, about that…I'm not so sure I'll be able to go because…."

"Stan, wait," Mr. Tourneau said, muting the phone. "Brad, your mother has already cleared it with the school administration."

"So, this is something you want?"

"Of course. I want to introduce you to my colleagues. You'll be their boss someday."

"Dad, I have finals coming up and all."

Mr. Tourneau was becoming agitated. "Look, Brad, it's one day. You can easily make it up. I want you…."

"You want," Brad interrupted. "I get that. What's in it for me?"

Mr. Tourneau was initially stunned at the brazenness, before realizing he was being gamed. He smiled. "What should be in it for you other than a chance to see the place where all this expensive education is leading?"

"A hockey game."

"What?"

"Don't try that delay crap with me, Dad. You heard me: a hockey game."

"Absolutely not!" his father thundered.

"Your call," Brad said, getting out of the car. "No deal."

"Wait, wait. You know your mother won't hear of it."

"I'll leave you to deal with your constituents," Brad smiled. "Come on, Dad. A crummy hockey game and your colleagues get to bore me to tears. Sounds like you're out a lot less than I am. Isn't that a win?"

Mr. Tourneau smiled, briefly. "Doesn't feel like a win," he said, nodding his head. "Stan doesn't know it yet, but his deal just got a lot pricier. Should I send the driver for you?"

"No, Joe's drivin'. Thanks, Dad," he said, his father waving him off. As he closed the door, Brad heard his father yell, "Okay, the deal's off, Stan!"

"Hey, B-rad!" Joe yelled, catching up with Brad as they ran up the front steps together. "What's shakin'? Goin' to the game today?"

"If I can lose the headache," Brad said, rubbing his forehead, hating that he even needed to game his own father.

"Your dad?" Joe recognized his friend's symptoms.

"Who else?"

BRAD HAD TO WATCH HIS TEAMMATES FROM THE STANDS, AS THE doctors had not yet cleared him to return to the team bench. It had been seven weeks since the injury and, though Brad had made a remarkably quick, and apparently complete, recovery from a broken jaw and several lost teeth, his medical team favored caution.

His mother favored an abolition of school-sponsored ice hockey altogether. Had it not been for her husband's diplomatic and insistent interlocution, his intemperate spouse may very well have brought the full force and effect of the legal system upon the heads of the school administration, coaches, referees, and family of the opposing player.

The player who had thrust the handle of his hockey stick up and through Brad's jaw while the referees weren't looking. As the two teams and referees skated away, he stood over a collapsed Brad who spit volumes of teeth and blood onto the ice of his crease.

"Stop that shot, shithead," he said before racing up ice in an attempt to conceal his unprovoked attack upon a defenseless player. He failed in that, however. He was first suspended, and later expelled, to forestall being indicted and sued by Mrs. Tourneau's lawyers.

But, the damage was done. Brad would see no more ice time as goalie of his high school squad, much to the chagrin of Brad, his coach, and his teammates, who sorely missed their varsity net minder.

Quince Harron, the JV goalie, a sophomore, had been pressed into service with the varsity squad and, though willing and appreciative of the opportunity, was no Brad Tourneau and would never be the instinctive defender Brad was.

It was obvious that the Prep squad's fortunes had taken a decided turn for the worse after Brad went down. It was also obvious why Brad would have been awarded a full athletic scholarship to Penn, had he not already received their full academic scholarship.

The best he could do for his team was watch, cheer, and provide analysis to the coaches and to Quince Harron, which he did, but it was not enough. Brad knew he would never be a coach. He needed to compete. He needed to tend goal. He firmly believed that instinct could not be taught. It could only be learned from facing competitors on the ice, as he himself learned every time he played.

Brad's jaw might have been suboptimal but, as he watched the action from the stands, his reflexes were still firing on all cylinders. Sadly, he saw, poor Quince Harron had yet to develop cylinders.

The kid was game, his heart was in the right place, and he tried very hard, but he was overmatched at the varsity level. Brad knew it, Quince knew it, and, unfortunately for Quince and the Prep squad, every other team knew it. Sixty minutes hadn't passed after the injury before the entire league learned that Brad Tourneau had gone down. Saint Joe's Prep, the league champion for the past three years with Brad in goal, was now ripe for the taking.

The Prep goal, for so long a stone-cold, lead-pipe lockdown by Brad Tourneau, now stood wide open, and virtually defenseless, to all comers.

"Maybe I'm turning my head too quickly to see if the puck is in the goal," Quince said to Brad after a particularly humiliating 8-2 defeat.

"I hadn't thought of that." Brad never looked to see if a puck had beat him. He didn't know how to respond.

"Yeah, I think I'll work on that," Quince said, convinced that he had hit on something important.

Brad wasn't sure how one went about practicing what to do after giving up a goal. But, if there was a most appropriate reaction, he feared Quince would have many opportunities to master it.

THE DAY BRAD HAD BEEN DREADING, BRING YOUR KID TO WORK Day, had arrived: his father's name for it, not the official title.

Brad started this day with his five-mile morning jog. Today, however, since he now knew that Tony Bench could see, Brad resolved to greet him. What could it hurt, and it might help, he figured. Today promised to be a disaster anyway. Maybe Tony Bench could provide a sort of antidote.

"Good morning," Brad said when, once again, he came upon Tony Bench.

"Bon jour." Tony Bench continued to look straight ahead as he spoke.

"I'm sorry. I don't speak French," Brad replied.

"Neither do I, really. Just a bit, but I'm not sorry, eh?" Tony said, continuing to stare straight ahead.

"Can you see?"

"Oui. Of course I can see."

"Then why don't you look at me?"

"I am."

"No, you're not. You're looking straight ahead. I'm over here," Brad said.

"My peripheral vision is fine. But I have Macular Degeneration so I can't see things straight ahead too well. There's a big ol' black hole in the middle of everything. You're on the edge of the black hole, but I can see you fine as long as I don't look straight at you."

"Oh. Sorry."

"Don't be. Ain't your fault, eh?"

Brad extended his hand. My name is...."

"I know who you are."

"You do?"

"Of course. You think I'd sit here every morning in the dark to watch someone I didn't know?"

"You've been watching me? Do I know you?"

"No, but I know you, Doc."

"Um, my name's not Doc."

"Yeah it is."

"I ought to know my own name. It's not Doc."

"I had a friend, a long time ago. He had the same name as you… Braddoc. He went by Doc."

"Wait. How do you know my name? Only my mom calls me Braddoc. Do you know my mom?"

"I do. My name's Desmoreau, eh? My friends call me Des. Well, they used to, anyway. Ain't too many of 'em around these days. Please, call me Des."

"Hi, Des."

"Hi, Doc. You mind if I call you Doc?"

"That's fine. I detect your accent. French Canadian?"

"Guilty as charged."

"Your friend, the other Braddoc, was he French Canadian too?"

"He was."

"But he's no longer alive?"

"Yes and no."

"Yes and no? How can he be both dead and alive?"

"It's possible."

"Um, no, I don't think it is." Brad sensed that Mr. Desmoreau was skating on dull blades.

"But you do think, eh? Ain't that what all this here running's about, thinking?"

"How do you know that? How do you know so much about me?"

"I'm psychic."

"Psychic?"

"Yep. I hear people's thoughts. I can also see things most people miss, especially when they come at me indirectly." Then, after a slight pause, he added, "Same as you, eh?"

"There you go again telling me about me."

"Am I right, or do I misspeak?"

Brad thought about some of the more difficult shots he had stopped. Shots that came at him, redirected in an instant, at an impossible angle, or when he was being screened by an opponent so he could not see a slap shot until the last split second. Oddly, the more difficult the line of sight, the better he seemed to see the puck. His instincts kicked in almost…almost as if he wasn't in complete control of his own response. As if, somehow, someone else, perhaps some puppeteer, was dictating that he kick here, or raise his stick there, or fall to his knees now, before he himself actually saw the puck.

"You're right," Brad agreed softly, after a moment's reflection.

Des screamed suddenly, slapping his thigh hard with the palm of his hand, making a loud clap, startling Brad. "Hah-hah! Of course I am! Des don't lie!" Then, continuing to look straight ahead rather than at Brad, he pointed a very crooked index finger sideways, at Brad, and said quietly, "and forget the puppeteer crap. What you do is all you and nobody else. You may not understand how you do it but that, my friend, is practically the definition of instinct. Don't go making up stories to explain what you don't understand. Don't sell yourself short, eh?"

Brad was stunned, yet again. This fey old guy, whoever he was, seemed to be able to read his thoughts. Perhaps he really was some sort of mind reader. Brad saw that Des lowered his hand now and rested it on his thigh, continuing to hold his crooked wooden walking stick with his other hand, looking straight ahead.

"Who are you?" Brad asked again.

Without facing Brad, the old man answered in a way that told Brad today's session was over, and that Des, though here, was somewhere far away.

"Name's Des," he replied, almost in a whisper. "And Des don't lie."

And Brad, who was nothing if not instinctive, immediately knew this was true. Des never lied. Looking around, Brad suddenly felt the undeniable aura. A glow, though faint and evanescent, seemed to emanate from the old man, brightening and warming ever-so-gently the early-morning dark that enshrouded them.

BRAD AND HIS FATHER RODE THE ELEVATOR TO THE TWENTY-FIRST floor of the worldwide headquarters of First Bank, Mr. Tourneau's employer. Exiting the elevator, Mr. Tourneau walked briskly, with Brad trailing, hustling to keep up, across the hardwood entrance and down a long hallway, past many offices, to a second reception area enroute to a large corner office beyond.

Mr. Tourneau was greeted by several employees along the way. As he marched to his office, Mr. Tourneau called over his shoulder to Brad, "Jane will take you around a little later and introduce you to these people." Brad was not surprised at his father's impersonal choice of words.

Mr. Tourneau's large corner office was impressive. It was meant to impress. Brad was drawn to the two large walls of windows, which met at the far corner of the office. His father placed his brief-case on an expansive mahogany desk, clicked open the briefcase, and withdrew several papers, placing them on the desktop. "Like that view?"

"It's awesome, Dad," Brad said. "I can see the Delaware River over there, and the Ben Franklin Bridge. Geez, I can see all the way over into Camden and South Jersey. There's the Aquarium and the baseball stadium for the Camden River Sharks. I can even see City Hall and Billy Penn over there," Brad said, looking hard to his right.

"Do you see the Prep?" Mr. Tourneau said, walking over.

Brad took a moment and looked down the perfect grid of city streets running east-west and north-south toward the neighborhood that housed his high school. "Wow, yeah, I see it. Right there," Brad said, pointing. "From up here it looks so close."

"Yep, it's a short trip from the Prep to where I sit, in more ways than one. That's why we sent you to the Prep. Anyway, today you'll start out with the compliance folks because they have the best understanding of how the various departments here coordinate.

They will introduce you to the leaders of several specific areas. You and I will then have lunch with several VPs and other members of the leadership team, before we meet with my boss, Jim Forester, the President and CEO. How's that sound?"

"Sounds pretty interesting."

Mr. Tourneau then walked back and pushed a button on his phone. "Jane, could you come in, please?"

Five seconds later, a forty-something woman opened the door to the office and entered. "Jane," Mr. Tourneau said, "This is my son, Brad. Brad, this is Jane Addison, my administrative assistant."

"Hello, Mrs. Addison," Brad said, uncomfortable addressing her as Jane.

"Hello, Brad. It is so nice to finally meet you. Your father has told me many good things about you."

"Thank you, ma'am."

"Jane, I've told Brad that he will be starting out in Compliance. Could you please take him there and we'll get this day started, okay?"

"Yes, Mr. Tourneau. Brad, are you ready?"

"I am."

"I will have him back here before noon," Jane said as they turned to leave.

"Thank you," Mr. Tourneau said, placing the headset on his head, as he sat in his desk chair and swiveled away from them, with his hands clasped behind his head. "Roger!" he exclaimed. "Did he bite?"

Brad's father was on his home turf, in his aerie, totally in control, confident and comfortable. As Jane Addison chatted away, leading him into who knows what, Brad was anything but comfortable.

It was a whirlwind morning and he did learn a lot. Mostly he learned that he knew absolutely nothing of any value. He was pretty sure that his four years of expensive Prep education had been a waste. His head was spinning. Debits, credits, mark-to-market, stocks, options, bonds, days to maturity, durations, were all terms he heard in the first hour of his tour but had never heard before.

People talked in acronyms all over the place. By the time he had finished listening to the legal group explain about contracts and registered representatives and vesting and beneficiaries and codicils and discretionary trading, his head ached.

After lunch with several of the AVPs, VPs, Senior VPs, and Executive VP, Brad and his father met with the President and CEO of First Bank, Jim Forrester.

"So, Brad, I hear you might be following in your father's foot-steps. Investment banking is a pretty nice career. Do you think you could succeed like your dad?"

"I think he and my mom have given me every advantage, sir. If I am successful someday, it will be a credit to them."

"We think Brad has narrowed his career choices down to investment banking and ice hockey," Mr. Tourneau said.

"Ice hockey! Sports?" Mr. Forrester asked Brad.

"I'm thinking about it, sir."

"Have you received offers from any teams?"

"I'll be playing for Penn while I'm there, sir."

"And after Penn?"

"That depends, sir."

"I see. Well, okay, you have time yet. I am sure your father has told you that an early start in our business is critical. You will want to begin building your cache of contacts even while you are in school; especially when you are in school. You will need to let your classmates know of your career ambitions, so they will know whom to contact when they need an investment banker. You may, some-day, inherit your father's file, but a portfolio that is not growing is dying, you understand? You will need to be adding to it soon after graduation. I'm sure your father will show you the ropes at the proper time."

"Count on it," Mr. Tourneau said.

"Yes, sir," Brad said.

"A bit of friendly unsolicited advice, if I may?"

"Please, sir."

"I understand that you are a young man, just starting out. Penn is a fine school and, oh, congratulations on your full ride, by the way."

"Thank you, sir."

"I daresay you are beginning to appreciate the fruits of your father's labors."

"And my mother's," Brad said.

"Ha-ha! Of course, of course. I meant no slight to the fine doctor." Brad, stealing a glance at his father, had his doubts. Mr. Forester, regaining his original line of thought, continued. "The odds of making it to the professional level in any sport are not favorable. But, should you make it, it will require your full dedication, as will success in any field. That would effectively rule out any hope of success in investment banking, where your most important relationships are formed in college and right after college."

"Yes, sir."

"So, I hope you appreciate that success as a professional athlete, should you attain that level, will come at a significant cost: the cost of lost opportunity. A successful athletic career will obviate a successful banking career. And banking is the lifeblood of business, of commerce, of leadership. It's what makes the world go 'round, as they say. The compensation of a top investment banker, like your father, will, over thirty years, dwarf any amount you are likely to earn as an athlete. And if you don't believe me, just ask your own father. Go ahead, tell him, John."

"It's true," Brad's father said.

"But, Dad, there aren't thirty-thousand people cheering you on every day, wearing your name on their jerseys, naming their sons after you."

"Brad. Son," Mr. Tourneau started. "Those things are important to you because you're seventeen, and healthy. As an athlete, you'll always be one serious injury away from ending your career and falling into obscurity with very little to show for it."

"That's why I got out of baseball," Mr. Forester said. "I actually made it to Single A, but I knew I could make more money in business. Best move I ever made."

"No regrets?" Brad asked.

"None. If I had it to do all over again, I would follow the exact same path. I am so glad I didn't choose sports."

"What did your dad want you to be?"

Mr. Forester seemed taken aback by this question, as he leaned back in his chair and put his fingertips together in front of him. He looked at Brad's father.

"I apologize, Jim," Brad's dad said. "I told him to ask questions, but…."

"No, no, that's alright, John. The only reason I hesitate is I actually had to think back and remember. It's a fair question." Then, looking at Brad, he said, "It's a good question, son. My father wanted me to become a baseball player, a great baseball player."

"But you chose your own path."

"That's true. I did."

"And it was the right path for you."

"Yes, it was."

The meeting wrapped up a short time later with Mr. Forester guaranteeing Brad full-time employment at the bank after graduation, working with his father. Mr. Tourneau was thrilled. Even Brad was impressed. He appreciated the excellent advice he had just received from two very successful men.

But, for Brad, the correct path forward just became even murkier. What was wrong with him? How could he even think of dismissing such well-intentioned aid? Most of his classmates would kill for the investment banking career being handed to him on a silver platter.

Later, Brad's father stopped by his boss's office. "Jim, I want to thank you for taking the time to meet with my son today. I think you made a real impression on him, and I appreciate that."

"Do you think it will make a difference?"

"I hope so. I sure hope so."

"I have to tell you, he caught me off-guard asking me about my father's wishes. He cut through all the malarkey and got right to the point, didn't he?"

"He is headstrong, Jim."

"And damn bright. John, look, he's seventeen. He's got to sort things out for himself. Don't beat yourself up. There's only so much you can do. In the end, it's got to be his choice. And, if he chooses hockey, maybe he is right – for him."

"If he's right, are we wrong?"

"I'm the CEO. I'm never wrong."

"Do I need to remind you about the seven iron?"

"Okay, I'm almost never wrong, wise ass."

"Thanks, Jim, really."

"He's a good kid, John. It'll work out."

At dinner, Brad recounted for his mother all he had learned that day. When he finished, he asked his father, "Dad, I never got the chance to ask you today, but what would happen if you weren't at work each day? Who would service your clients?"

"I suppose the bank would find somebody else or the clients would find some other bank."

"Please don't sell yourself short, dear," Mrs. Tourneau said. "I think the bank would sorely miss you were you not there."

"Possibly," Mr. Tourneau said, as he chewed his Chicken Florentine. "Some days, perhaps. Other days, I'm not so sure."

Brad considered this to be the most important lesson he learned all day. He maintained his "poker face" as his father had taught him, not revealing the twinge, the sting, upon hearing his own extremely successful and self-actualized father admit, in so many words, that even he was replaceable. If his father ever became unable to do his job, there would be other people and other banks to take up the slack.

As a young man determined to make a real difference in the world, as an idealist seeking to contribute a meaningful verse in the play of life, Brad, for the first time, became fearful. He had always assumed he would follow in his father's footsteps and he knew he could develop the tools to do so. He was about to embark on a new chapter in his life. This seemed a truly inopportune time to not know how to proceed. His father had always taught him that when swinging through the jungle of life, it's good to have one hand firmly on the next vine before relinquishing the vine you hold.

But how could Brad, in good conscience, just take a job, no matter how highly compensated, knowing that he'd be an insignificant cog in some massive self-perpetuating machine? Brad did not merely want to go along for the ride. Brad wanted to drive and, hopefully, even break new ground or do something important that no one else could do.

That night, when he went to bed, Brad suspected his parents were pleased with the outcome of the day's events, and more certain that he would follow in his father's footsteps. Brad was less sure.

And, despite all the managers, directors, vice presidents, brokers, lawyers, and accountants Brad met that day at First Bank, he was more impressed with the ancient, nearly blind, self-proclaimed psychic with the oversized walking stick, sitting on the bench in the dark. He couldn't get Des out of his mind.

DES WAS WAITING WHEN BRAD ARRIVED THE NEXT MORNING.

"Hello, Des."

"Hello yourself, eh?"

"Mind if I sit?"

"Suit yourself. Nowhere you gotta be today?"

"It's Saturday."

"Is it?"

"Yes. You didn't know I was happy for the day off? What kind of mind reader are you?"

"An old one. You get to be my age, and one day is pretty much the same as any other. Go ahead, sit a spell. What have you been thinking about while you were running today?"

Brad sat. "Once again, you're the mind reader. You tell me."

"Very well. Give me a minute. You just sit there and rest. Let me get my bearings. What have you been thinking…?"

Des stared straight ahead, as always. After a full two minutes of silence, Brad shifted his weight, as his rump was getting sore on the hard wooden bench. He wondered how Des could stand sitting still for as long as he did.

"Cuz me bum's as dead as Bob Marley, that's how."

Brad was stunned. "What did you say?"

"And they say I'm hard of hearing. You heard me. So, what do you think of all you heard at the bank yesterday?"

Brad jumped up. "Des, dude, how do you do that? You're spooking me, man."

"Sit, son, sit," Des said, patting the bench. "There's nothing to fear about me. I'm just an old, nearly blind guy who happens to be psychic."

Brad sat back down. "Are you really psychic?"

"Yes, sometimes. Everything else on me is falling apart, but that seems to get stronger as I get older, eh?"

"That's cool."

"You think so? I don't. Everything I treasure: taste, hearing, health, energy, and comfort are leaving me. The one thing I wish would leave, the psychic crap, seems to be taking over, growing like a weed. I can't get rid of it.

"If you believe in prayer, and if you don't mind, could you please pray for me? I could use all the help I can get. But, enough about me. Tell me about your day yesterday. Tell me about the big boss CEO. What's his name – Forster or something like that, but I can't hear it exactly, I'm afraid."

"Mr. Forester."

"Ah, that's it. Forester. Jim Forester, President and CEO. He's your dad's boss, right?"

"Yes. You know, Des, that's pretty amazing how you do that."

"A choking weed is what it is, trust me. So, tell me about Mr. Forester."

"I liked him. He's very sharp, and I think he's a good guy. It was nice of him to take the time to talk to me and try to help me. He even said I could work at the bank with my father after I graduate from college."

"Good. That's good."

"He said that banking is what makes the world go 'round. He said sports is just a diversion. It was pretty clear which he thought was more important."

"And what do you think?"

"I'm not so sure. I mean, Mr. Forester and my dad are very successful businessmen, and they are interested in me. I suppose I should listen to them."

"Yes, you should. Did Mr. Forester say anything else?"

"Yes, he said…." Brad stopped talking and looked at Des and smiled. "By the way, stop me if I happen to tell you something you don't know already."

"Hah!" Des' laugh burst out. "Good one. Okay that's a deal. But please. Go on. I do enjoy listening to you speak."

"Even if it's not necessary?"

"Even if it's not necessary, my good man," Des patted him on the knee.

"He said his dad wanted him to be a great baseball player but then Mr. Forester also said he was glad he didn't choose sports as a career because of the risk of serious injury, and because he was able to make more money as a businessman."

"Mm-hm, I see," Des said. "That's good advice. I might object to one thing there, though."

"What?"

"No one chooses professional sports as a career. Professional sports choose you."

Brad was stunned by this. He turned and stared at Des. The man certainly did have a way with words. Now it was Brad's turn to gaze straight ahead and say nothing as he let that thought sink in. No one chooses sports. Sports choose you. After a minute, he continued, "I never thought of that, but it feels right. But I just can't reconcile that with the advice I've received from two very successful businessmen."

"It's irrational," Des said.

"Yes, exactly. It's irrational to even consider wanting to play a game instead of making a fortune."

"You know, the great poet, George Bernard Shaw once talked about this very topic. You might want to consider what he had to say about it."

"What did he say?" Brad said.

"He said, 'The reasonable man adapts himself to the world; the unreasonable man persists in trying to adapt the world to himself. Therefore, all progress depends on the unreasonable man.'"

Yet again, and in the span of just two minutes, Brad was stunned by this ancient psychic. "Who are you?" he asked, mystified by the wisdom that seemed to flow from him like a clear Canadian spring.

"Since you ask, I'll tell you. I am an old friend of your grandfather. We were best friends. Actually, his father, your great grandfather, took me in when I was abandoned as a boy by my mother. Her Odawa Indian tribe thought I was evil because I was psychic. The Chief had her leave me on your great-grandparents' doorstep in the middle of the night as a three-year-old.

"Your great-grandparents raised me as their own, along with their son, your grandfather. His name was also Braddoc, but he went by 'Doc.' Doc and I grew up together in Canada. He was the greatest goalie I ever saw. We did everything together. We were on the same junior hockey team and were headed to the NHL. He married his childhood sweetheart, Mary. Then, when World War II broke out, Doc and me and a bunch of our friends enlisted together.

"One night we were camped out. I foolishly decided it might be a good time to teach my comrades a tribal dance. I was shot in the leg by a sniper for my trouble and couldn't walk. Your grandfather picked me up, with bullets buzzing all around him, and carried me to a jeep.

"He put me in the passenger seat, next to a driver who was to take me to a M.A.S.H. unit. Doc said, 'Rest easy, Des. You're gonna make it. They're gonna fix you up.' Then I said, 'Just another save, eh?' And he said, 'Best save I ever made. I'll come see you.'

"As he turned to leave, a sniper shot him in the throat. He fell down, slumped against the jeep. He was clutching his throat and couldn't talk, but he knew I could read his mind so he looked me in the eye and thought to me, 'Des, tell Mary I love her, will you? And promise me my son will be a great player.' 'I promise, Doc' I said to him, and he died right there in front of me.

"That was the last thing he ever said to me. He never saw his son, your father, who was born while we were deployed. I had nightmares for years after he died, and only by the grace of God and some great shrinks was I able to have some semblance of a life.

"I tried to keep my promise to Doc. I wanted to keep my promise, and I would have, but your grandmother blamed me, disowned me, and wouldn't let me anywhere near your father. She said I was cursed, evil, and a fool. Your mom doesn't care a whit for me either, by the way. But I guess it all worked out for the best. Your dad's done alright for himself."

Brad couldn't believe his ears. He stood and ran his hand through his hair, speechless. Des broke the silence. "Look, son, I hate to spring this on you, but there is not much time, I'm afraid. Just know that all the gray-haired and bald men in your life will have all kinds of advice for you. The problem is, none of them is seventeen, and none of them remembers what it was like to be seventeen.

"Every CEO, including Mr. Forester, will lead you to believe what they do matters, and it certainly does. But what they have forgotten, perhaps, is that there are many roads to your destination. Life is not about the destination, except to those old farts already there. It's about the journey."

Des paused briefly, as if trying to decide whether he should continue. Finally, he did. "To this gray hair, though, you do seem to be way up ice. Yes, way up ice, reaching behind you with your stick for the goal posts, but they're not there are they?"

"No," Brad said. "They're not."

"Too far up ice. Too far up ice," Des said again. "Time you got back in the crease where you belong, and where only you belong."

"Thank you, Des."

"Don't thank me. Thank Doc." This is the last thing Des said. He placed his chin above his hands atop his walking stick and seemed to stare wistfully, with an ever-so-slight smile forming at the corners of his mouth, straight ahead into the morning darkness. Seeing as only he could, perhaps behind the black hole in his vision, shadows of days, much better days, long gone.

Brad sat there for a few more minutes, staring at Des, before realizing his companion was occupying a time and place far removed from the bench upon which they sat. Just who is this remarkable man, Brad thought. Des' last words were ringing in his ears: "Don't thank me. Thank Doc." Was Des still trying to carry out his brother's dying wish, or had Des delivered a message just now from him?

"Take care, Des," Brad said, standing. "I'd better get going." He bent down and kissed Des on top of his head. "You're not evil, Des. Thank you. Thank you for everything."

Brad then started jogging home with Des' advice, or his grandfather's advice, he wasn't sure, in his ears. "Too far up ice. Too far up ice. Time to get back in the crease where you belong...."

He turned to look back at Des and stopped. Des's glow seemed dimmer this morning. It flickered as Des stood and waved a weary farewell, before turning and walking slowly in the opposite direction with the aid of his walking stick.

***

THAT NIGHT, AT DINNER, THINGS CAME TO A HEAD.

As the staff brought out the food, Brad's parents were ebullient, based on their perceptions of Brad's trip to work with his father the day before. Brad did not join in their excited exchange.

"Brad," his mother said, "are you okay? Why aren't you eating your dinner?"

"Sorry, mom. I'm just distracted. Finals are coming up."

"All the more reason to eat."

"Right. Could you pass the rib eye?"

"Your father and I were just wondering which department at the bank you'd prefer to start your internship," she said, passing a platter to Brad.

"Internship? What internship?"

"Your father has arranged for you to intern there this summer and each summer throughout college. That way, when you graduate, you will have gained a lot of experience in different areas, a lot of the managers will get a good look at you, and you will have a better idea of which managers are most capable."

"Dad, is that true? Did you arrange this?"

"Yes, I took the liberty. You'll also be paid well for your efforts. It's all arranged."

Brad was stunned. He looked down at the platter of steak and froze, panicked. Things were happening way too fast. His head started spinning.

"Isn't that wonderful, Brad?" his mother said. "It's all arranged."

Brad looked up, slowly, pained, and put the platter down, saying, "Mom, everything we do is arranged. We're Martinets for crying out loud. Have you noticed that? Everything we do: dinner, work, school."

"Is that so bad?" she interrupted. "It has worked well."

"For who?"

"For whom? For all of us, including you most of all. You have received the best schooling, the best preparation for life, the best contacts, and the best social circle. These are the people you want to associate with. These are the people who are going places, and you will go right along with them. The best home and food and clothes and possessions, and church. Even your precious ice hockey lessons, which I don't know how I ever let your father convince me were a good idea, cost a small fortune. You have to be able to afford the things you need in life so, really, I guess I don't see the problem."

"No, I don't suppose you do."

"Brad, be respectful of your mother," his father said.

"Oh, please, dear. Do let the boy speak his mind. Braddoc, what makes you so sure I can't see clearly?" Brad's mom tended to call him by his full name whenever she was upset with him.

Brad looked back and forth from his mother to his father before speaking. He was terribly uneasy about being put in this situation, but he was ready. This was no time for negotiations. This was not a game or contest to be won. He would not be manipulative, because he knew he did not have to be. He wasn't trying to win an argument. Brad did not care who won the argument. His mind was made up. This wasn't a time for winners and losers. This was the time for clarity. The puck stopped here, with him. This was a time for him to take a stand.

He looked at his father. "First, as Dad has always taught me, let's lay some ground rules."

"Ground rules? For what? To explain to me how I am delusional?" Brad knew his mother was nothing if not defensive.

Without responding directly, he said, "To agree on a favorable outcome here."

"Well, yes, I must say I would be thrilled to learn of all my shortcomings."

"Dear," Mr. Tourneau said, "it was you who said to let him speak. Perhaps we should hear what he has to say."

Mrs. Tourneau put down her fork, looked at Brad, and said nothing, for the moment.

Mr. Tourneau continued with Brad. "I suppose a favorable outcome might be for us to all agree on an appropriate course of action for you. Is that fair?"

"That's fair," Brad said.

"And would it be fair to assume that future might include ice hockey?"

"Yes."

"No!" his mother thundered. "That is not going to happen. Never! Over my dead body!"

"Why not, Mom?"

Mrs. Tourneau, always choleric and high-strung, was clearly agitated. "Why not!? Why not!? I won't hear of it, that's why not. Do you think we raised you all these years and gave you every good thing that money can buy so you could just run off willy-nilly and waste your life playing some ridiculous game? For what? So you can prove you can compete with some scurrilous, beer-drinking Neanderthals who would just as soon assail you as look at you?"

"Helen…," Mr. Tourneau started.

"And don't you start!" Mrs. Tourneau cut him off. "John, your mother must be turning in her grave just about now. Do you think she would stand for this? Do you remember how she felt about ice hockey? She was very clear that no Tourneau will ever have anything to do with that provincial element."

"What element?" Brad asked.

"The kind that gets you killed!" she yelled. "Tell him! Tell him, John," she implored her husband.

"Helen, hockey did not kill my father, regardless of what my mother believed. He died in the war."

"A war his hockey friends talked him into joining and then, when he tried to save one of them."

"Uncle Des?" her husband interrupted. "He's practically family."

"Please don't mention that name in this house, John. He's no uncle, and he's not family. Don't be so revisionist."

"Helen, take it down a notch," Mr. Tourneau warned.

Brad said, "Uncle Des?"

"Jacques Desmoreau," his father answered. "He was never legally adopted by my grandparents but they raised him as their own after he was abandoned as a young boy."

Mrs. Tourneau took a deep breath and composed herself before continuing. "It's just that even the thought of that…that…man who got your father killed for his trouble is just too much to bear. I will never get over it, John. Never.

"I can't be like you. I can't forgive them. He, and your father's other so-called friends, all returned home as pretty as you please without a scratch on their worthless hides.

"Your father, John! You never met your own father, because he risked his life for one of his prosaic rink rat rabble. Go ahead, tell him! Tell Braddoc where he is headed if he keeps this up. And don't forget to tell him what he is sacrificing in the meantime.

"Really, John, how can you abide such talk? Is this what you want for your son? Is this really what you want for our only son?"

"Mom, nice try, but it won't work this time." Brad had heard enough.

Mr. Tourneau slammed the table with the palm of his hand. "Brad, don't be insubordinate, do you understand me, young man?"

Brad stood and started walking across the room, away from his parents, turning to face them before leaving the room.

"No, Dad, truthfully, I don't understand you or mom, any more than you understand me. Know why? Because I can't climb into your heads. I can't see the world from behind your eyes. And you can't climb into my head to see the world from my eyes or feel what I feel from the inside out.

"I thought we agreed we were going to try to decide on the correct course of action for me. Yet, all I hear is mom ranting at me, screaming at me, telling me what I can't do over her dead body because someone who died before I was born wouldn't approve.

"How are you going to know what's best for me if you don't know me? And how are you going to know me without at least listening to the one person on this planet who can tell you about me? The one person who deserves at least a vote in determining an appropriate future for me?"

"But Brad," his dad said, "we're your parents. We've been around the block a few times and have the gray hairs to prove it. When you're older...."

It was Brad's turn to raise the volume. "The gray hairs on your head matter way less than the thoughts and feelings inside my head, Dad!"

Brad turned to leave.

"Where are you going?"

"Somewhere where I'm not outnumbered by people who disregard the rules of engagement. Somewhere where maybe, just maybe, people care about what I have to say. Don't wait up for me." Brad slammed the front door behind him as he left his parents, speechless and alone.

———

"Joe, it's Brad. Where are you?"

"Hey, B-rad. Sinamin's with Daly and Clark. Havin' some nachos. You comin'?"

"Yeah, I'll be there in a few minutes. Save me some nachos, will ya?"

"Sure."

"Later."

Brad closed his cellphone as he sat behind the steering wheel of his car and drove the ten minutes to Sinamin's Sports Bar & Grille. He needed to clear his head, get out of the house, and away from his folks, so he could think without pressure and be with his teammates. He knew this about himself.

As instinctive as he was physically and athletically, when actual forethought was necessary, he plodded. If he was ever pressed into military service, he liked his chances of surviving a dogfight or ambush better than his chances of carrying out any sort of sedulity. He liked his chances when the action was fast and furious, when the odds were stacked against him, and when there was little or no time to plan.

Joe, Daly, and Clark were sitting together in a large booth when Brad arrived. The waitress arrived with four large platters of nachos just after Brad sat down. He was not surprised.

"Dutch treat?" Brad asked his friends. Daly and Clark each looked at Joe as they shoved nachos into their mouths.

"Only if you're Dutch," Joe said, stuffing his mouth too.

"So, what? You were just going to sit here all night and not eat unless I came?"

Joe wiped his lips with the back of his hand before holding his hand up at Brad. Joe had, yet again, stuffed a bit too much food into his mouth. "No," he said, finally. "We had a backup plan in case you didn't show."

"Really, you goobers were actually going to pay for your own food?"

"No, we were going to play pool," Joe said, as he, Daly, and Clark laughed.

"No dough, no dinner," Daly said.

"No B-rad, no dough," Clark agreed.

"It's good to have friends," Brad shook his head.

"Oh, Come on, B-rad. It's only money. It's meant to go around."

"Correction," Brad said. "It's only my money that is meant to go around, apparently. Your money…do you guys even have an ATM card?"

"No, we have you," Daly said and the three friends laughed.

"Better than an ATM," Daly said. "You come with us," and the three of them laughed again.

"You knuckleheads are really pushing it," Brad warned.

"Oh, come on, B-rad," Joe said. "If any of us had full scholarships, we'd buy you nachos too."

"Yeah, what are friends for?" Daly said.

"You kumquats on scholarships…now that's a scary thought," Brad said, shaking his head.

"Here's to free nachos and kumquat scholarships," Joe shouted, piling a fresh load of nachos into his mouth, and all four of them laughed. Brad couldn't help it. These idiots were his friends and little did they realize how much he needed them right now. Nachos was a small price to pay for the mental break.

Later, as they shot pool, Clark said, "We sure miss you in goal, B-rad."

"Yeah, poor Quince is just way overmatched," Joe agreed. "Any chance you can play in even the last game?"

"No, Joe. You know that's not gonna happen."

"Too bad," Joe said. "I could have done a nice article about you for the Daily News."

"What?" Brad asked, surprised.

"You heard me. I'm gonna intern at the Daily News for the summer, before I head out to Penn State for four years."

"Really? Joe, that's great! So you're really gonna do it? You're gonna be a sportswriter?"

"That's the plan, Sam. That's all I've ever wanted."

Daly, Clark, and Brad all high-fived Joe, and Brad said, "Awesome, Dude. That's great! Really. But wait, who's gonna buy you nachos in Happy Valley?"

"I know where you live," Joe replied. "I'll send you my bill."

"Don't hold your breath. You're gonna lose a lot of weight. Better go with the meal plan."

"B-rad, old chum, you are my meal plan. Someday, I'm gonna be writing articles about you and you'll keep me and all your kumquat groupies in nachos forever."

"Don't count on it, Joe," Brad said, racking up the pool balls for a new game. "The Old Man practically has me working with him already."

"Really? At the bank?" Joe said.

"Yep. Clark, you break," Brad said. "Might be the best thing, Joe. Your nachos ain't cheap."

"Screw the nachos, B-rad. Give me something to write about and I'll get my own nachos."

"Ooh, big talk," Daly said, "for a guy who hasn't written anything yet."

"I'm serious, B-rad. Forget banking. You belong on the ice."

"You think so?" Brad asked as Clark broke.

"Absolutely," Joe said. "Plus, nobody wants to read about no damn banker."

"Right, I'll just explain to my folks how I can't become filthy stinking rich because you need to write about me wallowing away on some Godforsaken rink in junior hockey."

"I'll write about you and I'll give you one thing your Old Man can't."

"What?"

"A great nickname."

Brad looked at Joe and shook his head. "You don't know my old man. That ain't never gonna fly." Brad said, throwing two twenties on the pool table. "Sorry, guys. I gotta go," he said, as he walked out, realizing there were no answers to be found in Sinamin's Bar & Grille, for the son of Jack Tourneau.

Later that night when he went to bed, he turned on his side and said a silent prayer. "Please, God, let there be a path for me. Let me find my way. And, please, take care of Uncle Des. He's really suffering right now, and I think he's been suffering for a long time."

BRAD RAN EACH MORNING FOR THE NEXT SIX DAYS, BUT DES NEVER showed up. Every time Brad neared the bench hopefully, he was disappointed to find it empty. No Des. Brad hoped Des was okay, but he really had no way to find out. Des never said where he lived.

On the seventh morning, however, Brad saw a man sitting on the bench in the early morning, but it clearly wasn't Des. As Brad approached, the man looked at him and asked, in a French Canadian accent, "You must be Brad then, eh?"

"That's right. Are you a friend of Des?"

"Yes. He told me I would find you here."

"Wait!" Brad said, eyes wide, pointing, recognition dawning. "Are you...are you...Bernie Parent?"

"I am. Nice to meet you, son," Bernie Parent said, reaching out to shake hands.

Brad shook his hand. "I don't believe it. Bernie Parent. What are you doing here, Mr. Parent?"

"Please, call me Bernie, eh? Des is an old friend of mine. He asked that I talk to you."

"Is Des okay? I haven't seen him in a week or so. He used to be here every day."

"Have a seat, kid. We can talk."

Brad sat on the bench. Bernie Parent looked directly at Brad. "I'm afraid that I have some bad news. Des passed away a few days ago."

"What?! That's impossible. We sat here and talked every morning. He was fine."

"Des was never fine. He was troubled, as you probably figured out if you talked to him for more than five minutes. I can't imagine the pain of being rejected by one mother, let alone two. But, he's finally at rest, thank God, and the voices that crowded his head every waking minute have ceased. Des was a special man, a great man, but he was cursed for sure."

"Yes. I think so. How did you know him?"

Bernie chuckled a little. "Des and I go way back. He told me on several occasions that he had a promise to keep to someone, and he swore he would keep that promise even if it killed him. I never knew who he was talking about, but I figured he meant his brother, Doc.

"He always talked about Doc, eh? Des loved him. In his last testament, he told me you are Doc's grandson. He asked that I meet you and talk to you, and I am more than happy to do it, eh? He helped me when I was about your age, so I always have felt indebted to him." Then, getting to the point, he said, "He said your father is very wealthy."

"Yes. Giving up money is a hurdle if I am to pursue hockey

instead of business. My dad wants me to work at the bank with him after I graduate from college."

"Ah! Quite a dilemma eh? Money complicates things, that's for sure. Does money matter to you?" Bernie Parent asked.

"I don't know. I don't think so, but maybe that's because I've always had it and take it for granted. Did you have to choose?"

"Yes, but ignoring money wasn't one of my options. I never had a dime."

"So you did it for the money?"

"No. Money was never a consideration. I would've played hockey for nothing."

"Really?"

"Really."

"What if you'd failed?"

"I didn't think I would fail," Bernie Parent said.

"But weren't you worried that if you did fail, you'd have given up better opportunities?"

"To do what? Make more money? Look, kid. Money was not my motivation. It's never been my motivation. I didn't become a goal tender to make a fortune. I did it because, well, because I thought I could. I thought it was something I could do pretty well and I wanted to find out, eh?"

"But the odds are not good."

"That's true. I guess I thought, well, I'm young. I have time to make mistakes. If I wasn't any good, at least I would have taken my shot. I guess I thought it would be worse to grow old never having taken my shot. Always wondering, but never knowing for sure, you know?"

"There are no guarantees," Brad said softly, almost to himself.

"For sure, eh? No guarantees no matter which path you take."

"It's a little different for me, though. I'd probably make more money in business than I ever would as a goalie."

"Look, kid, we all have to choose our own path among many. I had different paths than you staring at me when I was your age but, still, I had to make my choice. It was difficult, as you are learning. Des talked to me then the way we are talking now. He helped me a great deal."

"What did he say to you?"

"He told me I had to do some pruning. I had to choose. He said, and I'll never forget this, 'Only when we prune does serendipity have a chance to shine through.'"

"Serendipity?"

"Unplanned goodness he called it. Great stuff, happiness and good fortune that happen when you prune, when you simplify, when you eliminate complications and are true to yourself."

"How do I prune?" Brad asked.

"Take money out of the equation," Bernie Parent said.

"Huh?"

"Take money out of the equation," Bernie Parent repeated.

"How am I supposed to do that?"

"How do you stop a breakaway, point-blank?"

"I don't know. I guess I just do it, that's all," Brad said.

"Exactly. Just do it. That's how you take money out of the equation. You just do it."

"That might work for you Canucks, but down here in the States it's a bit more complicated."

"I suppose that's true," Bernie Parent said. "Lots of opportunities for you Yanks. You have lots of options. Makes it tough. Don't forget, though, there's some Canuck in you too, otherwise you wouldn't be asking these questions. It's the Canuck in you trying to get out. It's the Canuck that's driving you right now. It's always been that way for our kind. It will always be that way. It was an itch I just had to scratch, I guess."

"So you really weren't concerned about the money? Amazing," Brad said.

"I can see why you would think that. After all, I suppose your parents have given you everything: the best education, plenty of money, possessions, and connections. But all I had were rocks and trees and lakes, some moose, and my buddies. We had to make do. So, maybe it's not so amazing that the best hockey players in the world are Canadian. I guess I figured, how much money did I really need to lace 'em up, chug a beer, and never let the bastards score?"

Bernie's eyes bore into Brad now, as he pointed an index finger at Brad's face and repeated for emphasis, "and never let the bastards score."

Brad sat dumbfounded, as Bernie Parent stood to leave. "So, you see, kid. It's in here," he said, patting his chest. "That's what's driving you right now, and it's priceless. There's not an old million-aire in the world right now who wouldn't give up a lot to have the opportunity your talent gives you."

"Really?"

"Tell you what, I'll give you a choice, but you have to choose just one. In this hand, there's $1 billion. Yours for the taking when you're forty, no questions asked. In this hand is your name inscribed in Lord Stanley's cup, maybe even multiple times. I don't need to know which you would choose, but you do. You answer that question for yourself and you will have the answer you seek."

Brad sat there, but said nothing right away. Finally, he stood and reached out his hand, "Thank you, Mr. Parent. I don't know why you and Des have gone to so much trouble on my behalf, but thank you very much."

"It's no trouble at all, kid. This is the way it's been done for generations, one great goal tender to another. Someday, I may be asking you to talk to some young stud, you know, to pass the torch like I'm doing now."

He stopped briefly to look around him. "Yep, this spot is defi-nitely off the beaten path. I can see why Des liked it here. The trees and hills remind me of home."

Words failed Brad. Bernie Parent, one of the greatest NHL goal tenders of all time, just said he was passing the torch to him. Unbe-lievable.

Brad's mind was set. He would have to break the news to his father. It wouldn't really be that difficult either, because he finally saw his path.

"Look, Dad, if you had your life to do all over again, would you choose a different career?"

"Honestly? No, I don't believe I would."

"So, you are happy with your choices?"

"I am satisfied with what I have been able to accomplish, yes."

"No regrets?"

"Well, maybe a few along the way, but that's life, Brad. I've made some mistakes but, overall, not too many regrets, no."

"So, what is it you enjoy most about being a successful invest-ment banker?"

"What is it I enjoy most? I would have to say I feel as though I've made a difference and have been richly rewarded for doing so."

"Uh-huh. The wealth is obvious, so talk to me about the differ-ence you feel you have made."

"Okay, well, let's see. I am in a very, very competitive business. It is truly dog-eat-dog, knock-'em-down, drag-'em-out every day and just about every hour of every day. I pursue deals. Big deals. Huge, mega deals. I have at least two dozen competitors breathing down my neck all the time. I may not know who they are, but I know they are somewhere, trying their damnedest to get the same deal done.

"So, I can't stop. I can never let up, because each deal I do is worth millions – to me and to us, your mother and you, too. If I thought for a minute that someone else had snuck in and stolen one of my deals because I had somehow failed, I don't know what I would do. Fortunately, that doesn't happen very often, if ever."

"You always win?"

"I like to think so, yes. I believe I always win."

"So the difference you have made is to amass a fortune that, if you hadn't, someone else would have."

"Exactly."

"What if there was no money?"

"No money? I'm afraid I don't understand."

"What if, after putting in all the time and effort to beat out your competitors and get some deal done, you did not receive a big pay day?"

"Brad, that's a pretty ridiculous hypothetical, don't you think? Can't we deal in reality?"

"Dad, I ask the question for a reason."

"Okay, well, if you insist. Let's see, I suppose if the compensation wasn't there, it wouldn't make any sense to do the deal."

"And if you weren't doing deals?"

"I'd be doing something else. Brad, c'mon, where are you going with this?"

"Sounds to me, Dad, the only real difference you have made is to get paid for doing something you wouldn't do if there wasn't any money in it and that if you didn't do it, someone else would."

Brad's father stared at his son. Brad continued. "I think that pretty much sums up the worldview of many burger flippers and Wal-Mart greeters."

"Except they're not multi-millionaires."

"Right. They aren't multi-millionaires."

"Look, don't start getting all sanctimonious."

"I'm not, Dad. I'm just saying you're in it for the money, that's all. You're great at what you do, and you get paid handsomely to do it, and you seem satisfied with that. But, Dad, that's not me. That's not enough for me. Being rich, owning things, doing deals, and beating out some jerks isn't what I care about."

"You say that because you're rich. You take it for granted. Let's see how you feel once you have to work for a living just to be able to afford a meal and a roof over your head and clothes on your back."

"Thanks to you, Dad, I will never have to worry about those things."

"Don't be so sure."

"I am sure, Dad. You worked a lifetime for me and mom, and you have no intention of sticking it to me just because I want to do something different."

"You're pretty damned sure of yourself. Remember, I write my will."

"Look, Dad, you do what you need to do, but don't threaten me. I'm telling you that I am not motivated by money. I will never be motivated by money, by things. That's you, Dad. That's just not me."

"And what are you, Brad? What is it you want to do that money is so beneath you?"

"Money isn't beneath me. Don't put words in my mouth. I didn't say that. I just said I'm motivated differently than you. I want to make a difference, whether I make a fortune or not. I want to make my mark and be remembered. I want to do something no one else can do."

"And what's that? Stop a damn puck? Your mother's right. Who really cares?"

"Yes, Dad. I want to stop a puck. I want to stop every damn puck. I care, Dad. And because I do, someday, maybe generations from now, people are going to remember me and talk about me and tell their kids about me. Not because I was rich, but because I followed my heart and did something no one else could do. And, because that's the way I feel, and because those people in the future will remember me.

"And because I can stop every damn puck, I will have made a difference. I will have left my mark."

———

JOE BILLINGSLEY DID BECOME A SPORTS JOURNALIST, WHICH surprised no one, least of all Brad, who quickly became Joe's favorite subject, and for good reason: becoming, by virtue of both extraordinary skill and an extraordinary name, prime fodder for Joe's creativity.

Just five short years after Des first called him Doc, and one year after graduating from Penn, Brad, all of twenty-two years old, became the starting goalie for the Philadelphia Flyers. When Brad goal tended to a shutout in his first NHL game, Joe's headline in the Philadelphia Daily News the next day immortalized Doc Tourneau with the greatest nickname he would ever create:

DOC TOURNEAU IS DOCTOR NO!

Thereafter, when every other fan base exhorted their team with chants of, "De-fense! De-fense!" Philadelphia Flyers fans upstaged them all with thunderous chants of:

DOC-TOR NO! DOC-TOR NO!

Brad heard them, of course, and became a goalie possessed. He thwarted every attack and parried every shot on goal. He won his second NHL game 1-0, turning away thirty-four shots, and stoning the opponent's best forward, one-on-one, in an overtime shoot-out.

As the crowd cheered, "DOC-TOR NO! DOC-TOR NO!" and the opposing forward skated away shaking his head, not believing the lightning-quick stick save he had just witnessed, Brad, surrounded by his joyous teammates, removed his mask and looked up ice.

For one fleeting moment, he could have sworn he saw a young

Des, in a Montreal Canadiens jersey, slapping a hockey stick on the ice, before dissipating, likely returning forevermore to those Halcyon days of rink rats and frozen Canadian lakes. In that moment, Brad did not know if he would become the greatest goalie of all time or merely a flash-in-the-pan. But he never had to wonder what would have happened had he taken his best shot at life.

He already knew

5

WE OF LITTLE FAITH

"Jeremiah, I need to see you in my office."

Bob Stevenson had seen enough. Through the partially frosted glass wall of his corner office, he couldn't take it anymore. He had patience and had been very understanding, he thought, of Jeremiah Zimmer, the program director whose work space was on the other side of the glass. This was the third consecutive day of Zimmer's ongoing conversations with…with… who, exactly, no one could say, as Zimmer was the only person sitting there.

The vice president of the company had just returned from clearing his proposed course of action with Human Resources. Stevenson hated the thought of losing his best and most capable technician right now, at quarter end, but others of the staff were going to have to pick up the slack until Zimmer returned.

"Yes, Mr. Stevenson?" Jeremiah Zimmer cowered in the doorway.

"Come in, Jeremiah. Come in. Please take a seat over at my table. I'll be with you in a minute," Stevenson said, buying a few more seconds to gather his thoughts and mentally prepare the points he was about to make. Though resolute, he knew he would need to be tactful, given Zimmer's recent personal problems. And it promised to be a difficult conversation for him because Jeremiah Zimmer, even with all of his problems, was certainly an ingenious team player.

Everyone liked him. Everyone cared about him, but enough was enough. Clearly, Jeremiah needed professional help to defeat whatever demons he had obviously been battling since his brother's recent death. Stevenson got up slowly from his desk and walked over to close his office door.

"Uh-oh, he's closing the door. This can't be good," Sasquatch said.

"Sasquatch, don't," Jeremiah whispered to the most mendacious of his seven demons who sat across the round table from him in one of the four chairs.

"What's that?" Stevenson said, walking over to sit at the table with Jeremiah. Stevenson, of course, saw and heard no demons.

"Um, nothing. Sorry, sir," Jeremiah said.

"Actually, Jeremiah, that's exactly what I wanted to talk to you about." Stevenson sat in another chair at the table.

"Dude, you are so screwed," Sasquatch said. "He knows." Jeremiah chanced a warning glance at Sasquatch, who added, "Oh, right. What are you going to do? Hit me? In front of your boss?"

Stevenson was wary of Jeremiah's odd glance and facial expression. "Jeremiah, what are you looking at?"

"Um, sorry, sir. Nothing, sir." Jeremiah felt that was the truth, technically.

"*Um, sorry, sir. Nothing, sir.* What a wuss," Sasquatch mocked.

"Jeremiah, are you alright?"

"Yes, sir. I'm fine. Did you like my report?"

"The financial metrics report? Yes. Thank you. It was fine. Better than fine, actually. It was quite good, as is all your work."

"Thank you, sir."

"Jeremiah, it's not your work that concerns me. That's not why I called you in here."

"Told you," Sasquatch said, and Jeremiah couldn't help but look at him again before quickly looking back at his boss.

"That's why I called you in here," Stevenson said, pointing at Jeremiah. "That look. The way you look away from me as if you're paying attention to someone else. Is there someone else in here, Jeremiah? Someone I can't see?"

"*No, sir.* Go ahead, say it. *No, sir,*" Sasquatch heckled Jeremiah. "Otherwise, he's gonna know you're cuckoo."

Jeremiah stole a quick glance at Sasquatch. It was hard for him not to. Sasquatch was bigger-than-life and very demanding, very controlling. He seemed to appear at the worse possible times, such as now, and much more frequently of late. Jeremiah looked at his boss, but did not answer. Instead, he looked around the office at all the awards, trophies, framed degrees and artwork adorning his boss's office before looking his boss in the eye.

Jeremiah had never lied and he was proud of that. He vowed always to be true to the memory of his parents, who taught him from an early age that nothing good came of lying. What they failed to mention was that, apparently, nothing good came of being truthful either. Still, he could not lie.

"Yes, sir."

"Oh boy! You did it now JZ. Crazy JZ!" Sasquatch laughed, and Jeremiah suddenly clamped his hands over his ears and looked down, clenching his teeth as a vein appeared on his forehead and a tear streamed down his cheek.

"I see," Bob Stevenson said. "That's good, Jeremiah. You have always been truthful and I appreciate that. It is admirable. But, son, I think we both know you need help."

"I'm seeing a shrink now, Mr. Stevenson," Jeremiah interrupted, looking up with red, tired eyes.

"I know. I know, son. And that's good. But, under the circumstances, I think it best for you to take some time off from work for a while, and focus on getting better. I know you loved your brother."

"He suffocated, sir. In his sleep. Twenty-seven years old. How does that even happen? He was the only family I had after my parents died. Now I have no one. No family."

"But you have many friends, Jeremiah. People who care for you. Your colleagues at work, me."

"Right, I know, but now I'm losing them too."

"No. You're not losing us. We will be here for you when you return, just as we are here for you now, telling you that you need to take care of yourself. Telling you to make your mental health a priority and return to work when you are able."

"But, I am trying, sir. I'm seeing a doctor and…."

"Jeremiah, you talk to yourself all day long and it's getting worse. Now you tell me you see people who no one else can see. Don't you think you should take care of yourself first before worrying about metrics reports and such? Aren't your mental and emotional well-being more important than financial reports?"

"Nope," Sasquatch said. "Go ahead, tell him how worthless you really are, Crazy JZ."

Stevenson was surprised by a sudden outburst from Jeremiah.

"Shut up! Just shut up, will you!" Jeremiah squeezed the palms of his hands over his ears and looked down once again, before realizing the implication of his outburst and looking up at his stunned boss. "Sorry, sir. Sorry, Mr. Stevenson. I didn't mean you, sir."

"I know, Jeremiah. I know."

As Jeremiah drove after work to his weekly appointment with Dr. Michael Scott, his psychiatrist, he was thankful that he only had to confess just one of his demons to his boss. Though

Sasquatch was the ringleader, Jeremiah had seven demons, at last count, and they all drove with him now.

"You should have seen him," Sasquatch said to the others. "He didn't even have the sense to deny me to his boss."

"Really?" said Ambler, the demon who constantly reminded Jeremiah that his mother never really loved him. "Idiot. No wonder your mother was ashamed of you."

"My mother loved me," Jeremiah said, both hands on the steering wheel, trying to concentrate on his driving.

"She loved your body, you little nut job," Con said. Con was short for Conshohocken. Con constantly reminded Jeremiah that his libido was evil.

Jeremiah's demons took the names of the towns in which Jeremiah first encountered them. Sasquatch first manifested in Canada, so even his name was location-based.

Philly was a teenage female troll who chewed and snapped gum incessantly. The only things she advocated were revenge, death, and general destruction.

Mal, short for Malvern, both criticized Jeremiah for not having enough money while, at the same time, complaining that everyone richer than Jeremiah was evil.

Dresher had an unquenchable thirst for beer, while Lancer, who first joined Jeremiah for a forgettable date in a local diner of the same name, preferred drugs.

"Shut up, Con," Jeremiah said.

"Jeremiah, why don't you just kill the little bastard?" Philly said.

"You really want him to do that?" Sasquatch asked. "Not that he ever would, or could."

"Right chemicals will do the trick," Lancer said. "He could experiment."

"Wrong prescription and you're history," Philly said to Lancer. "I like it."

"Or maybe you'd be history," Lancer retorted.

"Or all of us," Sasquatch said.

"Ooh, yeah, a total conflagration. We all go out in a blaze of glory. It'd be epic!" Philly's eyes lit up at the thought. "And maybe you'd get to see your folks on the other side, JZ. Your mom would love you for putting an end to all of us."

"She'd love his little angel body," Con said.

"Ain't gonna happen," Dresher said. "Boy ain't gonna do drugs."

"Dresher's right. He can't afford 'em," Mal said.

"But a couple of six packs with the right chemicals shouldn't be too expensive. That'd do the trick," Dresher said.

"So would a gun," Sasquatch said.

"Would you all just shut up!" Jeremiah screamed. "Please, just stop!"

The minivan fell silent for the next few moments, and Jeremiah was thankful for that. He was also thankful that Sasquatch was sitting in the back of the minivan. How did he know about the gun? "Wait. Minivan? What minivan?" Jeremiah looked around him. He didn't own a minivan.

"Yeah, nice wheels," Mal said. "You get a raise or a bonus?"

"No," Jeremiah said, almost to himself, confused. What happened to his Honda Civic? But, as he pulled into the parking lot of Dr. Scott's office, he didn't have time to worry about it.

"Hey, what the heck?" Sasquatch said. "Where are you going?"

"To see Dr. Scott. It's my weekly 7:00 p.m. appointment."

"How long is that going to take?"

"The usual. An hour."

"He's gonna get it on with Andrea," Con said. "She digs his body."

"An hour?" Sasquatch said. "And what are we supposed to do for an hour? Just sit here?"

"Why don't you all just take a ride somewhere and forget your way back?" Jeremiah suggested.

"You wouldn't mind parting with this fine set of wheels?" Mal said.

"It'd be a small price to pay to be rid of the lot of you. I left the keys in the ignition. If you're not here when I come out, I won't come looking for you," Jeremiah said, getting out, closing the door behind him. Mal immediately hopped into the driver's seat. Jeremiah called back over his shoulder. "I hear Nome, Alaska is nice this time of year."

"Alright! Nome, Alaska, here we come! Mal shouted, and Jeremiah heard all his demons whooping and hollering with glee inside the minivan, as it pulled into the street and drove away.

Jeremiah smiled to himself, breathed a sigh of relief and entered the medical building. "Good riddance," he said.

Andrea Lorenz, the psychiatric assistant, ushered Jeremiah into Dr. Michael Scott's office. "Make yourself comfortable," Andrea said. "Feel free to sit or lie down on the sofa. Dr. Scott will be in momentarily."

"Thank you, Andrea. I think I'll do that." Jeremiah reclined on the sofa as Andrea left the room and closed the door. He reflected on his day so far. The demons had begun to bother him at work now, ever since his brother, Noah, died in his sleep a month ago. This week was the worst, though, as they had been paying undue attention to him at his work desk, in the lunch room, in the men's room, and when he went for his walk at lunchtime.

Jeremiah's colleagues had initially asked if something was wrong, what could they do to help, etc. They had tried, but the demons had become so controlling that Jeremiah's friends at work had begun to avoid him. Things had gotten so bad, apparently, that even his boss had noticed, resulting in Jeremiah's involuntary six-week leave of absence, beginning tomorrow.

Jeremiah took a deep breath and placed his left forearm over his forehead. It was so peaceful here. He hoped Dr. Scott would stay away just a bit longer so he could just rest for a bit, without the demons hovering. Jeremiah decided he would chance taking a quick snooze before Dr. Scott appeared, and opened his eyes one last time to ensure he was still alone in the office.

No such luck. Jeremiah was startled to see Dr. Scott sitting in a chair, looking at him.

"Oh, sorry Doc," Jeremiah said, sitting up. "I didn't hear you come in."

"That's quite alright, Jeremiah," Dr. Scott said. "I didn't mean to startle you. You looked quite relaxed. How do you feel?"

"Never better, actually," Jeremiah said, smiling. "Like a million bucks."

"Well, that's good to hear."

"Yeah. The demons are gone."

"Gone?"

"Yep. They decided to take a drive to Nome, Alaska. They're not here."

"Nome, Alaska? Why Nome, Alaska?"

"Dunno. I suggested it and they were only too happy to oblige. They took the minivan." Jeremiah stopped suddenly and rubbed his forehead. "Wait, Doc. I don't have a minivan." Jeremiah looked up. "What time is it?"

"It's 8:15 p.m."

"8:15? You mean, I've been here an hour and a quarter already? Why are we getting started now instead of 7:00 o'clock? Why were you delayed so long? Have I been sleeping all this time?"

"Jeremiah," Dr. Scott began. "We started on time, at 7:00 p.m. Don't you recall we had agreed to try hypnosis to see if that could help relieve you of your demons?"

Jeremiah studied the hardwood floor at his feet. "Yes, now that you mention it," he said, realization dawning. "So, was it you who suggested Nome, Alaska?"

"It was."

"And the minivan?"

"Minivan?"

"Yes, I remember driving a minivan, but that was confusing to me because I don't own a minivan. I own a Honda Civic."

"Sorry, I cannot take credit for the minivan. That was all you. Perhaps your subconscious mind doesn't appreciate all your demons in a Honda Civic and conjured up the minivan to provide more room."

"Oh, good. So I still have my Honda?"

"Check your pockets. Your car keys should still be there."

Jeremiah dug into one of the pockets of his khaki dress slacks and retrieved the keys to his Honda Civic. He smiled. "It was getting ridiculous in the Honda."

"They seem to have grown quite fond of invading your personal space," Dr. Scott said.

"That's true. Hopefully, that's behind me. Do you think I'll run into them again?"

"Not if you stay out of Nome, Alaska."

Jeremiah smiled. "That shouldn't be too difficult."

"That's what I figured," Dr. Scott said.

"Wow, Doc, so that whole adventure I just had in the minivan was really you?"

"Jeremiah, I am not sure of everything you experienced. I cannot take credit for any conversations you might have had, or anything you might have heard. I admit, this treatment was risky, but I thought it was worth the risk. I did, however, suggest Nome, Alaska."

"Well, Doc, whatever it is you did sure seemed to work. I feel great. For the first time in a long time I feel really, really good. I can't believe you were able to get rid of all those demons, especially Sasquatch."

"Ah, your ringleader."

"Yes."

"Jeremiah, I know these demons all seemed very real to you, but you must know that they were all figments of your imagination. They were images your mind conjured up for some purpose, likely related to the stress of losing your brother and parents. They are not real."

"I know, Doc, but they sure seemed real to me. Especially Sasquatch. I can't believe you were able to get rid of him."

"Well, we'll keep our eye on things for a while yet. I want you to continue with our sessions for a few more weeks. I really think it would be best. Here's another one of my business cards. Keep it nearby. Call me at any time, day or night, if you need to talk to me."

"Will do, Doc. Thank you."

AFTER A LONG AND PARTICULARLY TRYING DAY, DR. MICHAEL Scott was on a hot seat of sorts. They had just started reading the bedtime story, Little Red Riding Hood. Seven-year-old Melanie Scott wanted to know if the Big Bad Wolf was real.

"No, dear," the Big Bad Wolf is not real. It's just a story and the Big Bad Wolf is make-believe."

"Oh," Melanie said, "like Santa Claus and the Easter Bunny?"

"Yes, dear. Now let's get back to the story, shall we?"

"And angels and devils?"

"Right, no angels or devils either."

"But why do stories have so many things that aren't real? Why do people believe in things that aren't real?"

"Well, they are just stories, and people like stories. Don't you like this story?"

"Yes."

"Don't you want to see what happens?"

"Yes."

"Well, that's why stories have so many make-believe characters. Because they're make-believe stories, and people like make-believe, just like you do."

"So, it's just for fun?"

"Exactly."

"And it's not real?"

"That's right. It's not real. It's just a cute story. Shall I continue so we can find out what happens?"

"Okay."

A few minutes later, when the story ended, Melanie agreed that it was a good story.

"But the Big Bad Wolf is just make-believe and he didn't really eat Grandma because it's just a story, right?"

"Very good. That's right. There is no Big Bad Wolf. But there is a tired little girl, and there is a bedtime."

"So no one ever really saw Santa Claus or the Easter Bunny or angels or devils, right? They're just make-believe too, right?"

Jeremiah Zimmer's face flashed through Dr. Scott's memory. "That's right, Melanie. Some people think they're real and think they see those things, but they don't. Some people just have a hard time telling real people from make-believe. Sometimes people think they see something when there is really nothing there to see. Some people see what they want to see, like angels or Santa Claus or leprechauns or unicorns."

"I'm glad I'm not like that," Melanie said. "I'm glad I don't see make-believe people and things that aren't real. They're scary."

"Now don't you worry your pretty little head over it, Melanie. They are not real, so they aren't scary at all. There is nothing to be afraid of, okay?"

"Okay."

Melanie pulled her blanket up to her chin. "Thanks, Mom."

"Sweet dreams, honey. I'll see you in the morning."

"Toodely doodles," Melanie said.

"Toodely doodles," said Dr. Scott as she turned off her daughter's bedside lamp.

She walked down the stairs and joined her mother in the living room.

"Mom, it's been a tough day for me, and I am pretty tired. I think I'll turn in for the night," she said, kissing her mother on the forehead.

"Okay, dear."

"Don't forget to turn off the TV before you go to bed and make sure the front door's locked, okay?"

"Yes, dear. Don't worry. I'll take care of everything. You just get to bed and get your sleep. You look exhausted."

"It's been a long day."

"Best cure for that's a long sleep. You go get started."

———

BUT IT WASN'T TO BE. DR. MICHAEL SCOTT'S BEDSIDE PHONE RANG at 3:45a.m., waking her.

"Hello," she managed to say into the receiver, having been startled awake from a sound sleep. She was almost awake, but very groggy.

"Dr. Michael Scott please."

"This is Dr. Scott. Who's calling?"

"This is Lieutenant Joe Carter of the Philadelphia Police Department, Dr. Scott. Do you know a Jeremiah Zimmer?"

Dr. Scott sat up straight in her bed, immediately wide awake.

"Yes. He's my patient. Is he okay?"

"No, ma'am. I'm sorry to tell you Mr. Zimmer is deceased."

"Deceased? No, that can't be. I just saw him last evening."

"You saw him last evening?"

"Yes, I'm his psychiatrist. It was a regular weekly session. We meet each Wednesday evening at 7:00."

"Yes, ma'am. I'm sorry, ma'am. Can you come to his house? We're here now. There are some things I think you might need to see. Maybe you can answer some questions for us."

After receiving the exact address and directing her mother to watch Melanie, Dr. Scott drove the 20 minutes from her home in Huntingdon Valley to the home of Jeremiah Zimmer in the Northeast Philadelphia neighborhood of Lawndale. There were police officers everywhere. She arrived just in time to see Jeremiah's body being removed in a body bag on a stretcher and wheeled to a waiting ambulance for transport to the city morgue.

Lieutenant Joe Carter met her just inside the front door, in the center hallway.

"Thanks for coming, Dr. Scott," he said. "We found your business card on his bedside table, which is why I called you. What you will want to see is upstairs, in the bedroom. Follow me, but please don't touch anything. The detectives are treating this as a suicide, but the lab's dusting for prints and taking photos. It's SOP."

"Okay," Dr. Scott said, and she followed the lieutenant upstairs. They entered the master bedroom.

"We found him slumped against the headboard. Apparently, he was sitting up in bed when he stuck his revolver in his mouth and pulled the trigger. We extracted the bullet from the wall above the headboard. You can see the blood stain there...."

Lieutenant Carter stopped talking and grabbed Dr. Scott who had slumped over and was retching.

"Sorry, Doc. Here, sit over here," he said, leading her to a chair in the corner. "You sit here until you feel better."

"I'm sorry, Lieutenant," she said. "This is all a bit much for me, I'm afraid. Jeremiah was a wonderful man. I'm just shocked that he would do this."

"You don't think he was capable of suicide?"

"I don't know. He was a tortured soul, for sure, but he never mentioned wanting to kill himself. He appeared to be making excellent progress, especially at his last session, last night. He never even told me he owned a gun."

"We checked. It's registered to him."

Dr. Scott shook her head. "It is surprising, I must say. Jeremiah did not strike me as being suicidal. He never evidenced that tendency to me. He was stressed due to losing his brother a month ago, and his parents last year, but he was coping. His employer placed him on involuntary six-week leave today, so that he could decompress. The poor dear had everything to live for, and he knew it. He was a fighter. He was one of the most honest people I ever met, and I firmly believe he was well on the road to recovery."

She leaned against the high back of the chair and stared at the blood-stained wall above the bed. Regardless of what she had just said, it was difficult to argue with the very graphic evidence that Jeremiah was not exactly who she thought he was. Still, she had a foreboding sense that something was missing. Some evidence was missing. For Dr. Michael Scott, things were not adding up.

Lieutenant Carter, studying the doctor as she gathered herself, seemed to sense this.

"You might want to take a look in the master bathroom through the doorway there when you feel up to it," he said, pointing. Maybe that will answer some questions for you."

"Okay," Dr. Scott said, standing. "I'm better now, I think. Let's see." She walked to the bathroom doorway, followed by the lieutenant. Looking into the bathroom, she froze and grabbed the door jamb to steady herself.

"Any idea what that means?" Lieutenant Carter said.

The bathroom mirror was on the wall above the sink. In big bold block letters, written with bright red lipstick, was one word: "SASQUATCH."

Dr. Scott's mind raced with the possibilities. Apparently Sasquatch had returned to pay Jeremiah a visit. But she knew that was virtually impossible. She had hypnotized Jeremiah and convinced him that all his demons, including Sasquatch, had been dispatched by minivan to Nome, Alaska. And, based upon his excited reaction, Jeremiah was convinced this was the new reality. It was not reasonable to think that Jeremiah would have conjured up his demons, in just a few hours, from such a distance.

Lieutenant Carter's walkie-talkie clicked to life. "Gotta go downstairs for a few minutes, Doc," he said. "I'll be right back to see if any of this rings a bell for you. Just stay out of the way of the detectives, okay?"

"Sure," she said, absent-mindedly, not really hearing what he said. She continued to stare at the mirror, recalling that Jeremiah had been most concerned about Sasquatch, and that he was most surprised that she was able to get rid of ringleader. Clearly, to Jeremiah, Sasquatch had been the most real demon of all.

"Don't blame yourself," a voice behind her said. She turned to see one of the detectives standing behind her. "The guy was messed up," he continued, looking at the mirror. "Sasquatch? Definitely messed up. Guess the poor slob had some demons, eh? Oh, sorry, Doc. I know you can't discuss your patients."

Dr. Scott turned away from him and faced the mirror again. "I hypnotized him," she said softly, almost to herself.

"Couldn't have been too difficult," the detective said.

"What do you mean?"

"I'm guessing the guy was pretty impressionable. Still, who isn't? I suppose hypnosis can be pretty risky, huh? Better left to a professional."

"Are you implying I'm not an experienced professional?" she turned to face the detective.

"I'm merely noting your patient wrote Sasquatch on his bathroom mirror with red lipstick before blowing his brains out."

"Look, Detective..." she hesitated, looking down at his name tag.

"Foote. B. Foote," he said.

"Look, Detective Foote. B. Foote?" she hesitated. What a coincidence.

He smiled, but his smile wasn't warm or friendly or ingratiating. It was…sinister.

"I wonder why a grown man would have red lipstick."

"Detective," she said, starting to object.

"Don't beat yourself up over that loser," he continued as if she hadn't spoken. "The whole adult world is hypnotized, anyway. In a manner of speaking, of course. The only clean canvases are kids. The only bright spots left. Gotta do something about that."

"What do you mean?" she asked, as the first rays of the morning sun filtered through the small bathroom window.

"You know. Make the world a better place. For me. Men are too easy. The world has never had a female-led genocide. But I am very patient and, unlike you, I have all the time in the world."

He sneered at her then and she became very afraid. He curled his one hand into a fist and shook it at her. She grabbed at her own throat as she started to suffocate.

"Maybe it's time to inspire a nice, fresh, ripe little girl. One who doesn't believe in demons, of course. Maybe an orphan," he said, as Doctor Scott fell to her knees, wheezing.

Detective B. Foote looked down and regarded her with contempt.

"Interesting that a suicidal patient would have a registered handgun you knew nothing about. Of course, you could have known, had you asked, but you didn't want to dig too deeply into the conversations he was having inside that minivan, did you?"

Dr. Scott looked up, stunned that he could know about the hypnotic trance, begging with her eyes that he help her breathe again.

"Why was that, Doctor?" Unconcerned with her distress, he fairly spat the last word as something insipid, distasteful. "Because you were running late and had to get home to Melanie? Is that the kind of caring professional you are?"

She shook her head in vigorous denial as she reached her hand into her mouth to clear her airway.

"Perhaps you were saving that conversation for a more convenient and um…billable time, hm?"

Doctor Scott fell backward onto the floor, then pushed herself up with one hand and grabbed the toilet bowl and seat, struggling to get back up. Panicked, she lost her grip on the toilet as she again grabbed at her constricted throat with both hands, and fell backward onto the floor.

Detective B. Foote tended to his hair as he considered his reflection in the mirror.

"That, as it turns out, was a truly poor choice for poor, good old, stone cold, dead Jeremiah, wasn't it? Had you only asked about the minivan conversation, he would have told you that I suggested the handgun, but you were too busy taking credit for sending us to Nome, Alaska. Weren't you? Such an amateur."

He looked down to see Dr. Scott grabbing at his ankles and pulling at the legs of his pants in an effort to have him help her.

"Oh, alright, it might be more fun to let you live through it anyway," he said, donning sunglasses. He waved his hand, releasing her from his otherworldly grasp as she continued to grovel on the bathroom floor, sucking air through her burning esophagus.

"Toodely-doodles, Doctor," he said.

Dr. Scott, understanding his meaning, and the implication for Melanie, stared at him in horror. "Sasquatch," she struggled to whisper.

He sneered at her, but said nothing more as he turned, crossed the bedroom and left. Dr. Scott heard his evil chortle as he disappeared, leaving her to understand, finally, why Jeremiah did what he did.

She broke down and cried like a baby on the bathroom floor, not knowing how she would ever be able to save her daughter.

Lieutenant Carter returned to find her sitting on the bathroom floor, crying. He looked at "SASQUATCH" on the bathroom mirror, and wondered what it all meant. In his many years on the force he had seen many things. He had seen man's inhumanity to man, and nothing shocked him anymore. He had become inured to the evil in the world, but not disbelieving. If anything, all the evil he saw on a daily basis had strengthened his own faith.

As he watched Dr. Scott, a grown professional woman, crying on the floor, he knew his next call would be to Father McIntyre, his parish pastor, and a very good person. At times like this, it helped to have faith.

It helped to believe.

6

LUIGI THE LEPRECHAUN

The year is 1960. A simpler time. Before we assassinated our leaders. Before drugs and rioting and Vietnam. Before computers and social networking and video games. It is a great time to be a kid in Philadelphia.

Hope springs eternal for most children – except for one kid I remember particularly well. Nice kid. Great big kid too, but he really had a defeatist attitude and upbringing which would have taken him nowhere fast. As luck would have it though, his fortune would change for the better, big time, the day he walked into Luigi's Bakery to buy ice cream – the day I first met him.

Luigi is a brilliant scientist, a former chemist for Rohm & Haas, who has retired at age sixty-five to start a bakery. Bit of a loner too, though he has taken a liking to me and Pop, who is Luigi's age.

Luigi says he came over from the old country, though he never specifies which old country. His dad was Italian, and with a name like Luigi -- well, my guess would be Italy. But, the old country may have been Ireland because his mom was Irish and Luigi is, um, a leprechaun.

Don't laugh. It's true. Luigi the Leprechaun, and he is the first

135

to admit it. Red hair, short, lucky, the whole nine yards. Except, of course, for the black beard, tan, and Italian accent. It's confusing. But one thing's for sure. Luigi is one heck of a fine baker.

His secret? Luigi has secret sugar. I call it pixie dust. It's a formula he concocted in his basement when he worked as a chemist, so he says. I think it's a recipe he got from his mom back in the old country. All I know is the stuff works.

***

MY TALE STARTS AROUND THE TIME POP AND I FIRST TEAMED UP with Luigi. When we first met him, Luigi was despondent due to his bakery's lack of clientele. I encouraged him to stick with it. I was actually his first customer and, in those early days of the bakery, I admit I bought enough Italian pastries to feed a small army. Pop and I ate what we could – it was all very delicious – but even we could not eat everything I purchased to support Luigi.

We froze many items, and donated much to several local soup kitchens. Eventually, the bakery began to see a steady stream of customers, and Luigi's Bakery became a successful neighborhood fixture. But Luigi always remembered that Pop and I were there when he most needed support. And Luigi, I would come to learn, was very loyal to those he liked. He has repaid the kindness many times over – in cannolis. But not just any cannolis. Luigi's special cannolis. Believe me, there is a difference.

Pop and I still reside in the same upstairs apartment where we lived back then, above the bakery facing Oxford Avenue in Northeast Philadelphia, about a block up from the Acme, or Ac-a-me, as the kids say.

I first met Luigi on the day the movers were moving his bakery equipment and furnishings into the store. My memory is so vivid because Luigi is so vivid. I mean, I had never met an older man with a full head of hair before, let alone hair that was bright red and wavy like Luigi's. In addition, I had never met a red-haired tanned man with a black beard, black moustache, green eyes, and bushy white eyebrows before. Yes, in appearance Luigi is quite unforgettable.

He seemed like a nice enough guy. Chatty, certainly, and hyperkinetic. Yes, definitely hyperkinetic. He still is, to this day, fifty-three years later.

Business was slow when he first opened up in the summer of 1960. Like Luigi, Pop was retired then also, but living with me. Mom had passed a few years earlier. Pop would go for walks when I was away at work. Usually, he would just walk with his oversized walking stick around the triangular city block on which we lived and visit the merchants downstairs: the barber, the deli, the hairdresser, the druggist, and, eventually, Luigi the baker.

Sometimes Pop would stroll across Oxford Avenue to the Acme to buy a few things, or just sit on a bench outside the Presbyterian church about a block up the street and chat with some of his old WWII buddies.

Pop knew everything that was going on in the neighborhood, and he knew most of the neighbors and their kids. The kids played outside in those days – the Baby Boomers had not yet been designated as such. Nonetheless, they were everywhere after school hours and during the summer breaks. Bikes, ice creams, stickball, Wiffle ball, playgrounds, stores – all were alive with a young populace. It was, indeed, a very good time to be alive.

Eventually, Pop befriended Luigi (Pop was friends with everybody) and would visit the bakery just as he visited the other shops. No one minded. In fact, I know they enjoyed Pop. He was quite a talker and, more importantly, a great listener. It was easy for him, though. He really was empathetic and interested in others. Plus, after all his years, he had become pretty wise, I think, such that folks would listen when he spoke.

But, once Luigi discovered Pop was somewhat of a chess

aficionado, well let's just say that Pop and Luigi had some world-class bouts. Luigi even set up a special table for chess, so he and Pop could play. And play they did. Just about every day.

Luigi's Bakery became a fixture in that neighborhood. People would hurry by in their cars on Oxford Avenue, commuting south to the city in the morning and back home in the evenings. And there would be Luigi's Bakery. The sign above the store sported a four-leaf clover and a flag of Italy. Through the large plate glass front window you could see the pastry counter, the ice cream counter, the tables with the red and white checkered tablecloths – each with a green four-leaf clover in the middle – and two older gentlemen, Pop and Luigi, playing chess.

***

"YOU THINK YOU'RE SO SMART, BUT YOU DON'T KNOW SQUAT." THE bell above the door tinkled as a rather tall teen came into the bakery, leading several of his friends. Pop and Luigi remained in their comatose state, not looking up.

"I know enough to know you ain't never going to Penn," one of the others retorted. "Face it, Jack, you're a football player, a jock. You gotta have smarts to get into Penn."

"Can I help you?" I asked. (I oftentimes filled in for Luigi when he was "busy.")

"Yessir, we'd all like to get ice creams," Jack said, apparently speaking for the group.

The boys stood in a group with their basketballs, pimple ball, and stickball bats. They continued to squabble among themselves as I took their orders and served them.

"Look, Gerry, I can too get into Penn. All I have to do is ace the SAT." Whereupon Gerry turned to the group, raising his hands in a questioning gesture, and everyone laughed. "Right, and all I have to do to play for the Phillies is become good at baseball," quipped one of the others.

"I'll put my money on Jack." More laughter.

"Speaking of money, pay the man, Butch – for once." Butch dug into his pockets for a quarter and handed it to me.

"I don't know, Steve, I can see Ruben playing for the Phillies before I could see Jack at Penn, and ain't no way Ruben ever plays for the Phillies."

"That's what I mean, Mike," Gerry said, licking his strawberry ice cream.

Scooping out the last of the ice creams, I looked up to see Jack roll his eyes before wandering away from the laughter and over to the chess match.

"Hi!" he said.

"Shh!" Luigi shushed him. "I'm trying to concentrate."

"What kind of checkers is that?" Jack asked.

"Hah!" Gerry laughed, joining Jack. "Ain't checkers, numbnuts. Ain't you never seen a chess game before?"

"Match," Luigi corrected.

"What?" asked Gerry.

"It's chess match, not chess game."

"Yeah, numbnuts," Jack said to Gerry. "Ain't you never seen a chess match before?"

"Very funny," Gerry replied.

"Jack, Gerry, you coming?" Ruben asked.

"You guys go ahead. I think I'll stay a little bit," Jack replied.

"C'mon, give it up, Jack. You ain't smart enough to learn how to play chess. Let's go shoot some hoops."

"Yeah, okay. I guess you're right," Jack said, as he rejoined his group leaving the bakery.

On his way out the door, Jack turned to me and said, "Thanks for the ice creams, mister."

"Big Dunderhead," Luigi said, after the boys had left.

"He seemed nice enough to me," Pop retorted.

"C'mon, Luigi, he seems like a good kid," I agreed with Pop.

"Maybe. But he's going nowhere fast if he keeps letting people put him down like that," Luigi said.

"Don't make him a Dunderhead," Pop said.

"Stupid jock," Luigi countered. "Nice enough, maybe, but that and a nickel...."

"Check!" Pop said.

"Damn!" cried Luigi. "How could I be so stupid?" He leaned his head on his hands and glared at the chess board.

"I presume that's a rhetorical question," Pop quipped.

"Must be contagious. Maybe I'll fumigate the store. Stupid kids," Luigi replied, ignoring Pop.

"Those stupid kids just spent a buck-fifty in your store. They're your customers," I reminded him, as I continued to wipe down the tables.

"Right, if it weren't for the damn customers and employees, running my own business wouldn't be so bad," Luigi said.

"Luigi, you don't have any employees, you cheap bastard. I do half the work around here. By the way, when do I get a raise?" I asked.

No response. Luigi was still stunned at being checked.

"Luigi? A raise?" I persisted.

"What?" Luigi asked, looking up, coming out of his trance. "Oh, it's coming."

"So is Christmas."

"By the way, you're fired," Luigi said, with a dismissive wave as he returned his attention to the chess board.

"Third time you've been fired this week," Pop said, looking up at me.

"A new personal record," I replied. "But I couldn't have done it without the help of my friends."

"Merry Christmas," Luigi mumbled, not looking up.

"I GUESS YOU FORGOT SOMETHING," I SAID, A FEW MINUTES LATER as Jack walked back into the store. Luigi, apparently, had worked his way out of a jam, and the chess match continued.

"Yep, my stickball bat. There it is," Jack said, pointing to the broom handle lying on the floor under the ice cream counter.

As he went to pick it up, he looked up at the pastry menu board on the back wall. "Does a can of lice actually cost five-hundred dollars?" he asked, pointing to the board.

"Check!" Pop exclaimed, moving a rook.

"Huh?" Luigi asked, turning from the chess board to see where Jack was pointing. "Can of lice? What are you talking about?"

"That's cannolis," I corrected Jack. "A cannoli is an Italian pastry. It's kind of like a cream puff."

"Idiot," Luigi mumbled under his breath, as he turned back to the board.

"Oh," Jack replied. "Does it really cost five-hundred dollars?"

"No, that must be a typo," I replied.

"It's no typo," Luigi corrected, turning to face us, agitated, yet again. "My special cannolis are special for a reason. That's why they cost so much."

"They must be pretty good, huh?" Jack asked.

"Give me five-hundred dollars, and you can see for yourself," Luigi replied.

"I don't have five-hundred dollars."

"Of course you don't."

"Check and mate," Pop exclaimed jubilantly, rising from the table and taking his walking stick.

"Damn!" Luigi exploded. "You!" he shouted, pointing at Jack. "It's all your fault! Take your baseball bat and get out!"

"It's a stickball bat," Jack corrected him, calmly.

"I don't care if it's a vampire bat, just take it and leave. You

made me lose the match. I couldn't concentrate with all your inter-
ruptions."

"Oh c'mon, Luigi. How about giving me a little credit," Pop
said.

"Credit? Credit?" Luigi sounded incredulous. "I give credit
where it's due. I'll give you credit the day you beat me without any
help."

"That would be yesterday," Pop laughed, "and every other day
this week."

"So you're on a bit of a lucky streak. Don't remind me. I'm
beginning to regret teaching you how to play."

"What! You teach me? You didn't know a queen from a pawn
before I showed up," Pop laughed.

"Okay, okay, enough you two old fools," I interceded. "Pop,
why don't you go back upstairs? I have to help Luigi clean up. I'll
be up to make dinner after I do. You two can play your games
tomorrow if you promise to behave."

"Hey, you watch yourself, you young whipersnap…."

"I need to go over to the Acme first," Pop interrupted. "I'll be
back in ten minutes."

"That's right, you go and run away, you old chicken," Luigi
continued. "You know I'll kick your sorry excuse for a German butt
in a rematch."

"No rematches now, Luigi," I said. "It's getting late. You boys
can play again tomorrow."

"Like I want to play the likes of him anyway," continued Luigi.
"I only play him because there's no real competition around here."

"Teach me."

It was Jack.

"Now why would I want to teach you?" Luigi asked.

"For competition. You just said Pop's not good enough for you.
Maybe you could teach me to play."

"Sorry," Luigi said, dismissively. "I can only tutor one student at a time, and I'm not done teaching him yet," Luigi said, thumbing at Pop.

"Go, Pop. Now!" I ordered as Pop raised his walking stick to begin what was surely going to be a long tirade. "I've had enough of you two for one day."

"Can I be white?" Jack asked, sitting at the chessboard, ignoring Luigi's protest.

"No, no," said Luigi. "House rules. I'm always white when we play in my bakery. White makes the first move," he said, sitting and positioning the pieces. "Here, set them up like this, except flip-flop your king and queen from the way I have mine. The king is the taller one."

"I'll be back in ten minutes," Pop said as he left the bakery. "Maybe you'll have made your first move by then."

"Go, you old fool," Luigi muttered, concentrating on the chess pieces once again.

"See ya, Pop. Be careful crossing the street," I said, as Pop went out the door. I walked over behind the counter to begin cleaning and closing up. Luigi, once again, was "too busy" to help.

"Hey, Luigi, am I still fired?"

"No, you're on probation. Now don't interrupt me."

"Figures."

"Hey, Jack, I thought you had a stickball game to go to," I said across the room.

"No, I can only stay for a few minutes. I have to go home and cram for the SAT exam tomorrow. I need to do better than I did last time."

"What score did you get last time?" Luigi asked.

"Just a 900, but I'll need a perfect score to have any chance of getting into Penn."

"What's a perfect score?"

"1600."

Luigi looked back at me, so Jack couldn't see his face, and rolled his eyes.

Then out of the corner of my eye, I saw the milk truck bearing down on Pop as he crossed Oxford Avenue. "Pop!" I screamed, as the truck veered at the last minute, missing Pop. But the driver lost control and the truck caromed at full speed right for the plate glass window.

Jack turned when I screamed, assessed the danger and responded quick as lightning to the truck now crashing into the store. In one fluid, superhuman motion, he threw the table aside, grabbed Luigi and threw him, literally, through the air and over the counter top where he landed next to me on the floor. In the following instant Jack went flying through the air and slammed into the far wall after the truck had struck him. The truck came to rest right over the spot where he and Luigi had been sitting just seconds earlier.

***

WHEN THE BAKERY BECAME QUIET, AND THE GLASS HAD STOPPED flying, Luigi and I peeked our heads up above the counter. Pop was standing on the sidewalk looking through the front wall of the store. The wall, door, and plate glass window had been thoroughly demolished. The truck driver pushed open his door, got out of the truck, and rushed over to where Jack lay in a crumpled heap up against the far wall, covered with shattered glass. Luigi and I hurried to join him. Amazingly, Jack was still conscious, though his arms, hands, and legs sustained some nasty lacerations.

"You all right, son?" the driver asked, kneeling down to help Jack sit up.

"I think so," Jack replied, as Luigi, the driver, and I breathed a collective sigh of relief. Jack winced as he tried to sit up. "I think I got cut up pretty good though."

"Come, come," Luigi said as the three of us tried to get Jack to his feet. "Bring him into the back room. There is a cot there where he can rest."

"I really need to get home to study for my test tomorrow," Jack said.

"Okay, okay, later. Right now, you rest on the cot here," Luigi said, helping Jack to the cot. "You just rest a few minutes first."

Four hours later the police had completed their questioning and the paramedics had dressed Jack's wounds and given him some aspirin. The Department of Transportation crew had removed the milk truck, and a handyman was busy boarding up the front of the store. The police also dismissed all the onlookers, except for Jack's parents, who now sat with him in the back room. It seemed like the whole neighborhood had turned out to see the commotion.

It was 7:00p.m. before the police and paramedics released Jack to his parents for the short walk home. It was clear to everyone, including the newspaper reporter who covered the incident, the police, the truck driver, Pop, me and everybody else, that Jack was a hero. He had literally saved Luigi's life. And no one knew that better than Luigi, who looked at me and then Pop with an extremely important, although unspoken, question. We each nodded our heads. "Okay then," Luigi concluded as he handed a cannoli to Jack.

"Jack, I wish to thank you for saving my life. It may not seem like much, but I want to give this cannoli to you. It isn't just a regular cannoli. It is a Luigi special cannoli."

"One of those five-hundred dollar ones?" Jack asked, as his startled parents' eyes went wide.

"It is."

"That's very nice, mister," Jack's dad laughed sarcastically, "but my son just risked his life to save yours and you want to give him a cannoli. Keep it. Let's go, Jack."

"No, no, I insist. House rules. It is not mine to keep. It is Jack's now. Oh, yes, it is Jack's."

Pop and I both nodded at Jack's parents. "Jack should take it," I assured them.

"And just how many of these five-hundred dollar cannolis do you sell?" asked Jack's dad.

"None yet, but they will be a big seller, I can assure you. In the meantime, I give them as gifts to those I choose. Jack, here, just take one bite before you leave and tell me if you've ever tasted anything as delicious as Luigi's special cannoli."

Jack looked at his parents. Jack's dad stood up. "Well, go on. We've got to get you home."

"Go ahead, dear," his mother said. "One bite and then we must leave. You need to get your sleep."

Jack took a bite.

"And?" asked Luigi, expectantly.

As Jack chewed, his eyes went wide. He took a second, much larger, bite.

"Ah, buono!" Luigi exclaimed. "That is good, no?"

In answer, Jack took another bite and then shoved the remainder in his mouth. "Good," Jack gulped.

"Don't talk with your mouth full," his mother said.

"All right, let's go." Jack's father helped his son to his feet, as Jack licked his fingers.

"Thanks a lot, Mr. Luigi. That was really good. I think it's worth five-hundred dollars."

"Hmpf," his father muttered. "Come on."

"One question, if I may," Luigi said, grabbing Jack's arm. "If you could have just one wish, what would it be, Jack?"

"That's easy. I'd wish for a 1600 score on the SAT exam tomorrow."

"Very good," said Luigi, closing his eyes and clasping his hands together. "You have wished well."

"Keep dreaming, Jack," Jack's dad said derisively. "Come on, let's get out of this looney bin."

But Jack had saved Luigi's life. He was about to learn just how lucky saving a leprechaun's life could be.

EVENTUALLY, THE STORE WAS CLEANED UP AND PUT BACK INTO working order. The chess matches resumed, as did the incessant banter of two crotchety old men, neither of whom would have it any other way. I am pretty certain their matches were less about chess than personal battles of wit. Some would say that's what kept them relatively young and sharp-witted for so long. Of course, we know better.

Anyway, Jack was one of the very first to sample a special cannoli, but there have been many others over the past half century or so – largely due to Jack or, to be more precise, due to the notoriety garnered by his heroics. It seems that Jack received his fifteen minutes of fame long before Andy Warhol coined that term. For Jack, however, the "fifteen minutes" were just the beginning.

So he was notable, to Pop, Luigi, and me, at least, for this reason, but also because even we, who should have known better, debated the relative importance to Jack's success of pure luck versus some personal trait.

That is, did Jack's subsequent accomplishments derive from an innate heroic ability, or from the cannoli? Luigi "knows" credit belongs squarely with the cannoli. In truth, he's probably right.

There have been quite a few Luigi's Special Cannoli customers over the years in Philadelphia. You probably know some of them: the local red-haired dear who rocketed to fame in "Annie," the two local brothers who built a luxury home empire, a boy who went on to make movies about a fictional boxer named Rocky, a female attorney-turned-successful crime novelist, dozens of lottery winners, and even the guy who played briefly in the big leagues before becoming an executive for Philadelphia's major league base-ball team.

But Jack was the first and the one who, at least in the opinion of Pop and me, would likely have succeeded without the cannoli. Luigi is quick to remind us, however, that without the cannoli Jack would not have scored 1600 on his SAT exam. Even Pop and I have to admit that is true.

And that 1600 score, as much as anything, seemed to allow Jack, finally, to overcome his father's negative influence and really start believing in himself. In that sense, then, Luigi's cannoli deserves most of the credit.

And, if that's true, then Luigi deserves the credit for turning Jack's life around. As is true with most successful people, Jack had help along the way from others. I in no way mean to denigrate Jack's subsequent accomplishments. He deserves credit for making the most of his abilities. I am just stating a fact. The cannoli helped.

The cannoli always helps.

Except for that first autumn, we rarely saw Jack. His father told him the bakery was cursed, that we were all crazy old men, that Jack wouldn't learn anything from hanging around "losers" like us, and that Jack would be better served applying to trade schools after he graduated from high school, should he be fortunate enough to do so.

Jack did return a few times to play chess with Luigi and Pop, and to eat cannolis, courtesy of Luigi who would never accept any payment from him.

In one of these visits, Jack mentioned that his dad left for good. Jack and his mom would remain in the neighborhood. His mom took a checkout job at the Acme.

Then, one day in mid-December, Jack came running into the store waving a piece of mail.

"I did it! 1600 on the SAT exam!"

He was so excited. We all gathered around and congratulated

him. As we sat and talked, we were surprised to learn that Jack also was the star running back for his high school football team. Jack mentioned this, in passing, as explanation for why he was unable to drop in to see us as often as he would've liked – he was tied up with football games, practices, and his homework. (The next day we subscribed to the Philadelphia Evening Bulletin, so as to stay up to speed on local developments.)

Jack said he had to go home to study for his school exams. As he left, Luigi gave him a cannoli. We would not see Jack again for fifty-three years.

WE DID, HOWEVER, FOLLOW HIS EXPLOITS IN THE LOCAL PRESS — first in the Bulletin and, later, after its demise, in the Philadelphia Inquirer. You see, the combination of Jack's heroic action in the bakery, and his athletic exploits, caught the attention of local reporters who sensed something special in Jack. Therefore, we were subsequently able to follow Jack's life in the newspapers. We clipped some headlines over the years:

- Local Running Back Earns Scholarship To Penn
- Local University of Pennsylvania Star Breaks School Rushing Record
- Jack Tanner, All-American
- Tanner Spurns NFL. Will Pursue Masters Degree.
- People To Watch: Jack Tanner Joins Commercial Real Estate Firm
- People To Watch: Jack Tanner Promoted
- People In The News: Tanner Named President of Goodson Commercial Real Estate
- Tanner To Take Goodson Public

- Goodson IPO Boon to Local Commercial Real Estate Market
- 30 Under 30: Spotlight on Jack Tanner
- Tanner Resigns From Real Estate. Starts Hedge Fund.
- Market Implosion Boon To Tanner's Fund
- 40 Under 40: Jack Tanner Contributes $1 Billion of Fortune To Local Educational Foundation
- Local Boy Makes Good. Tanner Makes Forbes 400 List of Wealthiest People.
- Tanner To Retire. Starts Educational Foundation.

Well, you get the idea. And with each headline, Luigi would raise the posted price of his Special Cannolis.

The most recent price is one-hundred thousand dollars. In fifty years, he has given away just about two hundred Special cannolis, though he has never sold one. Really, would you buy a cannoli for a hundred grand? Luigi knows no one will pay his posted price. But, he nonetheless wants to let the world know that he believes them to be valuable. He gives them freely to those he feels are especially deserving of good luck.

We have a special visitor today. In one of those truly inexplicable quirks of fate, fifty-three years to the day he walked out with his last cannoli, Jack Tanner gave his chauffeur the day off and drove the Rolls Royce himself to Luigi's Bakery. At this minute, as I sit at my PC and type this, I am watching him play chess with Pop and Luigi. Jack is, of course, surprised that we haven't aged.

"Forget apples," Luigi informs him. "A special cannoli a day keeps the doctor away."

"I suppose it's time I start taking chess seriously," Jack says. "I guess you can teach me a few things," he says to Pop, Luigi, and me, as he looks around. "Hey, Luigi, how's about I buy a round of your Special Cannolis, for old time's sake?" Jack says, reaching for his credit card. Then, as he looks up at the menu board, he says, "Whoa, one-hundred thousand dollars!"

"And worth every penny," Luigi counters.

"Actually, for what you get, that's pretty cheap," Jack replies.

"Aha! See, I told you, Pop," Luigi says loudly. "You underestimate the true market value of a Luigi's Bakery Special Cannoli!" Then, he says to Jack softly, as he pats his hand and hands the special cannoli to him, "Your money is no good here, my old friend. House Rules."

YOU'LL RECOGNIZE LUIGI'S BAKERY IMMEDIATELY. FIRST, THERE'S the Irish-Italian billboard on the front of the building. Second, there are the Irish-Italian tablecloth covers. Then, of course, there's the Rolls out front, as Jack has become a fixture too. So stop in and say hello. Bring your hopes, your fears, your troubles, and request a special cannoli. Who knows? It may be your lucky day.

7

____

DIME

J immy Dime, a freshman at Notre Dame University, was sitting in the school library on a Tuesday afternoon in mid-November, studying for his Investment Markets mid-term exam, when his cellphone buzzed.

"C me in 10. Imp."

The text was from the Special Teams coach for the varsity football team. Jimmy's eyes went wide. This could be big. Or not. Gathering his books, he tried to stay calm as he typed, "CU in 10."

Jimmy then made his way across campus to the stadium and the athletic offices there. He arrived within ten minutes – too soon, apparently, as Andrea, the administrative assistant listening on a headset, motioned him to a chair outside the coach's office.

"We're on a conference call. But it's wrapping up. Should be another minute or two."

Jimmy sat there as the "minute or two" went on for fifteen minutes. He wondered what could be going on; why Coach Allen wanted to see him, but he gathered little from Andrea's infrequent contributions to the call – matters of scheduling, as near as Jimmy could tell. He busied himself with his studies.

On the one hand, it wasn't difficult because he was learning about contrarian investment theory, and Jimmy, throughout his youth, had been nothing if not a natural-born contrarian in so many facets of his life.

On the other hand, concentrating now, even on a subject he loved, was difficult because Coach never called players to his office outside of designated practice times, until now.

Finally, Coach's door opened and several assistants filed out, talking among themselves, and headed down a hallway. They did not see Jimmy sitting there. Coach Allen was the last to appear at the door.

"Dime!" he said. "Thanks for coming over. Come in. Come in," he said, coming out to shake Jimmy's hand and motioning him into his office.

Once they were both seated, Coach Allen got right to the point.

"Dime, we just learned that Jack McHugh has a strained hamstring. His status is doubtful for our game Saturday, so we're going to need you to be ready to return kickoffs if he can't go."

"No problem, Coach, but what happened to Jack?"

"We're not sure. He probably pulled it in the third quarter of the game Saturday. The docs just confirmed it. He tried to hide it, but didn't do himself any favors. He may have just aggravated it further. That's bad news for him but an opportunity for you. We're going to need you to be ready, just in case he's a scrub. It seems highly unlikely he will be playing again anytime soon, in my non-medical opinion. I think it's worse than he's letting on. I think the docs will shut him down, at least for this game, and possibly several. So, I'm moving you up to the starting squad for Special Teams."

"Thanks, Coach Allen."

"Don't thank me. You've earned it."

"Still, I hope Jack's alright. That stinks for him."

"He'll be fine. He'll recover. Eventually. Happens all the time.

In the meantime, the team will need you to be ready. We're counting on you, Dime."

Leaving Coach's office, Jimmy decided to put his studies on hold for an hour or so. He would be getting his first start on Saturday, his first start as one of the Fighting Irish. Although it was just Special Teams, it was a lifelong dream come true. And, as such, it was worth celebrating.

Pop had always told him to celebrate the little things because, someday, looking back, you may come to learn they were the big things. This seemed to be one of those times.

Five minutes later, he stood in the end zone, hands inside the pockets of his winter team jacket, squinting out over the football field to shield his eyes against the late cold afternoon wind. He was the only one there, but the stadium would hold over eighty thousand cheering fans on Saturday. The moment wasn't lost on him.

This was big.

Which is why finally, *finally*, he permitted himself to reflect on his improbable journey.

Thanks, Pop. We made it, he thought, as the long-latent memories came flooding back, once he permitted them.

HE WAS BACK IN THE OLD NEIGHBORHOOD, AMIDST THE SMELLS OF the inner city under the blistering summer sun: asphalt, tar, gasoline. And the cracked sidewalks of North Philly. Bits of chipped concrete. Rubber gaskets from an old, rusty car, half in the street, half on the sidewalk, on cinder blocks. The Strawberry Mansion section of Philadelphia. A tough neighborhood whose better days were long gone by the time Jimmy arrived as a boy, years ago. Near Chalmers Street and Lehigh Avenue.

Stupid.

He had wandered too far from the orphanage on Hunting Park

Avenue. Way too far and had gotten lost. This was not the place to be if you didn't know where you were going. He was running for his life, a ten-year-old, undersized waif, down Hollywood Street.

The big kids were after him as he tore past the stoops of the many small row houses there. He knew he could outrun them. He could outrun anybody, even at a very early age. His speed had saved him on many occasions at the orphanage where, if you weren't big, you'd better be fast, if living to see tomorrow was important to you.

But even Jimmy had his limits. He certainly couldn't outrun them all day. At some point he was hoping he'd come across some familiar intersection or street sign that would guide him back to his own neighborhood.

So far, though, nothing. He'd been running, hard, for the past fifteen minutes, and he was starting to tire. The gang was behind him half a block. They weren't closing, but they were persistent. They weren't quitting. Where did all these kids come from?

Up ahead now, a new problem. Boys were coming at him. Apparently, they had decided to divide and conquer. Jimmy was scared now. Really scared. He was being pinched. On this narrow street he'd now need a miracle to escape. Half the gang was chasing him from the rear, but he knew he could outrun them. The others, however, were coming at him up ahead and closing fast.

Jimmy's eyes darted right as he ran, at the cars parked bumper-to-bumper forming a solid wall of sheet steel, and to the left, at the brick row homes and wooden front porches, one after another, stretching the length of the block, well past the attackers coming at him. A man, smoking a pipe, stood on his porch, behind the black wrought iron porch railing, watching the chase with interest.

Suddenly, Jimmy noticed a thin ribbon of sunlight cutting across the sidewalk just three houses ahead. Two houses were separated by a thin side alleyway. Without slowing, he darted left, between the rowhouses and down the alleyway to the rear of the row of houses, where a common alley ran the length of the block along the backs of the houses.

As he raced between the houses, he immediately saw that the alley dead-ended at a ten foot high wooden privacy fence of the house straight ahead.

Jimmy was just four feet ten inches tall, but he never hesitated, running straight at that fence, full-tilt. He leaped, planted one sneaker about halfway up the fence and vaulted himself up and atop the fence in one fluid motion. His other sneaker came down on top of the fence before he pushed off and leapt eight feet down to the concrete patio on the other side, just as the gang members arrived at the entrance to the side alleyway. They gave chase until they came to the privacy fence, not knowing which way to go. They decided, once again to split up – one half of the gang going right toward Chalmers St., the other half going left toward Lehigh Avenue.

Jimmy had just missed landing on the trash cans piled up on this side of the fence. He raced over and sat on the ground behind the large sycamore tree in one corner of the postage stamp rear yard. He was gassed, breathing heavily, and thankful for the opportunity to sit and finally stop running. He had been running hard for well over twenty minutes. He had held his breath when he heard the approaching footsteps and voices on the other side of the fence. He only exhaled when they had once again departed in haste.

But his respite was short-lived, as some kind of dog started barking ferociously inside the house. He saw a woman part a curtain in the rear window, and her German Shepherd bared its teeth when he saw Jimmy.

"Great," Jimmy said, as he stood and ran to the middle of the yard. He hoped he had enough time. He started running as the door opened and the dog tore straight for him. Jimmy was running too, toward the trash cans that he used as leverage to once again scale the fence as the dog lunged at him, missed, and crashed into the trash cans as Jimmy cleared the fence and landed on his feet in the alley.

Unfortunately, the dog barked and growled so loudly and consistently that it caught the attention of the gang members at either end of the alley who turned, as one, to see the cause of the commotion, and saw Jimmy run into the side alleyway back toward Hollywood Street.

The gang members then continued on to either end of Hollywood Street, once again hoping to pin Jimmy in the middle of the block.

Jimmy knew this too. He exited to Hollywood Street and turned right, running away from the gang members who would soon be coming from Chalmers Street at the nearer end of the block. He knew he wouldn't be able to get all the way to Lehigh at the further end of the block so, once again, he needed a miracle to escape. But this time, he knew, there would be no more alleyways, so he started looking for open windows and doors.

Nothing. He was trapped. The gangs would round the corners any second. He needed to disappear; so he immediately dropped to the sidewalk, and rolled under the car without wheels. It was raised up on cinderblocks, directly in front of the house where the man smoked his pipe.

The gang members rounded the corners and arrived at either end of the block at about the same time. Not seeing Jimmy, they ran toward each other, meeting at the middle of the block on the sidewalk in front of the man's house where they gathered to plan their next move.

"Man, where'd he go? He's got to be here somewhere."

"That little dude is fast, man. Disappeared, just like a friggin' genie or something."

Several of them were leaning against the car Jimmy was hiding under, holding his breath, and laying perfectly still. One of them looked up at the man on his porch and said, "Hey, dude. You hiding that punk?"

The man, standing on his elevated porch, surveyed the gang members looking up at him from the other side of the wrought iron railing. From his elevated vantage point he was able to see the outside of Jimmy's right leg and sneaker and bright orange sock under the car.

"Get off my car," he said to the gang members.

"That what this is?" one of them laughed. "Yo, Deuces, man says this here's his car. It look like a damn car to you?"

"Can't be no damn car, ain't got no wheels." All nine members of the gang laughed and high-fived Deuces.

"You boys should watch your mouths," the man said, trying to distract them from looking at the cinderblocks under the car and at Jimmy. "Clean up your language while you're in this neighborhood. We don't need none of your cussin' around here."

"That so, old man?" Deuces said, pulling out a switchblade, which made the characteristic swooshing sound as he released the blade. He took a step away from the car, toward the man. But Jimmy stuck out one of his legs and Deuces tripped and fell hard, face first, into the concrete sidewalk, breaking his nose, which spouted blood everywhere.

In the ensuing confusion and shock, Jimmy bolted out from under the street side of the car and ran as fast as he could up the street toward Chalmers. The teenage gang members all gave chase but Jimmy had a good head start and, although just ten years old, the God-given footspeed the others would never have. Jimmy ran a short block and turned left on 29th Street, immediately realizing that this would lead him straight back to the orphanage, about a mile away. He would have to outrun the gang for the mile, but he knew he could.

The man on the porch was stunned by what he had just witnessed. That little boy was not only smart, fast, and daring, but he changed directions faster than anyone he had ever seen. Or, more precisely, faster than anyone he had seen in many, many years. He turned, walked into his house and told Sarah, his wife, everything.

"Carl, he could be the answer to our prayers," she said when he had finished.

"What do you mean?" he said, as she continued, her back to him, to flip the hamburgers in the skillet atop the stove.

"I mean we tried for so long to get pregnant, but it wasn't God's plan for us. We agreed with Sister Muriel months ago to consider adoption. Maybe God tired of waiting on us. Maybe He sent this boy to us."

"To adopt? Sarah, we don't know that he's an orphan. We don't know anything about him. We don't even know where…," his voice trailed off.

"Where what?"

"I was going to say we don't even know where he lives, but I think I have a pretty good idea of where he lives."

She turned to look at him now. "Why?"

"Because he was wearing bright orange socks."

Sarah smiled. Brightly-colored socks were her thing. She had been making them and donating them to Sister Muriel at St. Anthony's Orphanage for years.

"I'll call Sister Muriel," Carl said, hugging his wife. "Maybe you're right. Maybe we should pay her a visit."

* * *

Jimmy had heard this story so many times, of the day he first came into his adoptive parents' lives. Standing in the end zone, he smiled, yet again, recalling it now.

The memory that presented itself next happened one year later, when he was eleven.

"What are we doing, Pop?" Jimmy asked.

"You are a natural-born contrarian," Carl said. It was the first time Jimmy had ever heard that word. "I think you need to learn how to take advantage of that."

"Contrarian?"

"Yes, Contrarian. It means someone who goes against the flow, against the grain. You tend to go left when everybody goes right."

"No, I don't."

"See? You're doing it now. Arguing for the sake of arguing, without thinking – which, actually, is instinctive. It's okay."

"I have no idea what you're talking about."

"Look, Son, the first time I ever saw you it was obvious you could run fast, very fast, much faster than those older boys who were chasing you. Yes, it was obvious. But that isn't what caught my attention."

"I know, I know, it was the orange socks. I've heard this story a hundred times."

Pop smiled. "No, not the orange socks. It was the way you cut down the side alleyway without slowing down and again, when you dropped and rolled under that old jalopy in a split second. Unbelievable. Most people just can't do those things, but you could, naturally, as a ten-year-old. It is a great gift."

They were standing about sixty feet from the playground fence that bordered Pop's junk yard. Jimmy was originally dismayed when he first learned that Pop owned and operated a junk yard.

"Why?" Pop asked.

"Because it's just junk," Jimmy said.

"Son, in the right hands, it isn't junk," Pop replied. This philosophy, as much as anything, defined Pop's outlook on so many aspects of life, including raising his son.

"What we are going to do today," Pop continued, "is begin to turn that gift into a competitive advantage."

"How? By climbing that fence?"

Rather than answer, Pop asked another question. "How long will it take you to run to that fence from here?"

"From here? Dunno, about four seconds, I guess."

Pop pulled out a stopwatch. "I'll time you. Ready, set, go, okay?

"Why?"

"You'll see. Ready? Set. Go!"

Jimmy sprinted into the fence.

"Three point six seconds," Pop said, stunned that Jimmy broke four seconds without even warming up first. But, he didn't say so. Rather, he lied, "Too slow."

"Too slow? Let's see you beat it."

"This ain't about me. Now get back here and do it again. You need to get this down to three seconds before we go on to the next step."

It took a year but the day finally came when Pop, holding his stopwatch, said, "two point nine seconds. Congratulations. Now we can move onto the next phase of your training."

Jimmy, for what seemed the ten thousandth time in the last year, had run as hard as he could and had slammed into the fence, exhausted.

Pop came up and hugged him. "Great job, Son. Well done."

"Thanks. What's the next phase?" Pop was pleased by this question, by his son's interest in continuing, even after a long year of repetitive, dull drills.

"Pretty much the same thing except with one little difference. Sub-three seconds, but without slamming into the fence."

Jimmy smiled. "Um, that's crazy, Pop. Nobody can do that."

Pop looked at him askance, eyebrows raised, as if to say, "Oh, really?"

"Really. Nobody can do that," Jimmy repeated.

"Jimmy, people can do that. Trust me. I used to be able to do it. I know what I'm talking about. You can do it."

"You used to be able to do it?"

"Sure."

"What happened? Why can't you do it anymore?

"What do you think? Old age."

"Pop, I don't understand. I thought you were going to teach me how to cut fast."

"I am," Pop said, but he said nothing more.

Jimmy recalled that Pop had always been a man of few words. Still, he remembered those lessons. They were like gold to him now. All those sprints at the fence when he failed to break three seconds, Pop always encouraged him with, "Champions are made when nobody's watching."

When Jimmy complained that everyone practices running fast but that no one practices stopping, Pop would say, "That's right. That's why you will be the greatest cutback runner ever. You need to build up those muscles and that instinct. Ten thousand stops should do it."

This took four years but finally, one day, fifteen-year-old Jimmy did run the sixty feet in two point nine seconds, successfully stopping just inches from the fence.

Pop smiled, and for the first of a thousand times, Jimmy heard him say, "On a dime."

Fast-forward one year. Sixteen-year-old Jimmy was the starting halfback for his high school football team, and he also returned kickoffs. He was already a local star, having broken the school record for most running yards, and most yards per carry by a wide margin. He also held the lifetime record for most kickoffs returned for touchdowns in the Commonwealth of Pennsylvania with one more season to play!

His team was playing in the state championship game in his junior year, but they were trailing late in the game. With just a few seconds left, they needed to score a touchdown to tie, otherwise their season would be over.

Their opponents had just kicked a field goal to increase their lead to six points, and now they had to kick off to Jimmy's team. Wary of Jimmy's unique ability to return kickoffs for touchdowns, they kicked it short, but Jimmy's teammates lateralled the ball back to him, knowing he was their only hope for a miracle.

Jimmy worked his magic once again, using his well-honed cutback ability to weave his way through the oncoming tacklers, and his speed to race down the left sideline toward the end zone. By the time he had reached midfield, and had avoided being tackled by the last opponent in front of him, the kicker, it looked like fifty yards of clear sailing to the end zone and a tie game.

But it wasn't clear sailing. The opposing team's defensive starters had been inserted onto the kickoff team to give them the best chance to stop Jimmy. As Jimmy raced down the sideline, the two best defenders in the league chased him, and they both had the better angles. Jimmy hoped against hope that he could out-sprint them to the end zone and he tried his best, running as hard and as fast as he could.

But angles are almost impossible to outrun, especially when the two players chasing you are seniors who had already won full rides to Division I universities for football.

Jimmy was tripped from behind on a desperation dive by the starting cornerback ten yards from the end zone, obliterated in a flying tackle by the starting safety, and knocked out of bounds just three yards from tying the game.

Three yards. Jimmy's team missed the state championship by three yards.

And Jimmy was hurt. But, he was often hurt, because he was undersized, and it would take many days for him to overcome his physical bruises, as it often did. But it took much longer for him to overcome the mental anguish of failure. He hadn't scored when his team most needed him. He had let his team down in the biggest game of their lives.

Two weeks later, it was Pop who brought him out of his funk. Jimmy, standing on the three yard line at Notre Dame, smiled to recall Pop's most important pep talk.

"Jimmy, we need to talk about the game. It's time," Pop said, sitting at the foot of Jimmy's bed two weeks after the crushing defeat at states.

"I lost. What's there to talk about?" Jimmy said, not turning away from his desk where he was preparing for his semester finals.

"The reason, for one thing," Pop said.

"I was too slow. That's the reason," Jimmy said.

"No, Son. You're wrong. That's not why you lost."

"Well, they caught me. I'd say I was too slow."

"Jimmy, I want you to look at me. Take a break."

Jimmy put down his pen, turned and looked at Pop.

"Son, look, winning is great. It really is. There's no denying that. But, as bad as losing is, there are lessons to be learned from it. Important lessons, but you need to be honest about what went wrong to be able to make the necessary corrections for next time."

"What next time? The season's over."

"For next year. For college. Look, that other team was full of seniors. They didn't win last year even though they had a very good team. It took them a year to learn from their mistakes. You and your team will most likely be back in states again next year. You'll all be seniors. But it's important for you to understand, really understand, what happened on that last play, so you can make the necessary correction. If you think you lost because you're too slow, then you will lose next year too, because you're not going to get any faster. You're as fast as you're going to get, but that's not the problem."

"Those kids were faster than me."

"Maybe. Maybe not. I didn't time them. Neither did you. But, you'd better get used to not being the fastest guy on the field because the longer you keep playing football, the better the competition is going to be until, finally, only the very, very best players will be playing.

"That's your real competition and they're all over the country. You may or may not be the fastest, I don't know, and neither do you. Not for sure. What I do know for sure, and you should too, is that you are fast enough. You will always be fast enough.

"But, remember, that's not your greatest gift. Your greatest gift is your cutback ability. That's what we worked on for years. Stopping on a dime. That's where you're better than everyone else. That's where you're the greatest."

"Didn't help me on that last play."

"That's right, and it's good you know that. Actually, that's what I really wanted to talk to you about, because the reason it didn't work on the last play is because you didn't let it."

"What do you mean?"

"I mean, you didn't stop. You thought you could outrun those guys. Why did you think that?"

"Because I thought I could."

"No you didn't. Don't lie. You knew they had the angle."

"But I was so close, just a few more feet. I should have made it."

"No, you shouldn't have made it, because those two were doing their job. They had the angle, and they knew it. Son, look, here's the thing. Out there, out on the field, there is a hundred-yard-long tunnel. It will take you from one end zone to the other, but you must stay within it. You must stay within the walls of the tunnel. If you try to break outside those walls, you will fail.

"Those defenders were the wall of the tunnel. You tried to outrun them or run through them, but it was wrong to do that. There are times when you take the game to them, and there are times when you let the game come to you. You have to learn the difference.

"Usually, when you hit a hole fast, that's taking the game to them. At other times, like when the defenders have the angle, there is no hole right away. You have to wait for it. It will appear. It always does, but you have to learn patience.

"That's what makes a great cutback runner great. He follows the tunnel, and the tunnel is not always straight ahead. In fact, it's almost never straight ahead. And, once you see it, to the left or right, you must take it. You must stop on a dime, and redirect like only you can. That's your game. That's why you will be great. Not because you bust through people, but because you stay in the tunnel they present to you."

Jimmy looked Pop in the eye. "I should have stopped."

Pop smiled and pointed at him. "The truth will set you free. Now that you have learned this lesson, let me be the first to congratulate you on being state champion next year."

Jimmy smiled, remembering that conversation. He and his teammates did indeed win the state championship in their senior year. Jimmy once again broke his own records from the year before, was named student-athlete of the year in Pennsylvania, and was admitted to Notre Dame University, his first choice, on a full scholarship for academics and athletics.

ON SATURDAY, JIMMY STOOD IN THE END ZONE. HE LOOKED DOWN to make sure his orange socks were under his white football socks. They were. He looked up in the stands. His mom and dad were pinpoints among the 80,000 cheering fans. They were visible to Jimmy because they were both twirling bright orange hand towels among the sea of white towels being twirled by every other fan.

Jimmy took a deep breath. He was ready. He had prepared his whole life for this moment. A minute later he looked up to see the football arcing towards him, descending from the perfect, cloudless, blue autumn sky.

He caught the ball two yards deep in the end zone and started running, following the wedge formed by his teammates blocking ahead. Jimmy would take the game to the opponents, right out of the chute, on the opening kickoff. But, once the tunnel shifted, he would stop on a dime and let the game come to him.

Five seconds later, his parents and 80,000-plus fans would never forget seeing the "Dime" with "10" underneath on the back of his jersey race down the left sideline, being chased by the last two defenders who had the angle.

With fifteen yards to go, Pop shouted, "Stop!" Jimmy couldn't hear him, of course, but he didn't have to.

He knew.

He suddenly stopped on a dime as the two defenders went flying by, and Jimmy followed his tunnel, uncontested, into the end zone for the first of many times in his collegiate and pro careers.

Back in Philadelphia about five-hundred people, including Sister Muriel, the other religious sisters and children of St. Anthony's Orphanage, and many neighbors attending the block party on little Hollywood Street, almost all of them wearing bright orange socks, erupted in a joyous celebration.

As Jimmy's teammates hoisted him on their shoulders in the end zone, the cheer arose from the stadium crowd. The same cheer that would fill the stadium every home Sunday for the next four years.

Notre Dime! Notre Dime! Notre Dime! Notre Dime!

8

FATHER & SON EXTERMINATORS

mma reached over to shut off the alarm clock. The bedroom was pitch black. The throbbing of her swollen left eye, and the sound of the television downstairs, confirmed a painful truth: she was still alive, but still trapped. At least Hank wasn't there. Silently, she thanked God for that.

She sat up on the edge of the bed, and reached out her hand to steady herself on the night table. Standing, electing not to turn on the bedside lamp, she walked slowly, carefully, through the dark toward the bathroom.

Pausing at the doorway, she squeezed her eyes shut, placed one hand over them, and turned on the bathroom light with her other hand.

Groping for the sink, she peeked through her fingers, and looked at herself in the mirror. The light hurt her eyes for a bit. Their swelling had subsided quickly, as it often did, and the stitches were no longer red; no sign of infection. Her left eye was still severely bloodshot, however. She'd be wearing sunglasses to work.

Emma showered and dressed for work. By 6:00 a.m. she walked down the hallway, noticed that Darrell was not in his bedroom, and continued quietly, gingerly, down the steps. The TV was loud enough. With any luck, she'd be able to get to the basement undetected, unmolested.

On the main floor, she saw Hank watching the morning news program. His back was to her, and he did not hear her as she walked away from the living room toward the kitchen, down the steps to the basement, and to her craft room.

She pulled the chain and the single ceiling bulb dimly illuminated her subterranean work space and a new, harsh reality. The small locked safe containing the costume jewelry she had designed and crafted for the past two weeks was gone! Frantic, she looked everywhere before realization dawned.

Darrell.

Breaking down in a heap on the painted and cracked concrete basement floor, face buried in her hands, she cried. She cried softly, for if Hank heard her, there would be nothing quiet about her suffering.

Suddenly, she saw a small form dart past her on the floor. Emma stifled a scream. Mice. She was terrified of mice. She rose quickly, gathered herself, and withdrew her ever-present handkerchief from her bra. She fussed at the folds in her skirt, brushed a strand of hair from her face, and adjusted her designer sunglasses.

"Gotta set some traps," she said, as she shut off the basement light and walked up the stairs to the kitchen.

Emma started a pot of coffee for Hank and Darrell, though she doubted Darrell was even there. Wherever he went, with any luck, he didn't take the car, otherwise she would have to take two buses to work.

Grilling the bacon, sausage, and eggs, she sensed Hank watching her before she saw him. Call it a survival instinct. Her first order of business each day was managing her husband and son so as to escape them for the workday, unharmed.

As the sole breadwinner, her job as a barber was critical to their keeping a roof over their heads, food on the table, a car in the driveway and, most importantly, her daily, all-too-fleeting reprieve from hell and chance to survive another day.

"Where's Darrell?" Emma said without turning around.

"Hell do I know?" Hank said. "Probably workin'. Makin' real money, not like you."

Since her survival demanded discretion, Emma chose not to remind Hank that their son hadn't made a dime in more than three years. Three years of hard time in prison, which meant nineteen-year-old Darrell had missed high school, but learned how to refine his illicit operation.

"Did he take the car?"

Emma turned when she heard the click.

Hank was pointing his revolver at her. The hammer was cocked. Secretly petrified, Emma belied no fear. Survival at times like this, at the many times the sadist threatened to shoot her, demanded she be cool. Hank was churlish, clearly, but he was also choleric and Emma knew not to feed the volcano.

She calmly turned back to the stovetop and emptied the eggs, bacon, and sausage from the frying pan to a plate, and reached the plate out to him.

"Eat. I'll get the coffee."

"About friggin' time," he said, putting the gun down, taking the plate, and sitting down at the kitchen table.

Emma breathed a silent prayer of thanks. *Even despots have to eat. If he ever learns to scramble an egg, I'm history.*

She continued to stand, leaning against the drainboard near the sink, rather than sit at the table with Hank. She preferred to keep a safe distance.

"Sit down over here," he ordered.

"Can't," she said. "Gotta take the bus. I'll be late as it is."

"Sit!" he thundered. "Don't make me get up."

Emma knew whatever little good luck she had enjoyed that

morning had just run its course. She walked over and sat across from her husband. She held the cup in her two hands in front of her. To all outward appearances, she was warming her hands. Actually, though, this was a defensive posture which might, might, permit her to parry the inevitable assault when it came. Survival.

"After I'm done eating, I want dessert. Go upstairs and get naked," he said.

"Hank," she began, "I can't, I've…" was all she could get out before he punched her savagely in the left eye again, opening the stitches anew. Blood splattered all over the table and Emma's full cup of coffee fell and crashed onto the floor.

Emma put her hand on her eye, grabbed her pocketbook, and bolted out the back door, before Hank could grab her. The pain was bad, but preferable to what Hank would have done to her in bed. Touching the side of her eye socket, she guessed she had likely deflected his punch enough to prevent an orbital bone fracture. Emma, bleeding profusely, in severe pain, and reaching again for her handkerchief, knew she had gotten off easy. This time.

Hank continued to eat as if nothing had happened.

"Stupid bitch," he said. Then, as he fingered his revolver on the table, he softly voiced a recurring thought, "Soon."

Emma walked quickly to the community hospital three blocks away. She checked herself into the emergency room, yet again, to have the stitches re-sewn.

The doctors there had long ago stopped believing that Emma had fallen down the steps, or walked into a cabinet, or banged her head on the car door, or was otherwise as clumsy as she let on. And Emma, for her part, had long ago stopped trying to convince them. She listened to their lectures, dutifully nodded her head, and thanked them for administering to her quickly so she could get to work.

Newly stitched, Emma was beginning to resemble a self-made woman. The flesh-colored bandage and designer glasses went a long way to camouflaging her injuries. She left the hospital and walked briskly past the avenue, shops, and bus stop, to morning Mass at the local parish church a half mile away.

She entered the church, blessed herself with holy water and proceeded to stand near an empty pew beside the stained glass window depicting the Annunciation. It was one of her favorite biblical stories. The Angel Gabriel announcing to Mary that she was to be the mother of God's son.

Steadying herself with one hand on the back of the pew, Emma winced as a bolt of pain seared her left eye. She applied the palm of her other hand to the eye socket and took a few deep breaths, waiting for the pain to subside.

Looking up at Gabriel, she smiled. Imagine being visited by an angel. How great must God love someone to permit such a thing? The bible teaches that Mary was afraid, but that the angel told her not to fear.

Emma did not think she herself would fear an angel, but was pretty sure she would never have the chance to find out. Still, she permitted her gaze to linger on Gabriel. How great would it be?

Sighing wistfully, she sat in the pew. She had a few minutes before Mass to pray. She pulled her rosary from a coat pocket, blessed herself and began to pray. She fingered the crucifix between her thumb and forefinger. Emma had crafted this rosary years ago. It was one of her favorite creations; her most prized possession.

She had made the crucifix from pewter and gold. The engravings on each were spectacular, she had to admit: true old world craftsmanship. Of all the mysteries upon which she could reflect while praying the Rosary -- the Sorrowful, Joyful, Glorious, and Luminous -- her favorite had always been the Joyful mysteries, basically because one of those mysteries was the Annunciation.

Reflecting on the Annunciation brought Mary and God and the

angels to life for Emma. And, if there was good to be found in this world, you didn't have to look much farther than to God, His mother, and His angels. She finished with a prayer to St. Michael the Archangel, asking that he protect and defend her.

She rose to leave church after Mass with a spring in her step, taking a minute or two to greet the other women she saw there every day.

Fortified against the challenges that awaited her outside this holy place, Emma reached to push open the church door. Another hand beat her to it.

Emma looked up to see a woman she had never seen before. She appeared, to Emma, to be almost a mirror image of herself. Of similar build and height, she was wearing the same type of head scarf and designer sunglasses that Emma wore.

They stood in the entry and looked at each other. Each offered that the other should go first, whereupon they both chuckled. The other woman then went through the doorway, and Emma followed.

Emma said, "Excuse me," and reached for the woman's arm. The woman turned and faced her, smiling.

"Yes?"

"Um," Emma hesitated, "I couldn't help but notice that we are wearing similar sunglasses and scarves. I've not seen you at morning Mass before. Are you new to the parish?"

"No, just new to the need for church," the woman replied.

"Oh…oh," Emma stammered, not knowing how to respond, creating an awkward, silent void.

Fortunately, the woman went on to break the ice. She lowered her sunglasses to display a horribly bruised black eye and scarlet blood-filled eyeball.

Pointing to it, she said, "My psychotic brother, if that's your real question."

Emma smiled weakly, tentatively. "I'm sorry, I didn't mean…."

"It's okay. I understand. And you?"

Emma looked right into the woman's eyes and understood she was asking not who beat her, but who had ruined her life.

"My son and his father," Emma answered honestly.

"Yes, there's a lot of that going around," the woman said. "I will keep you in my prayers. My name is Stella, by the way. Stella Sable," she said, extending her hand. "And you are?"

"Emma Mir-Crass," Emma replied, shaking her hand. "Thank you for your prayers. I will pray for you too, Stella."

"Thank you, Emma. Hopefully I'll see you here again."

"I'm here every day."

"Does it help?"

"Always," Emma said.

"Okay, well, thanks for chatting. It was nice to meet you. Have a good day," Stella said, turning to leave.

Strange, but in that split second, right there, Emma knew what she must do.

"Wait," she said, "just a minute. I have something I want to give you." Emma reached into her coat pocket and removed the rosary. "Here, I want you to have this," Emma said, holding the rosary out to Stella.

"No, no, oh no, I couldn't, really, that's not necessary…."

"I insist. Please," Emma said. "I want you to have it."

"Well, that's very nice of you," Stella said, taking hold of the rosary. "It's very beautiful. Very beautiful, but I am afraid I don't know how to use one."

Immediately, Emma knew she had done the right thing. She had acted impulsively, on a hunch, and was even surprised she had done so. It was not like her at all.

"There are booklets in the church," Emma said. "Or, I could teach you. It's not difficult."

Stella smiled. "Alright, I'd like that. It's a deal. But what are you going to do for a rosary?"

"I'll just make another one."

"You made this?" Stella was shocked. "Oh, I couldn't…." Stella offered the rosary back to Emma.

Emma smiled and pushed the rosary back at Stella. "No, I insist. I make lots of things: rosaries, jewelry, lamp shades, decorations. It's no bother at all, really. You will be doing me a big favor if you allow me to do this for you."

"But we just met. We're practically strangers. You don't know anything about me," Stella said.

Emma smiled as she touched her own swollen cheek.

"No, no. Not quite. I believe I know enough about you that matters, and you me. We're not really strangers at all, are we?"

Now it was Stella's turn to smile. "I suppose there's some truth to that."

"We're practically sisters," Emma said. "Sisters who have just met."

"You know, I could use a sister," Stella smiled.

"Me too," Emma said.

Emma walked briskly one half mile back to her bus stop on the avenue. As she stood there, waiting for the bus, she reached in to her coat pocket. The rosary wasn't there. She felt practically naked without it. It had been her companion, her sole comfort, for many years. She hoped it would now provide comfort to Stella. That woman needed it. It would not have been Christian of Emma to deny her the rosary.

She was suddenly aware of something metallic squeaking nearby in the strong March wind. Turning around she saw nothing behind her but the new car dealership. Looking down the avenue, on the other side of Knorr Street from the car dealership, she saw a wooden shop sign suspended above the large pane glass window of the retail store.

The wind was buffeting the sign, which swung back and forth on what, Emma supposed, was a rusty iron hinge.

Emma was shocked by the sign. It was painted bright yellow. In big, bold, black, block letters it proclaimed, "FATHER & SON EXTERMINATORS."

Emma was amazed. "If only," she thought. Then, immediately, "Forgive me, Lord."

The bus pulled up just then, and the front door opened. Emma got on, paid her fare, and sat down, looking out the window at the sign. It must be a new store, she thought. All the years she had waited at this bus stop she had never noticed the sign before. Maybe she would check it out on her way home.

After all, she had to do something about the mice in her basement workshop. A felon son and a homicidal, sadistic, abusive rapist of a husband she could handle. But it was the thought of mice in her basement that made Emma shudder.

<hr>

MARIO WAS NOT HAPPY. AFTER NINETEEN YEARS, EMMA COULD read her boss like a book. The barbershop was busy when she arrived twelve minutes late, at 9:12 a.m. Emma hung her coat on a hook, greeted one of her regular customers who was waiting for her, and escorted him to her barber chair.

Emma loved being a barber, and it was obvious. She engaged her customers, mostly men and boys but many women also, in conversation, and she thoroughly enjoyed experiencing their normal lives vicariously through them. It was cathartic.

Her customers loved her and were very loyal. Her colleagues also loved her because she was a business magnet. Emma's customers tended to tell their friends and acquaintances how much they appreciated Emma's skills, many of whom came to Mario's, some becoming the customers of the other barbers there.

Emma was skilled, personable, funny, attractive, and fast -- a killer combination for a barber. She was the consensus rainmaker. And, Emma was Mario's first employee after he and his wife had emigrated from Italy. Without Emma there would have been no Mario's Barber Shop, and nobody understood that better than Mario himself.

Still, Mario had decided that he had to talk to Emma, yet again, about her tardiness and about her obvious injuries. The first break of the day, when there were no customers in the shop, came only in the early afternoon.

"Emma, come with me," Mario called across the shop as he put on his windbreaker, "and bring your appetite. Let's get some lunch."

"Good luck," Yvonne whispered to Emma.

"It'll be fine," Emma whispered back, hurrying to put on her sunglasses, coat and scarf and catch up to her boss.

"We'll be a bit," Mario announced as he headed out the door, indicating it was going to be a long lunch.

"Ooh, vee go svanky?" Emma employed her native Russian accent as she ran after Mario.

"Cut that commie crap!" Mario shouted. "It's not going to work this time." His emphasis on "this time," concerned Emma. When they were both seated in the car, Mario said, "We'll do Mickey D's. Drive through. We need to talk in the car where no one can hear us."

"And such a beautiful, brand new Lexus it is too," Emma said. "Owning your own business pays pretty well, huh?"

"C'mon, Emma. Knock it off. If you're waiting for me to admit I don't need you and don't appreciate all you've done for me, you'll have to wait a long time. But this isn't about any of that."

"No, and it's not about a craving for Big Mac's either, so what is the bee in your bonnet, exactly? Why the cold shoulder all morning?"

"Three months, Emma!" he exploded. "Three friggin' months you've been showing up late every day. Everybody's talking about it. The other barbers, the customers, and now it's affecting the business. We're losing customers, Emma. Business is down.

"I get calls at night, at home. Customers aren't happy. They don't want to wait in the morning. When you show up late, they either leave or go to one of the other barbers."

"There's always a line waiting for me when I come in," Emma objected.

"Yes, I know. That's true. Some customers do wait for you, but some don't, and I hear from all of them.

"It's bad, Emma. It's gotta stop. You gotta start showing up on time or I'm going to have to...."

"To what, Mario? What are you going to have to do?"

"I'm going to have to let you go."

"Oh, pfft! Stop."

"Don't do that, Emma. I'm serious."

"Mario, please, can't we talk about something else? This conversation is ludicrous."

"Damn it, Emma! I'm serious! This time I mean it. You think I want to let you go? You think I don't know how big of a risk it is? It would jeopardize not only you but every other barber in that shop, including me."

"Then why do it?"

"Because you leave me no choice. I don't know what else to do."

"You know I have to go to daily Mass," Emma interrupted.

"I know it, dammit, Emma! I do! I'm Catholic too. I would never tell you not to go to Mass, but...."

"But what?"

"But that damned husband of yours...."

"Is my husband. And what God has joined together...."

"He's going to kill you, you know that, right? Someday, 9:12 a.m. is going to come and, and..." he stammered, "...and no Emma. You won't be walking in late. You won't be walking at all. But it will be too late, and there will be nothing I or anyone else will be able to do. Selfishly, that doesn't help my business but, more importantly…oh, never mind."

"What?"

"I'm seventy-two years old, Emma. I'm thinking about hanging 'em up. I need to retire but, to do that, I need to sell the business. I was hoping I could sell it to you."

"Me?"

"Why not? Who else would I sell it to? You are Mario's, after all."

"No, I'm not."

"Yes. You are," Mario said, with emphasis. "Everybody knows it."

"Mario, look, I'm flattered and all but I don't know anything about running a business and, even if I did, my husband.…"

"I know, Emma. That's what I've been trying to say."

"It's why I've never asked for a raise, not that I've ever had to. You have been very fair to me, Mario. More than fair. But if I owned your business, my husband.…"

"Would screw it all up," Mario concluded what they both knew was true. "I was hoping he'd be dead by now."

"Mario!"

"I'm sorry, Emma, but that man.…"

"Is still my husband."

"I could help you with that, you know."

"Mario! Stop!"

"I know people."

"Mario, please! We are married in the eyes of God. Would you interfere with God's will?"

Mario sighed. "You are a mule, an absolute mule. I wish I had your faith."

"And I wish I had your unbruised eyes, you dear, sweet man," Emma smiled, touching the side of his face.

"So, please tell me, my little Mother Theresa, why is it that God wills you to suffer and for me not to retire?"

"I'm pretty sure He doesn't will either of those things. I think He wills just the opposite. It's just a matter of time."

"Ah, time. Easier for some than others," Mario said, looking askance at her.

Emma got his meaning, but she wasn't at all certain which of them had the shorter timeline. She guessed Mrs. Mario didn't point loaded pistols at him.

As they continued to drive, in silence, Emma shuddered to recall how Hank had pointed the pistol at her that morning. She absent-mindedly reached into her coat pocket for the rosary, before recalling it was no longer there, and shuddered a second time. She thought a silent prayer. *"Lord, help Stella today, and Mario. He's a good man. And please help me. I don't have much more time."*

THE BUS CONTINUED UP RISING SUN AVENUE, THROUGH THE LIGHT rain and rush hour traffic, making stops every three blocks or so. It was a long, slow ride, but not long enough or slow enough for Emma. She feared going home every day, but especially today. If the bus had gotten a flat tire, it would have been all well and good with her.

But there were no flat tires today. The bus pulled away after she and some other commuters alighted at Knorr Street. Head down, umbrella up, Emma took a few rote steps to begin the long walk home, before remembering about the mice in the basement. Turning suddenly, she saw the large yellow sign through the rain, and turned back toward the avenue.

A small silver bell above the door tinkled as she entered. "Good day! Good day!" boomed the deep baritone voice of the tall, forty-something proprietor with salt-and-pepper hair who was watering plants on the front windowsill. He put the watering can down, hurried to take the umbrella from Emma and place it in the umbrella stand by the door, and ushered her inside.

"Come in, young lady, come in, come in, out of the rain. Bloody weather! May I take your coat?"

"Well, I don't know," Emma began. "I won't be staying long."

"Yes, yes, of course, but perhaps...um, if I might be so presumptuous, perhaps I could interest you in a seat there, by the fire, where you could warm yourself; dry off a bit?"

Emma stood transfixed, amazed at what she saw. She had expected a business office or typical retail storefront. What she saw looked more like a British sitting room or, at least, her mind's-eye version of what a British sitting room might look like.

There was a fine Persian rug over a beautiful oak-stained parquet hardwood floor, a floor-to-ceiling bluestone see-through fireplace and hearth toward the rear of the front room, separating it from an open space behind it, with gas-fired sconces on the two side walls.

Each side wall was covered with bold, bright, floral wallpaper bordered by a wide cherry baseboard and gleaming hunter green crown molding. Full-length velvet drapes framed the side windows; there was a partial wall of bookshelves to the right and, most surprisingly of all, two mint-green upholstered sitting chairs in front of the fireplace with a complete tea setting between them.

The whole room smelled of gardenia. How long had it been since Emma had experienced anything as wonderful, beautiful, and sensuous as gardenia?

"Emma, I hope you like Earl Grey." She was suddenly aware that he was touching her elbow, motioning toward the sitting area with his other hand. She noticed he had already hung her coat on the coat rack. When had that happened?

"Um, okay, I guess just a few minutes," Emma said, as she

began to walk toward the fireplace. "Wait. How did you know my name?" she said, sitting in one of the chairs. He sat in the other.

He pointed at her blouse, smiling.

Looking down, she fingered her name tag. "I forgot about that."

"Ah, an occupational hazard. I hope you don't mind me calling you by your name. I suppose that was frightfully forward of me."

"No, that's fine. It is my name, after all, Mister…."

"Lured. Oliver Lured, at your service, ma'am."

Emma had never before been called ma'am.

"If I may, please, call me Oliver. A spot of tea?" he asked, holding the teapot.

"Oliver," Emma said. "Um, okay. Thank you."

She really wanted to remove her shoes and run her toes through the rug. It looked sumptuous but, of course, she didn't dare. The fire felt so very good on her back and neck. She could feel her inhibitions melting away. What was this place?

He handed her a china tea cup and saucer. She placed the saucer on the table, warming her hands around the cup. She sipped at the tea, looking at Oliver Lured as she did so. Was he a proprietor or a host? She wasn't sure. But, the tea warmed her inside, and the teacup and fire warmed her outside, and it felt heavenly, absolutely heavenly.

The thought of trudging home in the rain to Hank and Darrell was fading fast. Looking around, Emma figured this is what a suite at a five-star hotel must be like.

"So, Emma, what is it that brings you to my humble abode on such an intrepid evening?"

"Um, mice."

"Mice?"

"Yes, I have mice in my basement."

"Mice?"

"Yes, mice. In my basement. I was thinking you might be able to exterminate…."

"The mice?"

"Yes, exactly. Or, at least, provide me with some traps."

"So, you came to Father and Son Exterminators thinking we could help you eradicate a few mice? Mice. I just want to make sure."

"Yes, mice. That is something you do, right? You are an exterminator, aren't you?"

"Very highly qualified, if I say so myself. Perhaps you noticed my professional credentials on the sign out front, MLS?"

"MLS?"

"Master Licensed Scotch. It's quite an archaic qualification today, I suppose, and there aren't many of us around anymore. Nonetheless, it is THE credential in our line of work. Quite first rate, I assure you. Today, it is better translated, Master Licensed Exterminator. I, myself, prefer Master Life Saver."

Emma smiled at that. "I suppose I could use a Master Life Saver."

"Indeed!" he said, sipping his tea. "Now we get down to it."

Emma wasn't sure what he meant by that, but she was beginning to think there was more to Oliver Lured than met the eye. "Are you the father or the son?"

"Neither."

"Neither?"

'Father & Son Exterminators' is just a name. Marketing. Somewhat ordinary, certainly. Hundreds of people will pass this storefront every day and never notice my sign, no matter how gaudy I manage to make it. And yet, to some it connotes…a…a…dare I say, solution."

"So, 'Father & Son Exterminators' is just you?"

"Quite right. No acolytes."

"Do you have any references?"

"Oh, yes, many. Thousands, in fact. Though, of course, they are all quite unable to speak so as you'd understand."

"They're foreigners?"

"No," he chuckled. "Well, to be accurate, some were, I suppose. But what I mean to say is each and every one of them was, as you might expect, a scurvy, mawkish parasite, altogether prosaic at best when they were drawing breath, but now quite altogether encumbered I am afraid."

"Encumbered?"

"Dead. Yes, quite dead, as a matter of fact. Oh, not to be maudlin about it. Is it even possible? After all, we are talking about vermin aren't we?"

"Vermin? No, I was asking about human references. Clients."

"Well, this is a new location for me. I only opened here quite recently, but…."

He put down his cup and saucer and stood, retrieving from the mantel over the fireplace some bright yellow materials Emma was pretty sure weren't there just a few minutes ago. Then again, she couldn't be sure of anything since she arrived. Who was this remarkable man?

"In lieu of the references you have every right to expect, perhaps I could give you something else. I want you to take these. They should be quite helpful. Yes, altogether helpful, I am sure. First, three mouse traps," he said, handing them to her

"They're bright yellow," Emma said.

"Yes. I have found that vermin of all stripes are drawn to yellow. And here, in these packets, is the bait."

"Yellow cheese," Emma said, accepting the packets.

"And, finally, for being my very first customer in this new location, a special gift," he said, handing a bright yellow ticket to Emma. "This is a raffle ticket. The auto dealer next door is raffling off a brand new sports car of some sort tomorrow and $5,000 for a year's supply of gas and maintenance."

"Well, that's very generous of you," Emma said, standing. "What do I owe you for these?"

"Tut, tut, my dear. No need. You have already paid me. You have kept me company, you are my first customer, and you are quite altogether lovely."

"But," Emma started.

"No buts. I insist," he said, handing her his bright yellow business card. She placed it, with the traps, cheese packets, and raffle ticket, in her pocketbook and stood as he ushered her to the door.

"You set those yellow traps and your problems will all disappear. But, guard that raffle ticket. It is payable to the bearer. Granted, it's just an American-made car, a Corvette, or some such meretricious vehicle, not a McLaren, Aston-Martin, Bentley, or Jaguar, but when in Rome, and all that."

He helped Emma with her coat, opened the door and her umbrella, and held the umbrella above her head as she went to step through the door. Impulsively, surprising even herself, she stood on her tip toes and kissed him on the cheek as she took her umbrella from him and clutched her package to her chest. There was something about him. Something she loved about him. "Thank you," she said, stepping out into the rain.

"Emma," he called after her.

She turned to face him. "Yes?"

"You were right."

"About what?"

"You weren't…," was all she could make out before the door closed.

She walked home three quarters of a mile in the rain and entered the house through the kitchen door in the rear. It would have been nice had Darrell not taken her car, but that would have required that he think about someone other than himself, which wasn't likely to happen anytime soon, if ever, she knew.

She noticed that the spilled coffee and broken cup were still on the kitchen floor. Home all day, contributing nothing to the household income, neither her husband nor her son had bothered to clean up the mess.

Emma shook her head. "So the evening begins," she said.

She opened the basement door and walked down the steps to get a mop and bucket. Back in the kitchen, she filled the bucket with hot water and Lysol, picked up the cup shards, and began to mop up the dried coffee and blood.

When she had finished, she carried the bucket and mop over to the stairway leading to the basement.

She was about to go downstairs to empty the bucket in the laundry tub before coming back up to prepare dinner, when Hank surprised her.

"Where you been?" he asked, appearing suddenly in the kitchen. "You're late."

"Yes, well, I would be making dinner right now but I had to clean up the mess you were too lazy to clean up."

It was a mistake, and she regretted it as soon as the words were out of her mouth.

"Oh, is that so?" Hank said. "Well, clean it up again," he said, as he rushed at her and shoved her hard down the basement stairs.

Emma went tumbling head over heels down the stairway, banging her head and limbs on the railing, stairs, and concrete wall on the way down before landing with a thud, banging her head on the concrete basement floor. The bucket, water, and mop tumbled down with her and landed loudly on top of her unconscious body at the foot of the stairs.

"Dude!" yelled Darrell, looking over Hank's shoulder. "What'd you do that for? Now who's gonna make us dinner?"

"Guess we eat out tonight," Hank said, turning away from the stairs.

"With what? I ain't got no money. You got money?" Darrell

said, still looking down the stairs. "Man, I think you might've killed her. She ain't movin' at all down there."

"She's young enough," Hank said. "She'll live. What d'you mean you ain't got no money? I thought you were doin' some big drug deal," he said, taking a beer out of the refrigerator.

"That ain't 'til tomorrow," Darrell said. "Don't drink all the beer," he said, walking over to the refrigerator.

"Hey, maybe there's money in here," he said, stopping to rifle through Emma's pocketbook. "Jackpot!" he exclaimed, taking three twenties from Emma's pocketbook. "And look at this. A raffle ticket for the drawing tomorrow up at Laramie Chevy. Maybe we'll win that yellow Vette. It's sweet."

"Keep dreamin'. Nobody ever wins those things. It's just a come on, a scam."

"Looks legit to me," Darrell replied, fondling the ticket. "Won't cost us nuthin' to check it out."

"Yeah, I guess. C'mon, let's get something to eat," Hank said, heading for the door.

"My treat!" Darrell said, following him out, waving the three twenties and the raffle ticket in the air.

"Great," Hank said, not bothering to close the door as they left.

Emma did not hear them leave, did not hear the mice running by her head, and did not hear anything at all as she lay unconscious for almost twenty minutes before stirring.

Moaning, the pain in her head exquisite, she was becoming vaguely aware that the chronic pain around her left eye was more acute than usual, if that was even possible. Then she remembered the Lysol, and she felt around her eye. The cleaning solution had spilled over her head and was dripping down from her hair, stinging her eyes and her wound.

She knew she was injured all over, but she wasn't certain where the most severe damage was. Everything hurt, but nothing seemed to be broken, until she tried to sit up. She screamed, as the pain in her lower right leg convulsed her.

Immediately stifling her outburst, she felt for what she was certain she would feel down by her right ankle: an unnatural protuberance, a broken tibia. But there was nothing sticking out of the skin.

"Good," she thought. "Maybe it's just a bad sprain. Well, pain is good. I guess my spine's not broken, thank God," she said, pushing away the bucket and mop and pushing herself into a sitting position on the floor with her back up against the first step.

"Sorry, Mario," she said, knowing that his sales would decline further were she to miss any significant time from work. "I should've kept my mouth shut. Stupid! Stupid! Stupid!" she shouted, angry at having mismanaged her husband.

She was always on pins and needles around him. Her survival demanded she be on stage and on her best behavior at all times. He was just a pack animal, a hunter, looking for any sign of weakness or vulnerability, and she had miscalculated badly. Stupid!

"Deal with it, girl," she said, pushing herself up to sit on the first step. The pain in her lower leg was intense, as it would be each time she moved up to the next step.

There were about twelve steps between her and the kitchen, and then another fourteen or so steps to the second floor, and a bunch of scooching around on her butt after she had climbed each staircase.

She didn't dare try standing on her right leg. There was definitely something wrong there, though she was pretty sure she could get through the night at home. She resolved to see a doctor in the morning, if things hadn't improved sufficiently by then. No one should have to suffer such abuse, she knew, but she did seem to be Built Ford Tough, as they say.

It took her half an hour to struggle up the basement steps on her butt. Up in the kitchen, Emma noticed her pocketbook on the floor. Moving gingerly by propping herself up onto her left leg and leaning on the kitchen table, chairs, and counter, she hopped over to the pocketbook, and bent to pick it up. Her money and the raffle ticket were gone, as she expected.

"Drinks on me, boys," she said, knowing where they would go for "dinner" and the implications for her once Hank returned.

She placed the pocketbook back on the kitchen counter and continued to hop through the kitchen and dining room to the front hallway and stairs leading upstairs. She went up the stairs on her butt again, then, once upstairs, used the banister to raise herself onto her left leg and hop into the bathroom.

She leaned over and started a hot bath, then hopped over and lowered the toilet seat top, sat down, and began taking off her coat and clothes. Everything she wore had been soaked through by dirty water, Lysol, sweat, and blood.

She soaked in the tub. The hot water felt glorious. Emma let her mind go blank. She knew she wasn't done for the day, there was more to come, as there was every evening with Hank, but she didn't think about any of that just now. She just wanted to relax, to feel clean, if only for a few minutes.

But, it couldn't be helped. Her mind had never done downtime real well. After a few minutes, Emma started to reflect on all that had happened to her that day.

She hoped Stella made good use of the rosary. Emma hoped it would help her with her brother. Then her thoughts went to the crucifix and to Jesus.

It was Lent and Emma began to reflect on the crucifixion of Christ, wondering if God had sent His angels to Him to help Him in His time of agony. "I hope so," she said, softly, to no one.

She thought about Mario, and said a silent prayer for him, that God would help him to retire. But, mostly, she thought about Oliver Lured, MLS.

What was it he had said as she was leaving? She was right. She was not…what? Emma vowed, once she was up and about, to go back to his store and question him. She felt as though she had missed something important and that bothered her.

An hour later, Emma had dried off, applied fresh makeup, put her hair up, changed into good clothes, and struggled back down the stairs. Her leg throbbed and she knew something was very wrong, so she called 9-1-1 and waited in the living room, with her pocketbook, and the mousetraps within, for the ambulance to arrive.

She would call Mario from the hospital tomorrow and let him know that she would not be coming in to work. She had no intention of putting up with a drunken Hank tonight, worrying whether he would rape her or shoot her or, most likely, both. She didn't even consider leaving a note for Hank or Darrell. They didn't care about her. She was done with them.

She looked around the room one last time, knowing she would never return. She didn't know where she would go, where she would stay, but she would figure that out later, and she trusted that God would help her.

"Forgive me, Lord," she said. "You joined us, yes, but Hank put us asunder a long time ago. Time to make it official."

EMMA WAS ADMITTED TO THE HOSPITAL THAT EVENING. THE admitting doctor quickly determined that her right leg was indeed broken and would require an emergency operation in the morning.

She slept peacefully through the night, for the first time in twenty years. In a dream, she heard what Oliver Lured, CLS, had said to her: "You were right. You were not afraid."

When Emma heard that, she awoke with a start – a good start, an excited start, similar to when she was young and dreamed she could fly.

Oliver Lured was, indeed, an angel, and Emma had been correct, he told her, when she believed she would not be afraid to meet an angel. She couldn't wait to go back and meet him again. It would be glorious!

Emma called Mario before going in for her operation. He promised to visit her that evening. By midafternoon, after the surgeons had reset Emma's tibia, she rested comfortably and watched her life change on TV.

The lead story on the 6:00 p.m. evening news concerned a so-called "Good News/Bad News" story. A crowd of about five hundred people had shown up that morning and waited for hours outside of the Laramie Chevrolet dealership at Knorr Street and Rising Sun Avenue.

As Emma watched the newscast, she could see the bright yellow 'Father & Son Exterminator' sign nearby. The winner of the brand new, bright yellow $50,000 fully-appointed Corvette Stingray was announced. It was a father and son, Hank and Darrell Crass. They were seen waving at the TV cameras as they drove their new car out of the dealership.

Two hours later, the scene changed to a rundown inner-city neighborhood about an hour away, where a drug deal had gone bad and the father and son, still sitting in their new car, had been shot and killed.

Emma was stunned, but the tears would not come.

The reporter on the street concluded the newscast from Laramie Chevrolet. She said this was a sad, sad turn of events, where very good news had become very sad news, in the blink of an eye.

Emma could not help but notice the 'Father & Son Exterminator' sign in the background as the camera focused on the reporter. She knew the reporter was wrong.

The 'blink of an eye' was more like twenty years, and the outcome, at least for Emma, was anything but sad.

Still, she did not smile.

"Forgive them, Lord. Have mercy on their souls." She shut off the TV and breathed deeply. This changed everything.

Thank God in heaven. This changed everything.

Emma did return to the house, after being released from the hospital a few days later. Technically, since she had been married to Hank, the Corvette now belonged to her.

Mr. Laramie, of Laramie Chevrolet, personally delivered a check to her for $10,000, as covered by the TV evening news: the $5,000 for gas and maintenance that her husband had won in the raffle, and an additional $5,000 to help with burial expenses.

Emma thanked him on TV but, privately, arranged for him to buy back the car for $40,000, an amount he agreed was fair value. Emma explained that she had no need of a sports car, couldn't afford one, and would not feel safe driving around the neighborhood in it.

She then listed the house for sale, buried her husband and son, and arranged with Mario to buy the barber shop, once her house sold, so that he could finally retire. She promised not to change anything at the store but the name. It would now be known as Emmario's and Mario was fine with that.

Emma also had plans to grow the number of stores via franchising, although she planned to maintain tight control over hiring and training. While she was a very gifted barber, she was only one person. She knew she could grow Emmario's by teaching more young barbers the secrets of her success, multiplying her effectiveness many-fold.

It was three weeks before Emma could drive her car, or walk around the neighborhood. Her first destination was the business address of her favorite angel, Oliver Lured – or, as more precisely stated on his business card, which Emma placed on the center console of her car, O. Goode Lured, MLS. "Cute," Emma thought.

When she arrived at the storefront, it was, as Emma had expected it might be, vacant. There was no business there.

Still, Emma walked up and peeked in the window. It was empty inside: no fireplace, no wallpaper, no sconces. Even the sign over the front door was gone, replaced by a realtor sign proclaiming a retail space and upstairs apartment for sale or lease.

Perfect. It would be the perfect location for a second Emmario's Barber Shop and home for her. No more buses and she could walk to church.

"Thank you, Gabriel," she said, for she had no doubt who O. Goode Lured really was and that he was still watching over her.

Her second destination was to the courthouse, where she changed her name back to her maiden name, Emma Mir. Mir was the name of one of the largest diamond mines in the world. Crass was a Russian name loosely translated as rough. Emma used to call herself a diamond in the rough, and she had been so for twenty years of marriage. Now, however, she would once again shine as the Mir she had always been.

As Emma drove off, Stella Sable was driving the other way on the avenue. They did not see each other. Stella was struggling to read, through swollen and blood-soaked eyes, the bright yellow sign she had never seen before, which read "Brother Exterminators."

"If only," Stella thought. Then, immediately, "Forgive me, Lord," as she glanced at the crucifix hanging from her rear view mirror. Still, she vowed to check out 'Brother Exterminators' on her return trip that evening.

9

THE SUPER-OUTLIER

Somewhere, an extraordinary man recorded the following on a CD-ROM. It will never be heard.

I am pretty certain I was not supposed to be born. I am a mistake. I would like to say I am fine with that, being as highly educated and cosmopolitan as I am. But, to be honest, it still hurts.

Were you to chart on a graph every human being who ever lived or will ever live, you would get a normal distribution. Most people are normal, clumped closely toward the middle of the graph.

Then there are those few to one side or the other of the average. They are the exceptions: giant or midget, wealthy or destitute, gifted or challenged, saint or murderer, etc.

Beyond these two extremes, further out on either side of the graph are the outliers – those extremely rare persons who seemingly defy explanation because they are so different from everyone else. These are the most famous, and infamous, of the human race.

Beyond this handful of outliers, however, is one super-outlier – the one who defies all explanation, the one who is extremely different from everyone else, including the outliers. That person is unique in a fundamental, one-in-a trillion-type way. That person may not even be a person at all. I am the super-outlier.

Mind you, I look pretty average, though nerdy. By all accounts, I am mensa-smart, but introverted to a fault. I think too much and talk too little. I am not overtly exceptional. In fact, I am eminently forgettable. My uniqueness lies therein. You could listen to me for an entire hour, and five minutes later you would not be able to remember anything I said.

Growing up, this used to bother me. It took years for me to accept it and, even though I now accept it, I still do not like it. It is sad. Nonetheless, I have managed to make lemonade from my life's bumper lemon crop. After all, I am a trillionaire, the wealthiest human in history and, I suppose, that counts for something.

A BIT OF BACKGROUND INFORMATION IS IN ORDER. I AM AN ORPHAN. I have no idea who my parents were. I can only assume I had parents, though at times I wonder. I was adopted by a wonderful older couple in the heartland. I attended Stanford University on a full scholarship. I am a gifted mathematician and software programmer. I invented a fifth-level quadratic equation known only to me.

I have used it over thirty years to exploit holes in inefficient investment markets all over the world – markets which, in the aggregate, are now short about a trillion dollars. World finance ministers know this, though the information has never been made public for fear of revolts, but they don't know where the money went.

It went to me. I picked their pockets – legally, of course. I am just smarter than they are and, well, goody for me, I suppose. Don't fret, though. I have, through my charitable foundations, taken steps to ensure my wealth is used for the good of future generations of children worldwide.

I have only come to accept being the super-outlier after several decades of heartache. It was difficult growing up because I was ignored by everybody, even those who cared about me.

It was only as I grew older that I understood they had no control over whether or not they could remember me and what I said or did. No one is to blame, them or me. It's just the way it must be. The Law of the Super-Outlier compels humans to forget or ignore me. Trust me. I am not paranoid. I used to be paranoid, but now I understand. It's not them. It's not me. It just is.

Many have seen me, but no one remembers. I might as well be The Invisible Man. As I walk toward people on the sidewalk, they either avert their eyes as they rush past, or seem to look right through me, as if I wasn't there at all. When they talk to me, they seem to suffer from ADD. They say things like, "What did you say?" or "Excuse me, hold that thought. I'll be right back," or "Do I know you?"

I even met The Beatles once. They forgot having met me but subsequently wrote "Nowhere Man." I am pretty sure I was their inspiration although, of course, they didn't know it.

Nature and society give clues to my existence, I believe. (Boy, I hope that doesn't sound too conceited. It may, but, trust me, there is no conceit in me. I can boast of nothing except being tired and wanting it all to end.) Alzheimer's, dementia, hallucinations, espionage, trade secrets, witness protection programs, and buried civilizations are all clues to the super-outlier – the person you cannot remember.

In my younger, rebellious days, I dealt with my circumstance foolishly, I must admit. I robbed a bank just to get caught. I was that starved for attention. Even though I walked away with over two million dollars, I was stunned to learn that the bank surveillance equipment had malfunctioned and eyewitnesses could not agree on my description. Some bank employees did not even realize the bank was being robbed.

Exasperated, I turned myself in to the police. I walked right into the precinct building and surrendered. I was in the middle of giving my deposition to an officer, when he excused himself to use the facilities.

When he returned, I began to resume my testimony, and he suddenly suffered a massive coronary and died right in front of me. That scared the bejesus out of me so I walked out of that precinct building. No one tried to stop me.

I then returned to the bank with the money in a bag and walked right up to the same teller I had robbed just two days earlier. She did not recognize me. I wore no disguise when I robbed her, and I wore no disguise when I returned. Still, she did not recognize me.

Amazing.

Anyway, when I tried to return the money, her phone rang. She excused herself to answer the phone, listened a bit, and reacted angrily to the caller whom, I presume from the conversation, was her husband. Five minutes later, she was still arguing, and ignoring me, so I left the bag of money at her window and walked out of the bank. That was thirty-five years ago. I still bank there, but no one has ever remembered me as being the robber. And they pride themselves on knowing their customers.

MANY PEOPLE HAVE SUFFERED SOME OF THE SAME SORT OF indignities I have. I am no different from others in this regard. However, some of the things which happen to me are pretty unique. I can say that without any hint of paranoia because it is true. Let me give some examples, and you can be the judge.

As I have said, I was orphaned. My mother gave birth to me in a hospital, but she did not take me home with her when she left. I am not certain whether she gave me up for adoption, or if she merely forgot to take me home. Ridiculous, you say? Not so fast. Consider the following.

There are times in school when kids feel as though the teacher shows favoritism to other students by calling on those other students repeatedly, rather than spreading the attention more democratically. We have all experienced the heartache of being overlooked by a teacher. It happens. When I was in sixth grade, I remember the teacher did not call on me for ten straight school days. Two whole weeks! I waved my hand like crazy, but she never called on me once.

Now, this would be a pretty remarkable streak for any kid, but especially for me. After all, I was a really good student. I studied hard, prepared well, knew the material, and got all A's on my report card.

In other words, I was the typical teacher's dream student. After two weeks of not being acknowledged in class, I went to talk to my teacher, Miss Patricia, about it. Guess what? She denied not having called on me and told me I was exaggerating. "Robert, you exaggerate," she said. My name is Andrew.

But, I came to learn later, Miss Patricia was not unique. It happened in seventh grade, eighth grade, ninth grade, and every grade thereafter through graduate school.

Then there was the time in Little League. The game was tied in the last inning, with two outs. We were the home team, and I had just hit a triple. I was standing at third base, just sixty feet away from scoring the winning run. If the batter could get a hit, I would score the winning run. If he made an out, then the game would end tied, because it was getting dark, and the field had no lights back then.

The batter took strike one, then strike two. He was not going to hit; I just knew it, and so I decided to steal home.

I took off. The pitcher stood on the mound with the ball and was looking right at me. I was terrified of making the final out, but I had no other choice. I ran as hard as I could and slid into home. Guess what? That pitcher never threw the ball. I heard him explain to his manager afterward that he never saw me and had forgotten I was at third. I had just hit a triple and he forgot I was at third. He was looking right at me when I broke for home plate yet, somehow, he did not see me!

Amazing.

So, you can see that being "invisible" can sometimes be a good thing. Sometimes you can steal home, win the game, and be a hero. More often, however, there are drawbacks.

For example, sometimes the coach can forget to pick you up for the team pizza party. Yes, it happened. Your friends, including your own date, can forget to pick you up when going out – to the prom, for crying out loud! Well, to be fair, they did remember as they pulled up to the high school, and then returned to get me. But, come on. My own prom date didn't notice that I wasn't in the car?

At my high school graduation, the principal forgot my name as he handed the diploma to me, even though I was the valedictorian. I can't tell you how many times people have sat on me, apparently not having seen me, on buses and trains, as I commute to work. Every once in awhile, some sexy young thing would do so, so there is an upside, I suppose. But for every bikini model, there were three "Biggest Loser" candidates, Sumo wrestlers, or offensive linemen.

So, having tired of being routinely crushed by overweight commuters, I decided to drive to work. This was a bad idea also, because drivers would cut in front of me as if I wasn't even on the road. Yes, I know this happens to all of us, but have you ever been rear-ended on three consecutive days while paying your toll at three different toll booths? I didn't think so.

On our first date, I took my future wife, Diane, to dinner at a French restaurant. She and I approached the maître d'. Diane requested a table and the maître d' asked if she was dining alone. "No," she said nodding in my direction, "we would like a table for two." "Very good," he replied, "does Madam wish to sit at the bar until her party arrives?"

I could go on and on. When we exchanged wedding vows, the priest asked Diane if she promised to love and cherish me in sickness and in health, etc., but he forgot to ask me. On our honeymoon, even Diane screamed when I walked out of the master bathroom, forgetting momentarily that I was in there.

It happens. In my world anyway. Sometimes, I swear I am on loan from another universe.

Please don't misunderstand. I am not a loser. I have amassed a fortune. In fact, I am the wealthiest man who has ever lived, by a lot. I have won at everything. I have been recognized by the greatest scientific organizations in the world, many times. I have been given great genetic gifts and I have maximized them for the benefit of mankind. I am satisfied, self-fulfilled, and have been faithfully loved and supported by my beautiful Diane these past thirty years.

I am the most successful man the world cannot remember. I feel certain that is by design. Not my design, certainly, as I would much prefer to be one of the masses. Even if I were just a lowly, nondescript, milquetoast, non-achieving, average Joe, I could handle it. More than merely handle it, however, I would prefer it. I would welcome it. I would love it. But, I have never been one of the masses, and I shall never be. I am the super-outlier. No one remembers me.

And now that my beloved Diane is in advanced stages of Alzheimer's, that has become an absolutely true statement.

I HAVE TOLD OTHERS OF MY SITUATION TO NO AVAIL. THE LAST person I told was a psychiatrist. He told me he thought I might be paranoid or delusional though, of course, he never used those terms with me. He prescribed powerful anti-depressants for me, though I never did purchase them (I don't believe in drugs), and ordered me to return to his office the next day at 11a.m.

Unfortunately, as I was driving to meet him the next morning, an Army helicopter, out on a routine practice run for the upcoming air show, crashed into his little clinic, which bordered the airbase, killing him, eight other employees, and two aides (who, I learned only later, had been called in to restrain and transmit his 11:00 a.m. patient,) totally destroying the clinic and all patient records in an impressive conflagration.

I concluded that I had better stop talking about myself – for the sake of my audience.

This, finally, brings me to you. Since informing anyone is verboten by the Laws of Nature or by God, do I imperil you by telling you? No, because you will never hear this, I am certain.

I record this as I sit a half mile below the earth's surface, in a secluded and occluded vein within an abandoned salt mine in Utah. If my sorry carcass is ever found, it likely won't be for another ten thousand years or so.

Those intrepid explorers of the future will also find this CD-ROM with more than two thousand years of advanced science, mathematics, engineering, and technology teachings, a nice bottle of chardonnay, a Colt 45, and a spent bullet casing.

Perhaps, just perhaps, that civilization ten thousand years in the future will finally hear my words. Perhaps, finally, someone will listen to me. Maybe, just maybe, I will be able to help that civilization not only to survive, but to thrive. Then perhaps, I will not have lived in vain.

THE CD-ROM, BULLET CASING, AND REVOLVER LASTED FAR MORE than ten thousand years. A seismic event caused that salt mine and, in fact, all of North America, to be covered in a mile-deep sheet of ice for millions of years. Upon the Great Thaw, a tremendous earthquake thrust those objects to a mountaintop, where they remained buried in the dirt floor of a forest for another one-hundred and fifty-nine thousand years.

Subsequently, a lightning strike started a forest fire that consumed that forest. Torrential rains caused massive mudslides that carried oceans of mud, trees, plants, and wildlife to the canyon floor, which had been crafted by the rushing waters of the melting ice sheet, six-thousand feet below.

One fine spring day, the tribe's advance scout saw something gleaming by the riverbed. He unearthed it with his massive right hand. It was a round, flat, silver disk. He sized it up quickly, sniffed it, and then rinsed it in the waters of the stream before eating it, which infuriated his ravenous fellow apes.

10

LEVI STONE

J ake Foley pushed his chair back from his dorm room desk. "Dude, it's done."

"'Bout time. Let's go get something to eat."

Jake leaned back, looked up at the drop ceiling, and ran both hands through his hair. "Chill, man. Let me think about this first."

"Just send it. Can't reign if you're not in the game." Ben Collier, Foley's roommate, was a budding urban philosopher. "Plus, I'm done too, for now. Can't read another friggin' word," he said, tossing the textbook aside as he rose up from the pillow and sat cross-legged on his bed. "What's there to think about?"

Foley was a freshman Computer Science major at Stanford University. He kept his prodigious programming skills sharp by designing and writing software in his spare time. His latest effort would wreak havoc on personal computers worldwide, and he knew it.

"This is the big one, Ben," he said. "Apocalyptic."

"Traceable?"

"Probably not, but who knows? Might take awhile, even for the big boys."

Foley was no stranger to federal surveillance. He was in Stanford at all only due to the good graces of a lenient federal judge and an accommodating school administration.

A gifted computer programmer, and a person Stanford seriously wanted as a future alumnus, his upside engineering potential was matched only by the extent to which he lacked ethics. He was a master programmer of the first order, and his latest effort would indeed do plenty of damage.

The only drawback, as he saw it, was that he was rarely caught, and rarely credited, for the toxicity of his viruses. He had infected over three million personal computers before his eighteenth birthday, though few people, outside the feds, knew who he was. Three million dead computers equated to about a six billion dollar chunk out of the GNP – not chump change. Jake Foley was a force. He knew it. Few others did.

Regardless, that was all about to change. Virus Me-239 would almost certainly put him in the programmer Hall of Fame. Hitting the send button now would kill a few million personal computers – maybe even ten million or more.

"So, we gonna eat or what?" Ben Collier asked.

"Don't rush me. I gotta savor the moment."

Seeing that Jake was zoning out again, Collier reclined, reapplied his ear buds, and buried his face in his textbook. "You're one seriously sick dude, Jakey."

As Jake stared at the keyboard, contemplating the destructive power at his fingertips, his palms became sweaty and a contemptuous grin took root. He stretched out his right index finger and held it just above the "send" key momentarily, closing his eyes to envision the havoc he was about to create. When he opened his eyes he inhaled deeply and depressed the send key.

Ben Collier concentrated on his text and music simultaneously.

It would be another twenty-two minutes before his stomach grumbled and he would look up to discover Jake Foley's lifeless body crumpled in a desk chair, one finger of his right hand welded to the send key.

HE SAT IN A ROCKING CHAIR ON THE SECOND FLOOR DECK OF THE rental cottage, on a hilltop overlooking Lac Saint Enfant, a large recreational lake about a hundred and fifty kilometers north of Ottawa, Quebec, Canada. It was just after 6:00 a.m., and the early summer morning fog was beginning its ascent from the lake surface.

His bare feet rested atop the deck railing, while Hugger, his Golden retriever pup, lay curled up a safe distance from the curved rockers of the chair. From his perch, he watched Mrs. Eva Henri as she walked to the 6:30 a.m. Mass, which she did every day, following the road that passed by the cottage, a hundred feet down the hillside embankment.

"Bon jour, Monsieur Desmoreaux," she called, waving.

"Bon jour, Mademoiselle Henri," he smiled and nodded his head.

"Je dirai une prière pour vous," she called, clasping her hands together prayerfully, as she did every day, to let him know she would be saying a prayer for him.

"Deux serait mieux," he offered pleasantly. Perhaps two prayers would be better.

His real name was Dr. Levi Stone. He was the greatest quantum physicist the world has never known, with Top Secret clearance at the U.S. Department of Defense, where he had been employed for thirty-five years. That was two years ago now, before Debra's death, his separation from his wife, and his self-imposed exile.

On the Web he could contact anyone and everyone, yet he

himself could be detected electronically by no one. The one-ounce crystalline Absorbium chip in his laptop computer ensured that. The one-ounce crystalline Absorbium chip surgically implanted under the skin of his left wrist ensured that his debit and credit card transactions could not be traced.

The two chips meant he was the proud, if technically illegal, owner of two-thirds of the crystalline Absorbium manufactured in the world. He was the "technically illegal" owner because although he was the inventor, he had been employed by the U.S. Department of Defense, the assignee of his invention. As possessor, however, he was invisible to all electronic detection.

Watching Mrs. Henri begin her ascent up the last hill to the Church of The Holy Child, Levi Stone turned to see the first rays of the rising sun glinting off the church spire.

"Okay, Hug, time for our walk," he said, rising, as Hugger rose with him, tail wagging in anticipation of another long walk in the brisk early morning Canadian air.

As he passed by the open door to his cottage, Levi Stone could hear the alarm beep on his computer. He wished the beeps would stop, the dying would stop, but that was out of his control now. The world would have to save itself from his Boomerang Virus.

LATER THAT DAY, COLONEL DAN MCGOVERN, U.S. Undersecretary of Defense, looked up from behind his large mahogany desk as his secretary ushered Mrs. Marion Stone into his office.

He knew this was not going to be a good day. Just three hours earlier, he was informed of the circumstances surrounding the death of a Stanford freshman Computer Science major, Jake Foley. The cause of death was apparently the same as in the deaths of six other

Computer Science students across the country in the past month: electrocution by computer.

All the victims had suffered third degree electrical burns to one finger – the same finger that had depressed the 'send' key on their computers. Apparently, some sort of charge surged through the key, melting it, and electrocuting the decedents, all of whom were found with one fried finger melded to the keyboard. He knew these deaths were not coincidental. Only one man in the world could engineer death-by-computer, and that man's wife had just walked into his office.

He would not disclose this top secret information to Mrs. Stone, of course, but he wanted to better understand Levi Stone and his motivations, before meeting with the Secretary of Defense later in the afternoon. He did not expect that meeting to be pleasant. Most meetings with his boss were anything but. It came with the territory. And since Levi Stone's whereabouts were currently cloaked by Absorbium crystals, Colonel McGovern and his staff were reduced to interviewing those who best knew him.

After exchanging pleasantries, Colonel McGovern, never one to mince words, came straight to the point.

"Mrs. Stone, we need to talk to your husband, but we don't know where he is, and we were hoping you might help us locate him."

"I assume finding him is urgent, since you've gone to all the trouble of bringing me here today."

"Yes, it is critical. Top priority."

Mrs. Stone sighed slightly, looking down at her hands folded in her lap, before looking up with sad, tired eyes. She was quite striking and an altogether attractive woman in her midfifties.

"Hm, top priority," she barely whispered, seemingly lost in thought.

"I'm sorry, Mrs. Stone, but do you have any idea where he might be?"

"Colonel, I do not."

"He never mentioned any special places he wanted to visit? Did he have any preferred destinations? Anyplace that he might go to be alone?"

"Yes, right here. This was his life. This building and the laboratories where he conducted his experiments. This is where he wanted to be and where he lived. If he is not here, I couldn't begin to tell you where he might be."

"Fair enough, but maybe you could tell me a little about his background. Something personal that he may not have disclosed to us. Something that would help me understand his motivations."

"Why? Has he done something wrong?"

The colonel smiled down at her. "Mrs. Stone, I, I …."

"Yes, I know. You can't say. I understand. You may be happy to know that Levi was top secret with me and Debra also. He divulged nothing. He was clearly happy in his work, but he never brought it home. All these years, I never had any idea what he was working on..." she said, looking away, her voice trailing off.

"Quantum mechanics, actually, Mrs. Stone. Levi is a brilliant scientist. I am so sorry for the loss of your daughter. According to Levi, she was a remarkable young lady."

"She was. Levi's only regret was missing her growing up. He tried to make it up to her later in her life and, in many ways, they were really very close – probably best friends. He was so proud of the fact that she became a science teacher and wanted to share her love of science with children. When the accident took Debra, he changed. I think when Debra died, some of my husband died with her. He was never the same after that."

"In what way did he change exactly?"

"Well, I suppose you know that Levi was born with a chip on his shoulder."

The colonel smiled. "That's not top secret."

"Yes, he did not hide it very well. He was so competitive in everything he did, but especially his work."

"Yes, Levi is driven," the colonel said.

"Driven? Haunted is more like it. By his father. He was always trying to please his dad. If Levi told me once, he told me a thousand times…" she hesitated, catching herself. "I never met him, but I believe Levi's father was a vengeful man who believed strongly in an eye-for-an-eye."

"Does Levi blame anyone for Debra's death?"

"The other driver, I suppose, but it was an accident, after all. The other driver ran a red light. Debra was just in the wrong place at the wrong time."

"Where was she exactly?"

"Exiting the parking lot at an electronics store. She had gone there to buy a computer because the computer she used for her lesson plans became infected with a virus. I remember how distraught she was. She went to replace it immediately, that same afternoon, unfortunately.

"If only she had waited a few minutes…maybe…maybe we would still have our baby." Mrs. Stone paused, as tears welled up in her eyes and her voice started to crack.

The colonel reached across his desk, touched. He offered Mrs. Stone a tissue, which she accepted.

"Thank you, Colonel. I'm sorry."

"Mrs. Stone, you are doing very well. I know how difficult this must be for you. I don't know what I would do if I lost my little girl."

"Thank you, Colonel. Yes, we lost our dear Debra. The loss was hardest on Levi. In the days after the funeral, he became even more distant, more remote, if that was even possible."

"Did he say or do anything unusual? Anything that might have been out of character?"

"Colonel, please tell me, is Levi in trouble?"

The colonel looked at her and smiled reassuringly.

"No, Mrs. Stone. Levi is not in trouble. It's just that we need to locate him," he lied. He chose not to divulge that her husband was the most wanted person in the country; that his actions posed an enormous security risk to U.S citizens, and that Levi Stone would, in all likelihood, be assassinated by the first U.S. government sharp-shooter to sight him.

"Well, in that case, there may be another person who Levi blames for Debra's death. You might want to locate whoever sent the virus that destroyed Debra's computer. In the days following Debra's funeral, Levi did call me. He said, and I quote, 'that programmer took our little girl, Marion. No one takes anything from Levi Stone.'"

And, just like that, Colonel Dan McGovern had the missing piece of his puzzle.

"Good morning, Colonel McGovern. Marion said you wanted to talk to me," Levi Stone began the call.

"Good morning, huh? So you're in the eastern time zone?"

"Yes, but – well, it's a big time zone."

"We'll find you, Stone. It's just a matter of time."

"I'm touched, Colonel. I didn't think you'd even notice I'd gone."

"Cut the crap, Stone. You think this is all a big game huh? Killing college kids."

"So, you know. Well, it was only a matter of time. The Department has always been pretty good about piecing information together. Kudos. Still, you will never find me. More importantly, your snipers will never find me."

"You're nothing but a common, low-grade murderer."

"Colonel, I think you and I both know there is nothing common or low grade about me – not that I'm much interested in your opinion. What can I do for you?"

"You can turn yourself in!" the Colonel snapped.

"That will never happen. If there's nothing else, I need to get my boat in the water. The fish are hungry and so am I."

"Why Stone? Why are you doing this?"

"They took something from me, so I take something from them. Pretty simple, really."

"Who took something from you?"

"Programmers."

"Programmers? What programmers? Who, specifically? These seven kids you've murdered all took something from you?"

"Not from me, but from somebody. Some programmer somewhere sent a virus that infected the computer of my Debra. That meant she had to get into her car and drive to the store to buy a new computer. She was then killed. Had she not had to make that trip to buy a new computer, she would still be alive today and so would those seven programmers. But, they make their choices and there's a price. I'm just collecting, that's all."

"You're one sick man, Stone. Your daughter was killed in a traffic accident. That is very sad, but it is a fact of life. It happens every day. What are you going to do, go kill everyone who runs a red light?"

"Colonel, you are missing the point. Yes, I would like to kill that driver, but I can't because he's in jail; he's protected. I would run a pretty decent risk of being captured or killed myself.

"Harming myself is counterintuitive, don't you think? I have no special advantage when it comes to fighting police. I do have an advantage when it comes to punishing programmers. And, make no mistake, I will punish some programmers."

"So, what, you plan to kill thousands of kids?"

"No, not thousands. Thirty-five."

"Thirty-five?"

"According to my research there are at any point in time only about thirty-five virus programmers in the world proficient enough to infect large numbers of computers. The kind of programmer it would have taken to cause my Debra to get into the car that final day of her short life. One of those thirty-five murdered my Debra. Unfortunately for the other thirty-four, I don't know which one."

"So, by your own deluded logic, all but one of those thirty-five kids will die needlessly."

"No, not exactly. While just one of them caused Debra's death, each of those programmers will be, statistically anyway, responsible for about ten vehicle fatalities each. Millions of owners of the computers infected will get into cars to buy replacement computers and roughly one in ten thousand of them will die in an automobile accident, which is the national average."

"You're mad, Stone, you know that? You are killing innocent people."

"They kill themselves."

"No, Stone. You kill them. Your virus kills them."

"My virus targets them, but only if they are repeat offenders. Three strikes and they're out, so to speak. They get two free passes. Their third offense, though, is suicide."

"No, not suicide. Murder. They don't want to die."

"So tell them," Stone replied.

"What?"

"You heard me, tell them. Warn them not to infect, so they won't run the risk of dying."

"That won't work."

"Why not?"

"It'll become a sort of Russian Roulette with them. Kids think they're invincible. If you tell them hacking is deadly, more of them will try it, not fewer."

"So why the warning labels on cigarettes?"

"Exactly. No impact. You make my point," Colonel McGovern

replied.

"Look, Colonel, the U.S. government – um, more specifically, you – know that hacking will be lethal, but you choose not to let people know. You are complicit."

"Stone, stop. Just stop, okay? Enough with the rationalizations here. You can stop it, and only you can stop it."

"Colonel, I'd like to oblige, but unless you can give my Debra back to me, I have a score to settle. That's how life works and you know it. Don't get all righteous with me about me being a murderer. That's your definition. It makes you the good guy and me the bad guy. If you could, you would pump me full of lead right now in the name of justice. Waging wars is justified. Capital punishment. All kinds of killing is justified by those in power. And those in power make the rules. Except, guess what? In this case, I am the power, and I make the rules."

"We'll find you, you know, and when we do, I personally will take great pleasure in blowing your brains to Kingdom Come," Colonel McGovern replied.

"And you would be justified, right?" Levi Stone asked.

"I wouldn't be breaking the law."

"In that case, Colonel, a friendly word of advice. When you and your posse try to track me down, you might not want to get too close to your computers."

"I don't take well to people screwing with me, Stone."

"Neither do I, Colonel. Neither do I."

UNDERSECRETARY OF DEFENSE, COLONEL DAN MCGOVERN, MADE his report to the Secretary of Defense, General George Moore who, in turn, had just finished briefing the president.

"Well, George," the President began, "I would say we have a situation on our hands."

"Yes sir, Mr. President."

"In the wrong hands, such a virus could hurt far more than thirty-five people. I would daresay millions would be at risk."

There was no need for General Moore to respond to the obvious.

"Of course, in the right hands, that virus would be a pretty nice defensive weapon, wouldn't it?" the President continued.

"Sir, its potential as a weapon or as a deterrent is unmatched. Levi Stone is a once-a-century brilliant scientist, gone bad."

"Well then, General, I suggest we had better rein in Dr. Levi Stone, and quickly."

"Sir, he is undetectable. We know only that he is in the Eastern Time zone."

"Well, General, short of nuking the entire Eastern time zone and the millions of us who live here, how do you propose we find Dr. Levi Stone?"

"Are you a religious man, Mr. President?"

"Yes, I am."

"Then I respectfully suggest you implore a higher authority."

"In God we trust?"

"We must, sir."

Levi Stone looked down and noticed Hugger was curled up, sleeping beneath the wooden bench upon which he sat. The bench was built into a wooden quarter-mile-long catwalk which ran along one side of the lake next to the road that fronted his cottage.

He gazed up and looked across Lac Saint Enfant at the white pines rising majestically from a series of islands toward the eastern side of the lake, about a mile away. The sound of the small waves rhythmically lapping at the shore in front of him caught his attention; he noticed a moving shadow that he knew wasn't there just a moment ago.

Looking to his left, he was surprised to see a young girl sitting next to him, swinging her legs. She couldn't have been older than five or six.

"Hello," she said pleasantly.

"Hello," Levi Stone replied. "Have you been sitting there long?"

"No."

"What's your name?" he asked.

"My mommy told me never to talk to strangers," she said.

"Well that's good advice. Is your mommy here?"

"No. She's at home."

"So, you're here with your dad?"

"Yes," she replied, continuing to look down at her legs swinging back and forth in front of the bench.

Levi Stone liked this little girl. She was adorable.

"But Daddy's sick right now. He likes to come here when he gets sick. The lake makes him feel better."

"It is a beautiful lake," Levi Stone agreed, looking out over the lake again. "Sun's coming up strong now. It's going to be a pretty day."

"Yes," she replied quietly.

"What's wrong with your daddy?"

"He is sick. I think they might take him away from us."

Levi Stone turned and took a good look at the girl now. She continued to look down at her swinging legs. Suddenly she stopped and looked up at him.

"I wish he would get better so they won't take him away from me."

"I'm sure your daddy will get better."

"Yes," she replied quietly and began swinging her legs again. Levi looked away to his right to see two men backing their motorboat into the water from a trailer attached to a pickup truck. "He will have to get rid of his virus."

Levi Stone turned abruptly back toward the girl. She was gone.

She had disappeared. His heart started pounding in his chest. Suddenly Hugger was licking his face as he awoke. Startled, he came to the realization that he had fallen asleep. He hugged his dog.

"It's all right. Good girl, Hugger. Daddy's okay."

Suddenly remembering the fishermen, he turned to look at them. They were gone, and the boat, trailer, and truck were not there either.

Looking back to the left now, Levi Stone saw rays of sunlight shining brightly off a bronze dedication plaque on a post supporting a wooden gazebo twenty feet away. He walked up to the plaque and read the inscription: "Dedicated July 26, 1918 to The Holy Child of the Lake."

Now Levi Stone, the great quantum physicist, was not at all a religious man. He did not believe in organized religion, or any religion, for that matter. Sometimes, though, religion believes in you.

You don't have to believe in two-by-fours but when one hits you in the head, they're kind of tough to ignore. Levi Stone had just experienced a religious version of a two-by-four upside the head. More than mere belief, he somehow knew that his dear Debra was talking to him through the Child of the Lake.

And for this reason, at that precise moment, Levi Stone knew what he had to do.

He and Hugger ran across the road and back up the embankment to his cottage. He immediately set to work dismantling the Boomerang Virus. Seven young men had already died at his hands, and he was now prepared to deal with the consequences, but no more must die.

After dismantling the virus, he spent the next fourteen hours reconfiguring it for a noble purpose which, he knew, would be a huge commercial success for someone, and he had one particular beneficiary in mind – a dear old friend. He then released the new, reconfigured software, and introductory letter, into the Internet cloud.

He awoke the next day and enjoyed a strong cup of coffee before getting his day started. And what a wonderful day it would be.

"Bon jour, Monsieur Desmoreaux," Mrs. Eva Henri called to him as she headed to the 6:30 a.m. Mass.

"Bon jour, Mademoiselle Henri," he smiled and ran down the embankment with Hugger. "May I accompany you to Mass today?"

"Why, Monsieur Desmoreaux, that would be wonderful," she said, as he took her arm in his and walked with her to the Church of The Holy Child.

After Mass, Levi Stone asked the priest to hear his confession. Father Coyle agreed.

Inside the confessional, Levi began by blessing himself, "Bless me, Father, for I have sinned. Father it has been many, many years since I have been to confession, so please bear with me as I may be a little rusty."

"Very good," Father replied.

"Father, I have committed some very, very serious sins. I am sorry for my sins, Father, and after I leave here today I plan to turn myself over to the authorities in the United States, and I am willing to place my life in God's hands. I also plan to try to do as much good as I can for as many people as possible. It won't help those I have hurt, but it is the best I can do."

"I see. And what is it you wish to confess?"

"Father, I have murdered seven people."

There was a long pause before Levi Stone broke the silence.

"I am sorry to heap this on you, Father. Truly, I am harmless. I was just confused. I went through a bad time after my daughter died, and I tried to avenge her death. I was wrong. I know I was so, so wrong," he broke off as he started to cry.

"I just wanted to see my baby again. They took her from me and I wanted to hurt them. I was wrong, Father. The Child of the Lake told me that unless I make amends, then I would not see my little girl in heaven. Father, I truly believe that is what she told me, and that is what I am trying to do. Please pray for me, Father. Especially, though, pray for those people I have killed and their families. I am truly sorry for what I have done."

"You must turn yourself over to the police. That is your penance."

"I promise, Father. I will. Very soon."

Then Father gave absolution as he blessed Levi Stone, "May God, the Father of Mercies, grant you pardon and peace, and I forgive you your sins in the Name of the Father and of the Son and of the Holy Spirit. Go in the love of Christ and sin no more."

"Thank you, Father. God bless you."

Levi called his wife on his cell phone from his Jeep, once he and Hugger were on the road for the twelve-hour drive back to Washington DC. He looked over at Hugger in the passenger seat, her ears flopping slightly inside the windy Jeep.

"Hugger, old girl, our lives are about to change, big-time. We're each about to get what we deserve, and you're going to love living with Mommy. She's a great lady." Then, turning back to focus on the road ahead, he said more to himself than to Hugger, "she's always been a great lady."

Marion agreed to meet with Levi that evening. Levi told her everything. Initially sad, she was not crushed, as Levi had feared. She was strong, even relieved, because Levi's sincere change of heart touched her deeply. They agreed that they would contact their attorney the next day and make arrangements for Levi to turn himself over to the authorities.

Within a year, Levi had been tried for the murders of seven young men, and was found guilty. Because of the enormous societal benefits of his new Levi Software, his willingness to return the

Absorbium crystals to the U.S. government, his discovery of the Levi virus antibody, and his voluntary surrender to the authorities, his life was spared.

But he was sentenced to seven consecutive life terms with no chance of parole. He would be consigned to living the rest of his life in prison, yet he was finally happy. Marion loved him more than ever and visited him four or five times a week, every week, for the rest of their lives. He lived in the hope that God would forgive him and that he, Marion, and Debra would all be united again one day.

The Levi Software was truly revolutionary. Based upon the same quantum mechanics as the Boomerang Virus, it was targeted at would-be harmful programmers. It invited them, and only them, to participate in one of the most grueling, yet financially rewarding scientific endeavors of all time. It was an online course which taught software engineering at quantum energy levels. It required twelve years to complete but its few dozen graduates every decade went on to become some of the most prolific and wealthy inventors of all time.

The course was endowed by Mrs. Marion Stone who was, in fact, Levi Stone's "dear old friend," and beneficial owner of the Levi Software and its billions in royalties.

Dr. Levi Stone died incarcerated as a very old man, after living the final forty-two years of his life in prison. He suffered much at the hands of other prisoners, and, as the years progressed and his health declined, various physical infirmities.

Yet, he did live to see many young graduates of his educational program, who otherwise would have turned to infecting the Internet with a wide variety of thousands of viruses, learn instead advanced quantum physics and make significant contributions to mankind including, incidentally, the total elimination of computer viruses worldwide.

He was awarded the Nobel Prize in Physics posthumously and became known as the Doctor of the Internet.

11

CRYPTIC

Sarge Tanner never needed to be told twice. He prided himself on being a man of action, a take-charge alpha male. A retired Special Forces veteran, he had learned the hard way, as always, and early in his military career, how fate rewarded decisiveness and punished timidity.

Timid was not a word anyone who knew Sarge Tanner would ascribe to him. And he couldn't abide it in others, especially the teams of men he had commanded through three tours of duty in Afghanistan, Pakistan, and Iraq. The cost of hesitation, he had seen over and over, was death.

Men who hesitated, died. He had seen enough of death to last ten lifetimes. This was his message to his men in the Army back in the day, and it was his rather ironic message to the staff he now managed at Holy Spirit Cemetery.

Sarge fidgeted at his desk in the cemetery office for two minutes, before standing and pacing for the last five. He kept eyeing his desk phone, annoyed.

"What's the holdup?" he wondered, walking over to peek through the venetian blinds at the torrential downpour pelting the one-floor cinderblock administration building, which housed the business office.

"Friggin' monsoon," he said before releasing the blind slats. "Helluva day for a floodin' funeral." He shook his head and walked back to his desk. Plopping down unceremoniously in his swivel chair, he once again eyed the phone. "Come on, Hank."

Hank Slater was Sarge's foreman. He was scheduled to report in by 10:55 a.m. It was now just 10:45, but Sarge had long ago made it clear that, although the official reporting time was 10:55, his expectation, even if not officially enforceable, was to receive a verbal report no later than 10:35, when possible.

Hank had always complied with his boss' wish. Always. Without fail, for over four years. Until now. This tardiness was unlike Hank. It was a surprise, and Sarge Tanner knew there were no positive surprises. Resolved, the man of action now reached for the receiver, a split second before the phone rang.

Sarge pounced. "You're late!" he shouted.

"Officially, I'm ten minutes early," Hank said, too calmly for Sarge. Hank Slater was, by nature, imperturbable. Not much riled him. Not monsoons and certainly not his demanding boss who, he knew, was over-reacting yet again.

"Don't even try it. You know what I mean. What took you so long? Everything okay?"

"Um, not really. You better get down here. We have a situation."

"What situation?"

"It's the reason I couldn't call. Depending on how you look at it, either the casket's too big for the crypt, or the crypt's too small for the casket. We've been trying to figure out how to get it in there, but we can't. That's why I didn't call before now. I didn't want to drag you out in this storm. We've been trying, but we can't do it."

"Which funeral?"

"Speaker, plot E-78."

"Geez, Hank, the funeral's not still there are they?"

"No, the priest, undertaker, and family hightailed it outta here about ten minutes ago."

"Good. What'd you tell them?"

"I told the FD the situation and he spoke to them. He made up some baloney about how it usually takes four hours to load a casket in a crypt and suggested they not stand around in the rain. Pretty quick thinking, really."

"The priest bought that?"

"Actually, I don't think so, but Fr. Alex is a cool dude. I think he saw what was going on, kept his mouth shut and let the FD handle it. Gotta tell ya, for the first time today, I was glad it was raining hard. I think that's why they agreed to leave."

"Which Home?" Sarge asked, sorting through a stack of papers on his desk.

"McPeak," Hank said at the same time as Sarge, who now held a contract up in front of his face.

"It had to be McPuke," Sarge continued. "Did you talk to him?"

"Yeah. He pulled me aside and told me to tell you, 'Forget it. Ain't happenin'. Those were his exact words."

"Cheap bastard," Sarge said. "He could have called first before ordering the casket. It's his fault."

Hank said nothing. After a moment's pause, Sarge said, "You sure there's no way it'll fit?"

"Come see for yourself."

"He's gonna pay. I'll make him deliver a replacement casket," Sarge said, unconvincingly.

"Whatever," Hank said. "I'm just the messenger." He knew Joe McPeak's well-deserved skinflint reputation as well as Sarge did. "You comin' or what?"

"Yeah, yeah. I'll be there in two minutes. We'll have to bring that body back to the fridge until McPecker replaces his casket."

"Or until hell freezes over," Hank said. "See you in two minutes."

Sarge hung up the receiver and threw the Speaker burial contract down on his desk. He walked across the room and grabbed his rain poncho and truck keys, when the phone rang again. He grabbed it.

"Tanner!" he said.

"Sarge, Joe McPeak. You hear about the Speaker burial?"

"I just did. I was just about to go down there."

"The casket's too long for the crypt."

"Yeah. That's what I understand. *Your* casket is too long for the crypt."

"Correction. Your casket, Sarge. I didn't buy it. It ain't mine. It now belongs to your dearly departed tenant, Mr. Speaker and his assigns."

"Look, McPeak, you screwed up. All you had to do was call me. I would have told you the size of the crypt which, by the way, is the only size crypt we have here at Holy Spirit. You should know that."

"Should I?" McPeak said. "Sarge, look, I arrange funerals all over the county, in easily two dozen different cemeteries, all but one of which could accommodate that casket. And I never have to call to confirm crypt sizes with any other cemetery. You need to upgrade your facility. I can't possibly be expected keep track of all the changes you and your competitors make."

"Save it, McPeak. Don't try peddling that line with me. That crypt is a standard-size small crypt."

"Was," McPeak interrupted. "Was the standard size. Ain't anymore, not in the latest fiscal year, not according to the revised tables from the NFDA."

Sarge, although unsure, gave away nothing. He replied without hesitation, "A phone call, McPeak. That's all you had to do was call. Now the family doesn't even get to see their loved one properly buried."

"I handled the family. They're fine – for now. But, they'll be back, soon, and they'd better find dear old dad resting comfortably in his expensive crypt. I suggest you get to work."

"That's just what I'm going to do. We're bringing him back to the freezer. Be here later today or tomorrow with a smaller casket, or I'll be forced to tell the family what really happened; how it's all your fault."

"You do and I'll sue," McPeak said.

"I'll counter sue," Sarge said, unflinching.

"Ah, a bark with no bite. Knock yourself out."

"I can't believe you'd rather pay attorney's fees than just replace the casket," Sarge said.

"Well, I won't be paying attorney's fees because we both know you're in no condition to sue. I'd beat you in court, and you know it. Just squeeze our boy Speaker in there. Make it work. Later." The phone line went dead as Joe McPeak hung up.

"Bastard," Sarge said, but he knew McPeak was right. The Board of Trustees of Holy Spirit Cemetery would never approve suing a Funeral Director. That would be really bad for business. Time to get the late Mr. Speaker inside and out of the rain. Sarge put on his rain hat, reached for a crow bar, extension cord, and tool chest, before opening the door and stepping out into a torrential downpour. It was going to be a long afternoon.

Hank and the rest of the crew were waiting for him as he arrived at plot E-78 a few minutes later.

It was a shallow crypt, a bit deeper than the casket was wide, and exactly as wide side-to-side as the casket lid was long. Which, in a nutshell, was the problem. The casket lid didn't need to be much smaller – just somewhat smaller than the crypt opening, but it wasn't.

The casket rested on a bier in front of the open concrete crypt. The hulking hinged concrete crypt door swung open, out of the way, off to one side. The sides of the casket lid evidenced scratches from where the lid scraped the side walls of the crypt opening before the crew gave up, retracted the casket, and replaced it on the bier.

Sarge approached the coffin and immediately saw the scratches on the lid, on either side. Rain water cascaded down the coffin lid, flowing like a waterfall off the front and back sides. He leaned down and traced the scratches on the right side of the lid with his fingers as Hank confirmed the bad news.

"Stainless steel," Hank shouted through the driving rain. "Sealed."

Sarge nodded. "Yeah," he yelled back.

He had been hoping against hope that it would have been wood or resin, but he knew better. Had that been the case, Hank and the crew would have already sheared the decorative molding down to fit the crypt. But, there would be no shearing down the solid steel molding. The Speakers had money, Sarge thought. Molded stainless steel coffins and concrete crypts did not come cheap.

"Want us to load the coffin in the truck, Sarge?" Hank yelled.

"No. Change of plans. McPrick ain't payin'."

"No shit," Hank shouted, sarcastically. "So, what're we gonna do, boss? Can't shave steel." He and the rest of the crew pulled on their poncho hoods to shield their eyes and faces from the worst of the rain.

"Nope. That's true," Sarge shouted, standing back up and looking Hank in the eye. "We'll have to cut the concrete."

"With what?"

"There's a drill and generator in the bed. Diamond bits too," Sarge shouted through the torrent. "Here," he yelled, handing the ignition keys to Hank. "Back the truck down here so we can use the generator. I need to take a look inside," he said, jerking his thumb at the crypt. "Bring me the level too. It's in the cab." He turned and walked around the coffin and into the crypt.

Before heading to the truck, Hank directed his three crew mates to drape a nearby tarp over the coffin and secure it against the wind.

It took just two minutes for him to back the truck up close to the coffin.

He joined Sarge in the narrow crypt, thankful for the brief respite from the driving rain, and watched Sarge drag his work boot across one section of the concrete floor.

"Here's the level, Sarge."

Sarge took it.

"Thanks." He then looked down. "Coupla high spots in the floor."

"Can't really tell," Hank said. "Think anyone will really notice once the coffin's in here?"

"No, but if the coffin can't sit level I'm gonna have to cut a wide groove to make sure the lid fits."

"Ah! Good call. Yeah, now I see what you're sayin'. More work."

"Yep. Look, why don't you get the boys to set up the drill and connect it to the generator while I do this? Then you all wait in the truck, out of the rain. It'll take me a while before Mr. Speaker can finally rest in peace."

Hank left and Sarge got to work. He used the level and a carpenter's pencil to mark a line on the side walls where he would be cutting the groove.

He was focused on the task at hand and, with the deafening sound of the pounding rain, did not take note of the rising voices outside. When he had finished, however, and turned to retrieve the drill from the truck bed, he couldn't help but notice the oldest of the four men yelling, facing the others from a distance and pointing at them.

He said something in Spanish Sarge did not understand. Whatever he said must have been pretty funny, Sarge thought, because Hank and the two other men began laughing loudly as the old guy got into the truck and slammed the door shut.

Sarge caught Hank's eye. "What's up?"

"Guillermo, Gil, asked what 'Speaker' meant and we told him. Now he doesn't want to have anything to do with the coffin. He said it's a sign."

"A sign? Of what?"

"Who knows? He's just a whack-a-do. Good worker, but who can say what runs through that ancient brain of his? Probably thinks the corpse is gonna sit up and start talkin' cuz his name was Speaker," Hank concluded, wiping the rain from his face while shaking his head. "Crazy old fart. I told him to go sit in the truck. We can load the coffin without him."

Sarge looked at Guillermo peering through the rear window of the pickup's cab, eyes wide, staring past Sarge at the coffin, cowering, as if he really expected a ghost to rise up. Sarge followed his gaze, turned to look at the rain running off the tarp-covered coffin, and sighed.

"Whatever," he said, almost to himself, before carrying the drill and dragging the extension cord around the coffin to the crypt where he immediately got to work cutting a groove in the right side-wall of the crypt.

Even with the diamond drill bits, it was difficult and strenuous work. It took twenty minutes to drill a groove sufficiently wide enough on the right side wall, and an additional twenty minutes to drill another wide and level groove on the left side wall.

When he finally finished he was covered head to toe in a fine mixture of rainwater and concrete dust. He removed his protective eye goggles and his golden honey-brown eyes shimmered brightly through a hoary mask of hair, eyebrows, beard, and moustache; a truly ghoulish apparition.

Guillermo, staring out the rear window of the truck, was apoplectic at the sight, terror-struck, dropping down and cowering on the truck seat, arms over his head. To his horror, he imagined the newly-resurrected 'Speaker', suddenly unencumbered by the sealed coffin, now possessing Sarge's body and looking demonically, with cold, icy, dead eyes, right at him. It was all too much, at least for his aging bowel.

Guillermo knew he would never live down the taunts should he pollute the truck in this way, so he bolted outside, slammed the truck door, and ran up the road back to the equipment garage, and the bathroom there, trailed closely by a wretched odor undetectable in the monsoon inundating the cemetery.

"Gil!" Hank shouted after him. "What're you doing?" Guillermo didn't turn around, didn't stop, but continued running away from the ghastly Speaker he knew, just knew, was now pursuing him.

Sarge watched all this with bemusement. Hank turned, looked at him, rolled his eyes making a circular motion with his index finger next to his temple.

"Crazy old Gil," Hank shouted to Sarge while walking to him.

"What's with him?" Sarge asked.

"Who knows? With Gil, could be just about anything. The boys say he hears voices and sees things that ain't there. Probably superstitious is all."

"Or schizo."

"Could be. Wouldn't doubt it. Baby Boomer and all, and a vet to boot. Probably drugs in there somewhere."

"Yeah, I suppose," Sarge said softly, almost to himself.

"Hey, Sarge, you're a vet. Ever have PTSD? Ever hear voices and stuff?"

"What's it to ya?"

"Nuthin'. Just wonderin'. Wonderin' what runs through his head mostly. Scary dude, sometimes, to be honest. Thought you might have some advice."

"Why? Am I a scary dude?"

"No, you're cool. Just tryin' to understand 'im is all. Somebody's gotta help 'im."

"I ain't no shrink. Maybe the VA can help. Tell you what,

though. When I start hearin' voices I'll make sure you're the first one I tell. Okay?"

"Sorry boss. I didn't mean nuthin' by it. Shouldn'ta asked."

"Forget it."

"You ready?" Hank said.

"Yeah, call your guys. Let's get this over with."

It would prove easier said than done. Hank and his two helpers removed the tarp before all four men positioned themselves around the casket, two on either side. Sarge and Hank were on the side closest to the crypt. They would back up toward the crypt as they carried the casket. The two other men faced them from the other side of the casket. They would walk forward.

Together, they lifted the coffin from the bier and proceeded the few steps to the crypt entrance, placing the leading edge of the coffin on the concrete floor, and taking care to align the longer coffin lid, which overhung the coffin a few inches on each side, with the newly cut grooves in the side walls of the crypt.

Fortunately, Sarge had located the grooves perfectly and it at first appeared that there would be just enough room to maneuver the coffin into the crypt. However, it was also clear that, once the coffin was slid all the way into the slender crypt, the lid would effectively be locked in place by the upper edges of the grooves.

"Won't be able to open it once we get it in here," Hank said, immediately feeling foolish not only for having stated the obvious, but for having given voice to a non-problem.

Sarge looked at him. "You really think he's going somewhere?"

"No, I guess not."

The arduous task of positioning the heavy casket became even more difficult the further forward it slid on the uneven concrete floor.

"The damn floor ain't level," Sarge said at about the halfway point, straining with Hank and the others to force the casket where it clearly no longer wanted to go.

"Gotta cut the grooves wider. Back it up," he said and the men reluctantly obeyed their leader. They backed the coffin out with great effort, groaned as they hoisted it on the bier, and fastened the tarp again while Sarge resumed his cutting.

Twenty-five minutes later, they were back at it, trying to slide the coffin lid along the grooves. This time, finally, it worked and the coffin was pushed to its final resting place. True, the forward edge of the coffin, closest to the rear of the crypt, was higher than the side of the coffin facing the opening, but both sides rested on the uneven floor.

The coffin lid, as Hank had noted, could not be opened in this position, embedded as it was in the wall grooves. But, this would not be immediately obvious to future visitors. The crypt door had a large opening in the upper half, fitted with a steel grill. Visitors could see into the crypt, could see the coffin; but, with the crypt door closed, the wedging of the coffin into the side walls would not be noticeable at all. And no one would know that the coffin tilted ever so slightly on the uneven floor.

Or, would they?

Sarge and Hank had to climb over the casket to exit the crypt. Passing by on either side was impossible, of course.

Outside the crypt, the four men paused to catch their breath. Suddenly, the rain stopped. The monsoon departed as quickly as it had arrived earlier that morning, and the clouds started to break up as the sun began, here and there, to slice through the gloom.

"You guys load up the bier and the drill while I close up the crypt," Sarge said. The men did as he said, placing the drill and the bier in the bed of the pickup before piling into the cab to wait for Sarge to finish up.

Sarge walked to the side of the crypt, placed both hands on the stone door, and released the large wooden block wedge with the toe of his work boot. As he began to swing the door, it squeaked loudly on its hinges. Halfway through the closing arc, Sarge stopped, moving the door back and forth slowly, slightly, to test the hinges. The hinges continued squeaking in response to each small movement.

"Gotta oil those hinges," Sarge said softly, still holding the door in his gloved hands, as he tried to look more closely at the hinges.

"I'm tilted." The voice was muffled.

Sarge looked up, at the coffin. His eyes went wide. Did he just hear Mr. Speaker talk to him? A nervous smile. A slight head shake. A quick look around to see if anyone else was there.

What should he do? If Mr. Speaker spoke, he surely was alive, right? But how could that be? He had been confirmed dead by the coroner five days earlier and had been in cold storage and embalmed in the meantime.

Impossible! Plus, Sarge was dog tired. It had been a long day. All that stuff with Crazy Gil, combined with the pounding rain, and the overexertion necessary to rectify McPeak's mistake were taking their toll on him.

Speaker was as dead as he was ever going to be. That's all there was to it. And, first chance he got, Sarge was going to have a tall cold one, a thick steak and a hot shower, and turn in early to put this God-awful day behind him.

But, he had heard the voice. He had definitely heard Speaker. Sarge was a decorated vet. He couldn't just bury a man alive. Momentarily frozen, he didn't know what to do. He looked around to see if the men were watching him. They weren't, thank God.

So, what? What should he do? Call the men to pull the casket out so he could look inside to make sure Speaker was dead? But, of course he was dead! How would that look? The boss has them pull out a casket they had just slaved to put in to peek in and see that the corpse was really dead?

Oh, that'd go over real well! They'd be talking about that, behind his back, forever. Crazy Sarge. Hears voices. Don't get stuck on a detail with him unless you really like to bury the same body two or three times!

Nonetheless, beads of sweat started rolling down his face, and from his armpits under his gear. He could feel his heart quicken. He froze as if stricken. He didn't know what to do.

"Am I cracking up? Losing it? Is this PTSD?" he asked himself as a ray of sunshine broke through the clouds and bathed the coffin in bright light.

At that precise moment there was no mistake. A voice came from the coffin.

"Shut the damn door!"

Sarge Tanner, man of action, a take-charge alpha male, never needed to be told twice.

He shut the damn door.

12

CHRISTMAS KINDLING

I was nervous. Even a drive cross country from the west coast didn't afford enough time to prepare for the sudden onslaught of emotions engulfing me as I turned onto Boyle Street and saw my parents' house again for the first time in thirteen years.

The memories came flooding back. There was Mrs. Curran's house, the Flynn's house, old man Becker's place, Randy and Zach's house, and three dozen or so other twin homes that stood as masonry sentinels on either side of the city street lined by sycamore trees, bare for the winter.

I was certain I could recall the name of each and every family on Boyle Street – at least every family that had lived there thirteen years ago. There was the oak tree where I broke my arm as a seven-year-old on an ill-conceived rope swing, and the concrete steps rising up with the lawn embankments from the common sidewalk to the individual walks fronting each house. The faux gaslight street lamps were in remarkably good repair. The mailboxes were still at the corner bus stop.

Still, time had clearly marched onward. The makes and models of cars parked in the street were different from those of my childhood. There were many more mid-priced imports now. Facades on the homes had been upgraded. Folks had built covered patios in the front, and wooden decks off the rear, of their houses. The supermarket at the end of the street was larger than in the days when I played stickball there with my friends. The store had expanded from side to side at the expense of the landlocked parking lot surrounded by row homes. There was no room for stickball anymore.

I parked the Jeep in front of my father's house and sat there, petrified. Koufax seemed to sense my uneasiness. He rose up from his seat, looked out the window and then back at me as if to say, "What?" He whined softly and wagged his tail slightly. I petted his head. "It's okay, Boy. You're not the one Dad will have a problem with."

I WAS DREADING THIS MOMENT. THIRTY YEARS OLD AND CRAWLING back to dad, Sol Silverstein's prototypical Giving Tree. Could there be a worse feeling? Failure, remorse, sorrow – for what I had done, and had become, yes, but also for what could have been, for what should have been, and for what I had put my parents through. *Been all through this a million times*, I thought. *What's done is done.*

"In for a dime, in for a dollar, Koufax. Rock bottom's getting kind of old anyway, don't you think? Come on, let's get this over with, Boy," I said as I leaned across and opened Koufax's door.

Koufax bounded out of the Jeep. I walked around and joined him on the sidewalk. The house was decorated for Christmas. As old as my dad was, I somehow knew he would still have the place decorated for the holidays. The red, white, and green strings of electric lights were unique. I remembered as a boy going to Sears with my dad to buy individual boxes of red, green and white lights because that exact combination of colors was not sold as a set. But my dad had insisted that this particular combination of colors was the "true" Christmas presentation.

Every year the light display was the same – red, green, and white lights. And only my dad's house displayed that combination. I often wondered why the rest of the city hadn't gotten the same "Official True Christmas Light Colors" email that my dad had apparently received. Still, I had to admit, I was fond of the lights. They did look festive. Uniquely festive.

We approached the house and I noticed the real Canadian balsam Christmas tree in the front window with the white lights – two more Pickett family traditions that, apparently, had survived.

I pushed the doorbell, but I didn't hear it ring. I pushed it a second time.

Still no ring.

I knocked softly on the vertical window pane next to the door, followed by a slightly louder knock a few seconds later.

Hesitating, momentarily fearing that my father might be avoiding me, I tried the doorknob. It turned and I pushed the door inward a few inches. Koufax pushed through the opening; his paws padded softly on the hardwood floor of the foyer.

Dad never used to lock the doors. *Apparently some things never change*, I thought, following Koufax into my childhood home. Though I had no right to expect it of him, I hoped my dad's kind heart was also one of the things that hadn't changed.

"Dad?" I called. No answer. I looked around and noticed that the furnishings had changed only slightly over the years. The television, recliners, sofa, chairs, and end tables in the living room were the same as I remembered. The mantle over the fireplace was trimmed with a pine rope garland and two red Christmas stockings, with the names in gold sparkle lettering, hung there: one for me, and one for Jenny.

"Jenny? Who's Jenny?" I asked Koufax softly. A third, identical stocking was hung also, but this one displayed no name. *"Probably Dad's,"* I thought.

The rugs were newer and the walls had been painted in earth tones, though the baseboard, chair rails, and crown molding sported the high-gloss white enamel my father always favored. The hardwood floors had been recently stripped and finished. They looked good. The whole house looked neat, clean, and smelled wonderful.

I walked through the dining room and into the kitchen, where pans of freshly baked Christmas cookies sat cooling on the kitchen table and counter top. Koufax appeared to savor the aroma. His big brown eyes pleaded for a sample.

"Sorry, Bud. No freeloading in this house. This isn't our home."

I returned through the dining room to the foot of the stairs and called up,

"Hello! Anybody home?"

A door squeaked open upstairs.

"Coming. Coming," a voice called, and when I recognized my father's voice, my heart almost stopped.

"Steady, Boy," I said to Koufax – more to steady myself than him. He looked up at me and wagged his tail slowly. My heart racing, pounding in my chest, I looked up the stairs and almost didn't recognize my father. He had aged markedly. The once tall, proud, former athlete was now stoop-shouldered, bent at the waist, walking slowly, with a cane. Almost totally bald, thin wisps of white hair had replaced the full head of thick salt and pepper hair I remembered.

IN THAT INSTANT, A FLOOD OF MEMORIES RUSHED AT ME. EVERY memory my brain was able to conjure up, of momentous occasions spent with my father, flashed as a kaleidoscope, as I stood on the lower landing, two steps above the hallway floor. This was the moment of truth, the moment I had been dreading. How would my father react?

And how ought my father react? To seeing his loser son scurrying back home, beaten, defeated, humbled by a world that placed no stock in also-ran, washed-up, former minor league ballplayers?

How many times had I refused to return, to admit defeat, to face the man who had sacrificed everything for me. How many months and years had I wandered aimlessly, hopelessly, bitterly, from one sub-par job to another, only, in the end, to be crushed, as I was, by the weight of the dead dreams-turned-living-nightmare? How many times had I considered just ending it all?

Many, many times. The only thing that stopped me was the knowledge that in doing so I would be taking the coward's way out and would inflict another in a long line of wounds upon my father, who deserved much better.

It would've been so easy for me. This was harder, much harder. But I have never been a quitter. I never took a shortcut and I wasn't about to start now.

As difficult as facing my father would be, I would go right on trying, for what it was worth, to do the right thing. To "pound the strike zone." That was my father's pitching parlance for, "don't nibble around the fringes of life. Go for it!" If the hitter beats me, if life beats me, I would make sure it would beat me as I tried, as best I could, to win. To throw strikes. To pound the strike zone of life.

Overcome with regret, I watched my dad descend ever-so-slowly, one step at a time, with his cane, looking down at each step, not looking up, being exceedingly careful. Not seeing me, he called again, "I'm coming, I'm coming." I couldn't recall ever being as tense as I was now. Not even my memory of the head-on automobile crash, which ended my playing career and almost ended my life, frightened me as much.

I wanted to say something, anything, so my father wouldn't be startled, but I just couldn't. Fear gripped me, and I couldn't speak. It was all I could do to keep from turning, running out the door to my Jeep, driving and never coming back.

Anxiety squeezed me like the green Black & Decker hardened steel vise on my father's ancient workbench in the garage. I felt my heart thumping in my head, in my chest. I gripped the banister with a sweaty hand to steady myself, raising my head to look into my father's eyes. Koufax whimpered softly behind me.

Two thirds of the way down the staircase, Dad looked up and saw me for the first time.

"Pick? Pick? Is that you? Can it be?"

My father faltered and clung to the banister. Recovering quickly, he began to hurry down the remaining few steps. "Pick, it is you. Pick, oh Pick. Oh my God and Father in heaven! Pick!" he yelled as he reached the landing, dropped his cane, buried his head in my chest and wrapped his arms around me.

"Pick, you've come home. You've come home. I knew you would. I knew you would come back. Oh, how I prayed, Pick. You have no idea. How I prayed that you would return. And you have. Saints be praised, Son. Good God in heaven be praised!"

I wiped my tears on my jacket sleeve and held my father at arm's length, as Koufax barked furiously.

"Dad, I am so sorry, so sorry…."

"Pick, Pick, it's okay, it's okay," my dad interrupted as Koufax continued to bark at him. "Good looking dog. What's his name?"

"Koufax."

"Koufax, huh? Great name." Dad smiled, stooping to pet Koufax's head. "The best." Koufax stopped barking, still wagging his tail rapidly, as he licked my dad's outstretched hand.

Standing back up, and facing me, Dad continued. "Here, here, let me look at you, Pick. You have really grown up, haven't you? Last time I saw you, you were…," he hesitated with his hand held up to my chin. "Look at me going on. Come, come, you must have come quite a distance. Let's sit in the living room and talk, shall we? There's so much I want to hear."

I wrapped my left arm around my father's shoulders. "Sure, Dad, I'd like that."

"Care for some cookies, a beer, or something else to eat or drink?" he asked.

"No, I'm good, Dad. I can wait a bit. We need to talk," I said, stooping to pick up the fallen cane, and supporting his frail hand on my arm as we walked into the living room.

My father sat in his lounge chair and I sat, facing him, on a ladder-back chair I had pulled over. Koufax laid at my feet, resting with his head on his front legs stretched out in front of him, but attentive. I used a handkerchief to wipe my eyes and blow my nose. I then leaned forward on my knees and held out my hands to my father, who joined hands with me.

"Dad, I don't know where to begin, so let me first tell you how sorry I am," I began.

"Sorry? For what?" my father asked, and I realized then that he was still the Giving Tree.

"For everything, Dad. For running away, for thinking only of myself, for hurting you and Mom, for ruining my baseball career – for everything. For being a world-class jerk."

"Pick, Pick, Son," my dad began. "Trust me, it wasn't all you. There is enough blame to go around here."

"What?" I asked, incredulous.

"Pick, it was me who pushed you into baseball. I encouraged you to become a professional athlete when, all along, I suppose, I knew you had the heart of an artist. It was me who broke your mother's heart."

"No, Dad. No. I won't let you do this. I won't let you be the fall guy here. You cannot hold yourself responsible for my decisions and that's what they were. My decisions. I chose sports. It was my decision and my mistake."

"But I encouraged you...."

"Dad, you were being a dad, that's all. What father wouldn't want his son to be a professional baseball player?"

"But it's different with me, Pick. Of all the knuckleheads in the world, I was your father and, as your father, I think I always knew what was best for you. Just as your mother knew. And she was right. I was wrong for encouraging you the way I did, Pick. You were, um, are a gifted musician and artist. I had no right to interfere with that."

"Come on, Dad, you had no way of knowing I would get into that car...."

"Doesn't matter. You should never have been put into a position where getting into that car was an option. Had I listened to your mother, you'd have had a fine career in music."

"You don't know that, Dad."

"Yes, Pick, I do."

"There are no guarantees."

"I am your father, Pick. Next to your mother, I know you as well as anyone ever has. And I know the gift you can bring to the world. It is so obvious. But I was blinded by the thought of my son being a professional pitcher. I just wish I hadn't been so stupid."

"Dad, look...."

"I know this may come as a surprise to you, Pick. I know you feel terrible about leaving home the way you did and I can't deny that it hurt. It did. But Pick, that's life. You were just a kid. You needed me to advise you and I let you down. My advice was influenced by the promise of fame for you and, probably to some extent, by the chance to be the father of a famous son. But, were I the father I should have been, I wouldn't have been influenced by any of that. I should have been able to do what came so naturally to your mother. I should have considered your needs only. Not mine.

"And you, first and foremost, have always been an artist, Pick. I think you know that now – perhaps you always knew it. You feel deeply, Pick, and through your music, you express the feelings of many. That is your great gift. Not a ninety-five mile-per-hour fast-ball which is here today, gone tomorrow, but art and music. And your art, your music, can live forever. I just wish I hadn't interfered with that. Can you ever forgive me?"

I was stunned. My father sought my forgiveness! All these years I had blamed myself, and correctly so, regardless of what my father believed. I had no idea he harbored such guilt.

"Dad, if I lived a thousand years, I couldn't begin to imagine the need to forgive you for anything. Truly, Dad, you are mistaken. But, yes, anything I can do for you, I will. If I can forgive you, as misguided as that concept seems to me, I do forgive you.

"But Dad, you have to listen to me now. I have traveled a long, lonely, and troubled path to get to sit here with you today, look into your eyes, and tell you how sorry I am for everything, and how much I love you. I do forgive you, Dad, but please, please, can you find it in your heart to forgive, really forgive, me for running away, for neglecting you and Mom, for thinking only of myself, behaving the way I have, hurting people, hurting myself, and failing the way I have? I hope you can, Dad, because I can't."

"You must, Pick. You must forgive yourself the way I do. And yes, Pick, I do forgive you – totally and unconditionally. So did Mom. It is only then that you will be able to get on with your life and make the artistic impact of which you and I both know you are capable."

"Do you really believe that, Dad?"

"Yes, Pick, I do. And because I believe that, I hereby release you from my dream. You are now, at this moment, free to begin living your own dream, whatever, whenever, and wherever that is, without qualification or approval from me. It is your life, Son, and I need you to take charge of it and start making it the life you need it to be."

"You see, Dad, the problem is I have no idea what that life looks like. What I'm supposed to do. I keep praying for a sign."

"Pick, there are signs all around you. You just can't see them because you put blinders on. Let the artist out, Pick. Listen to your heart. It's a good heart. See with your inner eye, with the eye of your soul. If you do that, you will clearly see the signs all around you. And once you do, once you understand and make up your mind, remember what I always told you."

"Pound the strike zone?"

"Yes. In pitching, of course, but in everything. In music, in art, in life. Go for it, Pick. You set the course. Don't let me or anybody else set it for you. You have many great gifts, Son. Use them. And please, don't worry about me or Mom. We've had our lives and guess what? We had a truly great and loving son. That's more than most people may ever have and that's enough.

"Oh, and one more thing. You say you love me, and I know you do. But you must know that I have never stopped loving you. It wouldn't be possible, Pick. You mentioned a thousand years. Well, a parent's love for his child, my love and your mother's love for you, will outlive us. It will never die. I will always be there for you. Don't ever doubt that. Don't doubt that even for a second."

I looked at my dad and smiled. The idea that my father would not want me to return home seemed now to be a distant, silly, baseless, and ridiculous one.

"I won't, Dad. Not anymore. Thanks. Look, how about I take you up on that beer now?"

"In the fridge. Help yourself," he said. "Then get your butt back here and we'll decorate this tree. It's Christmas Eve, after all. Besides, Jenny will be home in a few hours."

"Ah, the stocking. Who's Jenny?" I asked.

"You remember Jenny Barnes, don't you? She used to live next door."

"Of course I remember her. She was three years behind me in school. We practically grew up together."

"Jenny bought the house next door from her mom, who retired to a smaller house near the shore. Jenny was a teacher, but was laid off when the state cut back on its education funding. Anyway, once she lost her job, she couldn't keep up with the mortgage payments. The bank foreclosed and I agreed to take her in until she got back on her feet. It didn't take very long. She returned to school to study nursing. Excellent nurses are always in demand, it seems. We agreed that she would live here, rent free. In return, she keeps the place spotless, as you can see. It's too much for me to handle anymore and Jenny has done a nice job keeping it ship-shape. She prepares all the meals too. She's a great cook. Real nice kid."

"Uh-huh," I responded. "So, what do you do while Jenny's working and cooking and taking care of the house?"

"Well, you know, I write, but I'm not nearly as productive as I used to be. It takes me forever to write anything anymore. Still, I believe it's important for me to keep at it."

"By the way, how did you know I was coming home? You hung my stocking," I said, fingering my hanging stocking.

"I have always hoped you would come home, Pick."

The phone rang and Dad answered it. "Oh, hello. Yes, everything's fine. I'm fine. Just sitting here talking with a visitor. Can you guess who it is? A clue? Um, do you like baseball? Yep, that's right. Pick came home. Yes, isn't it wonderful? Okay, I'll tell him. See you soon. Bye."

"I suppose that was Jenny?" I asked.

Dad smiled, hesitating. "Wait 'til she sees you after all these years," he finally responded. "She'll be so surprised."

I returned from the kitchen with a cookie, a beer, and Koufax. "You okay, Dad? Can I get you something to eat or drink?"

"No, Pick. I'm good. I think I'll just sit here and rest a spell.

Watch you decorate the tree. The decorations are in those boxes next to the tree. I never get tired of watching other people work."

I smiled at my father's oft-used self-deprecatory remark. "You know, I used to wonder why you would always say that. You have out-worked a hundred average men in your lifetime, and you and I both know it."

"Yeah, well, if I was a good writer, maybe I wouldn't have had to work so hard at it. Hey, could you turn on the radio there? I could stand a little Christmas music."

"Sure." I switched on the radio under the television on the entertainment center and sounds of Andy Williams' "I'll be home for Christmas" filled the room.

"Ah, how apropos," Dad smiled, as he leaned back in the recliner, raised the footrest, and stretched out his legs. "It doesn't get any better than this."

"So you approve of the way I'm decorating the tree?" I asked.

"Absolutely. Which is to say, you're doing it, and I'm not. I definitely approve."

An hour later, I was finished hanging the ornaments and garland on the tree. My father had fallen asleep before Andy Williams finished, and he managed to sleep through Frank Sinatra, Perry Como, Josh Grobin, Mariah Carey, Amy Grant, Johnny Mathis, Nat King Cole, Celine Dion, the Chipmunks, Gene Autry, Barbara Streisand, Burl Ives, and the entire Mormon Tabernacle Choir. But, as any good father is inclined to do, he awoke as soon as I sat on the sofa.

"Tree looks great, Pick."

"Thanks."

"Wanna get a fire going in the fireplace?"

"Sure, I'll give it a shot," I said, as I rose from the sofa. "That's always been your thing though. I've never been very good at it."

"Ah, that's because you don't have much experience at it. It's like anything else, you know. Practice, practice, practice."

I opened the fireplace screen, reached over for some logs and started to place them in the grate.

"You'll need more logs," my father said. "If God didn't want us to stay warm…."

"I know, He wouldn't have given us a trillion trees," I concluded.

"That's right."

"But that doesn't mean we have to fire up a trillion trees in this fireplace," I said.

"True, but the more you use, the less you'll have to do it. Don't forget the kindling. It's there in the bag. You'll need kindling to get a good fire started."

"So, that's been the secret all these years. Kindling," I said.

"Yep, that's the secret."

"So practice, practice, practice, but kindling helps, eh?"

"You know, I like that," he replied. "Because, of course, you always need the right tools for the job. Yes, I like that. Practice, practice, practice, but kindling helps. Nice touch."

So after I had a roaring fire going, I returned to the sofa. We sat in the room while the fireplace glowed, the tree lights twinkled, the Christmas music played softly in the background, and we got caught up on the past thirteen years, the lost thirteen years.

Finally, after three more hours, and after I had drunk three more beers, but Dad had had nothing to eat or drink, I said, "Dad, are you sure I can't get you something? You haven't had anything since I've been here."

"No, Pick. I'm fine, really. Don't worry about me. I'm afraid I just don't eat or drink much anymore. Old age, I guess. But you eat up. Anything we have in there is yours. And I want you to stay here tonight. Can you do that?"

"Sure, I'd like that, if it's not too much trouble."

"Trouble? Goodness! It's no trouble at all. Having you here is a blessing, an absolute blessing."

"Back at you, Dad. I'll stay the night then."

"Good, and we can share Christmas day tomorrow with Jenny. I know she'd like that. She's a good kid, Pick."

"So you've said."

"I did expect her to be home by now. It's getting late," he said as he rose, walked to the window, parted two slats of the venetian blinds, and looked outside. "Oh dear, it's snowing. I suppose that might have slowed her down a bit."

"Dad, I'm going to take Koufax out in the back yard. We'll be right back."

When Koufax and I came back inside, I found my father standing with the aid of his cane.

"Pick, I'm going to be going to sleep now. It's way past my time, I'm afraid. I thought for sure Jenny would be home by now. Do me a favor, will you?"

"Sure."

"Could you wait up for her?"

"Certainly."

"Good. Don't lock the doors. I'm not sure the locks work anyway. After she comes home, you can have the middle bedroom upstairs – the guest room next to the bathroom. My room's the front room, of course. Jenny sleeps in the back bedroom, okay?"

"Okay. Thanks. That's great."

"Come here, Pick. Give me a hug."

I wrapped my father in my arms and held him. "I love you, Dad."

"And I love you more than you will ever know. I always have. So did Mom. And we never stopped loving you for a second. You mean the world to me. I am so proud of you."

Then, stepping back, he continued. "You know, Pick, there is no blessing known to man greater than love. To love, and to be loved, is the greatest gift there is."

"I know, Dad."

"Well, okay then. I just wanted to make sure," he said, poking his cane at me. "Sometimes, you can be pretty bull-headed."

"Good night, Dad. Do you need help up the stairs?"

"No. I'm good. I'll get there, eventually. You go enjoy the fire. Merry Christmas, Pick."

"Merry Christmas, Dad. Sleep well. See you tomorrow."

I watched my father ascend the stairs slowly, one step at a time. Halfway up, he said, without turning around, "And make sure you wait up for Jenny."

"Aye-aye, Cap'n," I responded.

"She's a good girl."

"So you've said."

"She'll do you a lot of good."

I smiled, but did not respond.

"You could do a lot worse than to listen to your father."

"I know, Dad. Merry Christmas."

"Mark my words, this will be the best Christmas ever. Merry Christmas, Pick."

I turned and walked back into the living room. Koufax was curled up in a ball in front of the fireplace. I sat down cross-legged next to him.

"Pretty cozy, hey Boy?"

Koufax's tail thumped the hardwood floor softly. I stared at the fire for a few minutes, thinking about all that I had experienced that day. If miracles existed, I was sure I had just experienced one in my father's forgiveness.

I brushed a tear from my cheek as I thought about how unconditionally my father and mother had loved me, even after all of the hare-brained things I had done; how I had messed up my life. My dad thought I should pursue my writing, art, and music. That much was clear. But was he right? Was that the best course for me? I didn't know.

"Dear God," I whispered, "don't let me screw up anymore.

Please show me the way. Give me a sign. If you can possibly still love me, please give me a sign. I don't blame you if you don't love me, but I know you must love my dad. Even if it's just for my parents' sake, could you help me? Could you give me a sign – if not for my sake, for theirs? I promise I won't let you down anymore and I won't let them down anymore."

Then I shifted my weight, raised my left knee and leaned on it for a few minutes, gazing more intently at the fire before looking down at Koufax.

"Pretty funny, hey Boy? Me praying. Like God has time to worry about me. You stay here. I'm going to sit on the sofa."

I got up and sat on the sofa as Koufax laid his head back down and went to sleep. After another ten minutes, I laid down on the sofa and eventually drifted off to sleep also.

———

THE GRANDFATHER CLOCK NEAR THE SOFA CHIMED AT 8:00 O'CLOCK Christmas morning, waking me with a start. I sat bolt upright.

"Where am I? Koufax?"

But Koufax wasn't there. I rubbed my face in my hands and looked around, slowly becoming reoriented to my surroundings.

"Koufax!" I called.

"In here," came a woman's voice I did not recognize. Her voice seemed to come from the kitchen. I tossed the blanket aside, stretched my arms way above my head, and began to walk slowly toward the kitchen. My back was stiff from sleeping on the sofa, and I tried to loosen it by flexing as I walked. I could smell the aromas of coffee and bacon coming from the kitchen.

"Merry Christmas, sleepy head." A gorgeous, tall, twenty-some-thing strawberry blonde with a smile to set the world right, greeted me as I entered the kitchen.

Her hair was pulled back in a ponytail, and there was a flour smudge under one of her light hazel eyes. I was awake enough to see that this Christmas morning was definitely off to an excellent start. She wore a Christmas apron and was mixing batter in a bowl, with a spatula. The cookies from the night before were arranged neatly on a cookie tray in the middle of the kitchen table. Two place settings had been set. French toast, scrambled eggs, bacon, sausage, coffee, and orange juice were waiting.

"Merry Christmas. Jenny?" I asked.

"Guilty as charged." Her slightly husky voice may have been borderline too sexy for Christmas. Koufax jumped up and put his paws on me. Did he sense my interest? Was he jealous?

"Hey, Koufax," I said, scratching behind each of his ears. "Down, Boy."

"Did you sleep well?" Jenny asked.

"Apparently," I responded, waving my arm at the kitchen table. "I didn't hear you come in or prepare any of this."

"Yep, a regular Santa Claus I am," Jenny smiled. Good God, what a smile!

"Well, Koufax chose to stay with you when I called him just now. I am duly impressed."

"As well you should be," she beamed. There was a pregnant pause then, which made us both a bit uncomfortable. Jenny made the first move. She wrapped her arms around me and said, "Welcome home, Pick."

I hugged her back. "Thanks, Jenny. It's good to see you too. You look great."

Stepping back, she said, "Come on, let's eat. I hope you like french toast."

"I love french toast," I said, sitting. "Thanks for doing all this. Heckuva spread you've got here."

"No problem. I figured you might like something to eat. I just didn't know what you liked, so I thought I'd make a little of everything. Care for some coffee?"

"Perfect. Thanks."

All of a sudden, Koufax started barking upstairs.

"Geez, I guess he's sleeping later nowadays," I said, placing my coffee cup on the table and hurrying towards the staircase.

"Koufax! Koufax!" I shouted up the stairs. Koufax appeared at the top of the stairs and looked down.

"Come here, Boy. Come on, come on down here." But Koufax turned, ran to the front bedroom, and resumed his barking. I called up, "Shh, Boy. Quiet!"

Jenny, standing next to me said, "It's okay. He won't wake anyone."

"He'll wake my dad," I said, before running upstairs.

Koufax sat at the far end of the hallway, barking at the closed front bedroom door. I hurried after him and stooped to calm him down.

"It's okay, boy. It's okay. Be quiet now." Immediately Koufax stopped barking and began to whine softly.

I stood and knocked at the bedroom door, as Jenny approached. "Dad? Dad, time to get up. It's Christmas Day," I called through the closed door.

"Pick, you okay?" Jenny asked.

"I'm fine," I replied without looking back. I turned the doorknob and pushed the door open.

The bedroom was empty, and apparently it had been unoccupied for some time. Sheets covered every piece of furniture, except the bed, and there was a fine film of dust on everything, including the floor. There were no sheets or blankets covering the bare mattress and box spring. It was immediately obvious that no one had slept in this room in quite some time. I turned to Jenny. "Isn't this my father's bedroom?"

Not waiting for an answer, I said, "I must have made a mistake." I pushed past Jenny and hurried to the middle bedroom. This was the guest room, where I was supposed to have slept the night before.

It was smaller and spotless. The made-up bed was undisturbed. No one was in the room.

"What the heck," I said and hurried to the last remaining bedroom, the back bedroom.

"That's my room," Jenny said.

"I know. That's what he told me," I replied, walking over and opening both closet doors.

"That's what who told you?"

"My father. He told me the back bedroom was yours, the middle bedroom was for guests, and the front bedroom was his."

"That's correct," Jenny confirmed.

"Well, where is he then?"

"Where is who?"

"My father! My father! Where is he?" I asked face-to-face now with Jenny.

"Pick, really, are you okay?"

"Yes. I'm fine. I'd be better if I could find my dad," I said, as I hurried past her and back toward the front bedroom again.

"Pick!" Jenny shouted.

I turned to face her. "What?"

"Your father's not here. He hasn't been here for six years."

"You're crazy!" I shouted. "He was here just last night, with me. We sat down in the living room and talked for hours. Then he came up here and went to bed. In fact, he answered the phone when you called last night."

"Pick, I didn't call last night."

But my father had said Jenny called, hadn't he? I tried to recall the conversation:

"I suppose that was Jenny?"

"Wait 'til she sees you after all these years. She'll be so surprised."

Okay, maybe I had assumed incorrectly. My dad had not exactly answered my question directly yes or no. Was that intentional? My head started to swim. I ran into the front bedroom again and opened all the closet doors.

"Dad!" I shouted. "Dad, where are you?" Panicked now, I stood incapacitated in the middle of the bedroom and looked over at Jenny who stood in the doorway. "Where is he, Jenny? Where is my dad?" I pleaded.

Jenny walked over and sat on the bed. She patted the mattress next to her. "Come here, Pick. Sit here with me. There's something I need to tell you."

I sat next to her. "Where is he?"

"Pick, I'm sorry but I guess I just assumed you knew."

"Knew what?"

"Pick, your dad passed away six years ago."

Initially defiant, I bolted to my feet and faced Jenny. Jenny did not back down, but looked up at me. I looked into Jenny's eyes, and the artist subjugated within for so long saw the truth there. I raised my eyes and looked at the room as if seeing it for the first time. And, suddenly, I knew. It all made sense.

My father had stopped writing to me six years ago not because of anything I did or didn't do, but because he had died. I walked slowly over to my father's writing desk. His walking stick leaned against it. I took it in my hands as my father's words rang in my ears: *A parent's love for their child, my love and your mother's love for you will outlive us. It will never die.*

Time seemed to slow down and the bedroom now appeared to be so stark, so empty, and so cold. The heating vents had been closed to conserve energy, I reasoned. That made sense. All the furniture in the house, including the pieces in this room, hadn't changed, likely pending my own return and decision, as sole heir, to its disposition. It was all so clear now, as was the path I must take.

"Pick, there are signs all around you," my father had said. And with those words my father was foretelling how I would come to soon understand the significance of the conversation we were

having. Indeed, my prayers had finally been answered. I had been granted my sign: one final conversation with my long-dead father, who had no need of food, and who Koufax was also able to see, apparently. I smiled slightly as I gingerly, almost reverently, looked at the walking stick in my hands before I leaned it back against the desk.

"He always hated long good-byes. How did he die?" I asked.

"Cancer. I'm so sorry to be the one to have to tell you this, Pick."

"No, Jenny. It's okay. You did good. It's not right that you were put in this position and I am the one who needs to apologize for frightening you just now. You had no way of knowing I was unaware that my own father had died. It's my fault. I dropped out and no one knew where I was or how to contact me. Come on. Let's go back downstairs. There's nothing up here." I pulled the door closed as we walked out of the room.

Back in the living room, we sat on the sofa. I told her everything that had happened the night before. I recounted every detail I could recall of the conversations I had with my father. I said it was clearly a miracle, the sign I had sought for so long and, to my surprise and delight, Jenny agreed. "I always thought this house was magical," she said. "Actually, I don't know if I thought this house was magical or if you and your parents were. You were always just so happy and into so many different things. This was a happening place."

"So you really believe I saw my dad?"

"Yes, I do."

"But how could you? The whole thing sounds so crazy. Doesn't it sound crazy to you?"

"Special, yes, but crazy? Not necessarily."

"Really? It sounds crazy to me. How can you just believe that I spent hours conversing with my dearly departed dad?"

"I'll tell you how. Pick, your dad was like a father to me, the father I never had. You know my dad abandoned my mom when I was only a year old. I never remembered him, and never saw him once he ran out on Mom.

"After Mom moved and then passed away, your father took me in. Make no mistake, that's exactly what he did. He helped me greatly at a time when I most needed help. I don't know what would have happened to me if it weren't for your dad. I tried to repay his kindness by keeping this place nice for him, cooking, being here for him when he suffered his stroke and later, with the cancer."

"Thank you, Jenny."

"Don't thank me. It was the least I could do. I only wish I could've done more. Anyway, I also used to take your dad to church – initially on Sundays then, when your mom died, daily, because that's what he wanted. He tried to get me to go to church also, but I don't believe. Never have. I felt bad for him, because he so wanted me to believe, to have faith but, honestly Pick, I can't say that God has ever been especially good to me. If I believed in anything, or anybody, it was your dad. He was one of the few people who was good to me just because. He never asked for anything in return. He was just a great man.

"On the morning of the day he died, I wanted to move him into hospice, so he would receive the professional medical care I was not qualified to give. He refused. He insisted on staying in his bedroom. He said he would never leave this house until the day you returned home. I remember saying what if you never returned home. He told me to have faith. I responded that I had faith – in him.

"He became cross with me and started coughing. When he calmed down he told me I must have true faith. He really wanted that to happen. He knew he was dying but was okay with death, because he knew he would soon see Myra."

"My mom," I said.

"I said, 'Yes, I know you will.' But he smiled and said, 'Don't patronize me. You don't believe. What will it take for you to believe?' Being the wise-ass that I am, I said perhaps a phone call from Myra. Your dad closed his eyes. I thought he went to sleep, but he opened his eyes, smiled, and said, 'Done. Myra agrees. She will call. Will you believe when she calls?' he asked me. I said I would.

"A few hours later, just minutes before he died, I was crying. I thought he couldn't hear me anymore. His breathing became very labored, and he hadn't opened his eyes for a long time. I thought I was talking to myself. I said, 'There is so much I need to say to you. And so much I need to learn from you.' Then he opened his eyes and said, 'Like what?'

"I knew there wasn't much time. I was beside myself with grief and couldn't think of anything. Finally, I said something really stupid; the only thing I could think to say. I said, 'Like, how to start a fire in the fireplace.' And he answered me. The last thing he ever said was, 'I will tell you, but then you must believe.' Then he died. Those were his last words.

"He was laid to rest. I never received an answer to my question and Myra never called, so I never believed. Until today."

"Why today? What changed?"

"Myra did call. She called your father last night. You thought it was me calling, but it was your mom keeping her end of her bargain with your father. Remember, he said, 'See you soon.' Who else would he be saying that to, but your mom? And telling you about using kindling to start a fire. Your dad knew you would tell me. He was talking as much to me as he was to you. Yes, Pick, I think I have received my answers, just as you have."

After considering all that Jenny had said, I finally responded, "I suppose we could both be crazy."

"Or, we could both be blessed," Jenny countered. "I choose to believe. Finally."

Suddenly, Koufax started barking. Jenny and I walked into the hallway where Koufax sat barking at the front door.

"Quiet, boy," I said as Jenny opened the main inside door, but no one was there. There was, however, an envelope which had been placed between the closed aluminum storm door and the now-opened main door. Jenny retrieved the envelope and opened the storm door to see who had left the envelope. No one was outside.

"Funny," she said.

"What's funny?" I asked.

"There's no one there, and no footprints in the snow. How'd it get here?"

"Open it up. Who's it from?"

Jenny opened the envelope. There was a Christmas card inside with a handwritten message. Jenny handed it to me. It read,

Dearest Pick,

You've come home. Now, your mother and I can rest.

Always remember two things: 1. Kindling. 2. Jenny.

With any luck, they could be one and the same for you.

Merry Christmas.

I love you always,

Dad

P.S. It took me all night to write this card. Best thing I ever wrote.

I showed the card to Jenny. She read it, smiled, and looked up at me. I now stood pointing to the mistletoe suspended from the chandelier over our heads. "May I?" I asked.

"I thought you'd never ask," Jenny replied, as I held her and kissed her.

"Correction. This *still is* a magical place," she said, flashing that killer smile again.

"There is one thing I don't understand," I said.

"And what might that be?"

"If my dad isn't here, and you didn't know I was coming, why did you hang the three stockings?"

Jenny looked back at the three identical red Christmas stockings with white trim hanging from the white mantle over the fireplace. "That's easy. I didn't."

"What?"

"I didn't hang three. I hung one, for me. I just assumed you hung the other two, one for you and one for Koufax."

"You assumed I just happened to bring two more stockings identical to yours?"

"I figured you bought the same Wal-Mart specials I bought," Jenny replied, as I walked over to the stockings.

"Jenny, I didn't bring any stockings," I said. I noticed the stocking on the left said Jenny, the one in the middle said Pick. The stocking on the right had no name on the front. I turned it around. "This is the one you assumed was for Koufax?"

"Yes. Isn't it?"

"Not quite." I stepped aside to show the name in gold sparkly lettering: "Dad."

Jenny's eyes went wide with wonder. "Like I said: I believe."

Once again, Koufax started barking at the open doorway. I took Jenny's hand as I led her to the door. No one was there.

As a strong gust of wind rattled the storm door and swirled the snow around outside, I held Jenny in my arms.

"Right. Kindling. We got it. Thanks, Dad. Merry Christmas."

ABOUT THE AUTHOR

William Norbert McCambley, Jr., was born and raised in Philadelphia, the first son in a family of seven girls and two boys. By the age of seven, he was regaling his younger sister and brother with the madcap adventures of Harry & Sam, the first of many characters to spring from his fertile imagination.

In addition to storytelling, he loved all things baseball, especially the Philadelphia Phillies. Eventually, he made room for basketball, football, hockey, and soccer. But a good line drive could always take him back to his little league and sandlot days on the pitcher's mound.

Upon graduating from college, he married the love of his life, who gave him four wonderful children with whom he could share his stories, both real and imagined, and his tremendous faith in all things good and kind.

* 9 7 9 8 9 8 7 2 5 5 6 0 5 *